Cloaked

by

Taylor Hobbs

This is a work of fiction. Names, characters, places, and incidents are either the product of the author's imagination or are used fictitiously, and any resemblance to actual persons living or dead, business establishments, events, or locales, is entirely coincidental.

Cloaked

Cover Art by *Debbie Taylor*

The Wild Rose Press, Inc.
PO Box 708
Adams Basin, NY 14410-0708
Visit us at www.thewildrosepress.com

Publishing History
First Tea Rose Edition, 2018
Print ISBN 978-1-5092-2151-6
Digital ISBN 978-1-5092-2152-3

Published in the United States of America

"Please, whatever you are," Henry begged, "don't hurt us. Please."

There was no answer, but Charlotte heard the rustle of fabric and a felt a light breeze on her skin as the shadow whisked by her. She whirled around to face the cell across from Henry's. Through the haze of her torchlight circle, Charlotte watched as the shadow knelt down, freeing a hand holding a key from the depths of a long, black cloak. With the telltale rasp of iron on iron, the door to the other cell creaked open.

The stranger crept soundlessly inside, returning seconds later with a body slung over its shoulders. The body emitted a low groan, and the shadow lowered its burden to lean against the wall. With unexpected care, the shadow crouched over the emaciated prisoner and murmured softly to him.

Seeing this spark of humanity gave Charlotte the courage she needed. "Help us." It was a statement, not a question.

The cloaked figure remained kneeling next to its charge, and a man's voice finally spoke in a low rumble. "But you have nothing to offer me."

Charlotte hesitated at his unexpected statement, trying to decipher its meaning. "Free my brother, and you can have anything you want."

Dedication

For Conor

Chapter One

Naked as the day she was born, Charlotte felt the earth's grip tighten around her with an unyielding hold. Fighting claustrophobic panic, she tried filling her lungs with as much cold, damp air as her narrow confines allowed. Her ribs scraped against the rough stone, hands raw and oozing from dragging her body up from the sewers like an earthworm struggling to reach the surface. The tunnel was too tight, and her shallow breaths would not be enough to sustain her, to keep her conscious.

Charlotte winced as her elbow caught a stone's razor edge, and the warm blood that welled up caused an involuntary shiver as it trickled down her body. *Maybe it will help get me unstuck*, she thought, grimacing.

By that point, the scrape only added one more to the hundreds of cuts that marred her skin, but the pain did nothing to make her regret the decision to forgo clothing. It would have gotten in the way, and scars didn't bother her. None of it would matter if she died there anyway, lodged in the drain, as tight as a cork in a wine bottle. Charlotte wondered how long it would take for someone in the castle to discover her body. Probably weeks, if ever, because the smell of her tiny, decomposing figure would blend in with the rancid aroma wafting up from below.

Curling her toes, she tried to find purchase to scoot herself forward up the diagonal slope. With trembling muscles, Charlotte willed herself to concentrate as she fought off another threatening cramp. A thick blanket of absolute darkness pressed against her eyeballs, making her head throb in confusion as she tried to figure out how much further she needed to go.

What if I miscalculated? she thought. *I should be there by now.* She blinked hard, vision straining for a hint of light. Still nothing.

Charlotte bit her lip, wanting to scream in fear and frustration before realizing that a strangled yell would only waste precious energy. Blood filled her mouth, refocusing her rage as she spit it out to mingle with the surrounding filth.

Move or die, she told herself. And she really didn't want to die.

Reach, pull, reach, pull. It might have been Charlotte's imagination, but it seemed that the confines of the drain were widening ever so slightly. This hope spurred her on as she clawed faster, the cold reduced to a memory as sweat slicked her skin. When her lungs expanded enough to take in her first deep breath, she almost cried with relief. The faintest hint of light appeared in front of her, a gentle flickering that shone down into the drain from above.

With the promise of freedom so near, it took all of Charlotte's self-control to maintain her quiet approach. If she got caught, then her journey would have been for nothing, and she might as well have sent her brother to the hangman herself.

Finally positioning herself under the grate covering the top of the drain, Charlotte listened and waited for her opening. She could hear the shuffling of other people but was unable to distinguish if they were prisoners or guards. The sound of quiet sobbing reached her hiding place. Thunderous steps slammed on the grate overhead, startling a tiny squeak out of Charlotte's mouth. She fervently hoped it sounded like a mouse.

"*Boy!*" a man roared.

The prisoner hiccupped once, and then the crying ceased, already anticipating the rant that followed.

"Shut yer trap, or I'll do it for ya. Jus' have to tell the duke you accidentally choked on yer own tongue. He won't be pleased, but I wager he can still get some sort of information outta you tomorrow." He chuckled. "Standin' duty for an old fool and a whelp. Keep me up all night, and fer what? Not like they're goin' anywhere…" The guard's footsteps faded away, and Charlotte heard a heavy door slam.

Now or never, she thought, and braced herself for the next part of her plan.

With just enough room to crouch in her hiding place, Charlotte reached up to her plaited hair and pulled a long, lethal pin out of the tangles. Clenching the weapon in her hand, she pushed her shoulders up against the heavy grate with a bowed head, willing it to give. After the long crawl, her arms were next to useless. The metal groaned but remained in place.

Undeterred, Charlotte contorted herself to press her bare feet up against the last barrier to the outside world. Pins and needles pricked her legs as blood flow shot to the muscles. All the fear and uncertainty of what lay beyond disappeared as she pushed the barrier with all her might, forgetting to care that it opened into a dungeon.

The grate conceded the struggle, popping into the air before landing on the stone floor with a reverberating clang. Cringing at her stupidity, Charlotte remained frozen in the drain, clutching her weapon. She waited for the guard to return, determined to do some damage if he laid a hand on her.

"What was that?" a familiar voice asked.

Henry, please, for once in your life, be quiet, Charlotte prayed. She imagined her brother's wide eyes looking around in panic for the source of the noise. How anyone could ever think he was capable of treason, espionage, and the rest of the numerous charges brought against him, Charlotte had no idea.

As the moment stretched and the guard still hadn't appeared, Charlotte's heartbeat slowed. She raised her head, and her eyes sparkling in the torchlight gave the only evidence of her location. While she stood up slowly, her damaged body merged with her surroundings, the dirt and filth and mud camouflaging her within the prison. She threw one leg over the edge of the drain and clambered up.

Charlotte shook off a wave of dizziness that threatened to overcome her as she stumbled forward. Pools of blood formed at her feet, leaving bloody tracks as she made her way over to her brother. The boy crept forward in his cell, propelled by a morbid curiosity to see the person mad enough to break into a dungeon through the sewers.

"Henry," Charlotte whispered.

At her voice, her brother stumbled backward onto his rear. He was thinner than when she had last seen him, even though it had been a mere four days. His lips were chapped, eyes red from crying, snot ran down in rivulets from his nose, and Charlotte had never seen a more wonderful face.

Henry crawled to the bars of his cell and pulled himself upright. "Are you real?" he asked, reaching for her.

Charlotte closed the gap between them, clasping his hand within her bruised and bloody one. She felt for broken bones in the hand she gripped, and was relieved to find none. That was good; it meant the duke hadn't started on the torture yet. From the information she had gathered earlier in the week, Duke Belaq rarely deviated from his preferred routine with the prisoners—namely, leaving them to imagine all the horrors he would inflict before personally administering them.

"How did you get here?" Henry asked. "They said they were going to torture me tomorrow! Why won't they believe me? I've already told them, I don't know what they're talking about!"

"Keep your voice down," Charlotte hissed. "I'm here to get you out."

"Out? Escape? How are we going to escape? This place is a fortress."

Charlotte pursed her lips as she pulled away from her brother, her attention already on the cell lock keeping them apart. Kneeling down, she slipped her metal hairpin into the mechanism. Her deft fingers searched for the right touch that would spring the lock, but it eluded her. Every passing second increased the possibility that the guard would return, and Charlotte's adrenaline began to betray her. Her hands shook, and she slipped again. "Blast!"

"Charlotte?"

"What?"

"I think I heard something."

Charlotte froze, ears straining as she realized her brother was right. She slowly removed the pin from the lock, hardly daring to breathe as they both stood, terrified, wholly unprepared to face whatever came through the door.

But instead of the guard barreling through to apprehend Charlotte, the door opened with hardly a creak. A shadow glided into the room, sweeping over to extinguish all but one of the torches with a seamless movement. The dungeon plunged into darkness, save for the small circle of light that surrounded the siblings.

The warm light that still illuminated Charlotte was anything but a comfort. Acutely aware that the mystery shadow could now see her while she couldn't see it, she whipped her head back and forth. She risked a glance at Henry, who opened his mouth to speak, but she cut him off.

"Whoever you are, j-just leave us alone," Charlotte said, cursing herself internally for the tremble in her tone. Her order sounded less than menacing, and she could only imagine how she looked in her vulnerable state, unable to at least orient herself to face his attack.

"Please, whatever you are," Henry begged, "don't hurt us. Please."

There was no answer, but Charlotte heard the rustle of fabric and a felt a light breeze on her skin as the shadow whisked by her. She whirled around to face the cell across from Henry's. Through the haze of her torchlight circle, Charlotte watched as the shadow knelt down, freeing a hand holding a key from the depths of a long, black cloak. With the telltale rasp of iron on iron, the door to the other cell creaked open.

The stranger crept soundlessly inside, returning seconds later with a body slung over its shoulders. The body emitted a low groan, and the shadow lowered its burden to lean against the wall. With unexpected care, the shadow crouched over the emaciated prisoner and murmured softly to him.

Seeing this spark of humanity gave Charlotte the courage she needed. "Help us." It was a statement, not a question.

The cloaked figure remained kneeling next to its charge, and a man's voice finally spoke in a low rumble. "But you have nothing to offer me."

Charlotte hesitated at his unexpected statement, trying to decipher its meaning. "Free my brother, and you can have anything you want." Desperation clouded her judgment, but Charlotte was out of options.

Her original plan hadn't been strong to begin with, and this stranger offered the chance for her and Henry to actually get out of the situation alive. The only plan Charlotte could come up with in four days was to crawl through the sewer, free Henry with her hairpin, evade the guard, and then run like hell through the castle until they stumbled upon a way out. There was a strong possibility it was a suicide mission, but Charlotte wouldn't have been able to live with herself if she hadn't made every attempt to save her little brother.

Her definitive statement must have piqued the shadow man's interest, because he shot up onto his feet, toeing the line of her illuminated circle. She refused to shrink back, and held her ground while he towered over her.

"It is not wise to make open-ended promises," he

murmured, face cloaked in his hood. "Then again, you slipped into a dungeon of your own volition, so maybe wisdom is not your strength."

Jutting out her chin, Charlotte said, "Maybe not. But I'm not letting you leave here until you open Henry's door." She swore she heard him chuckle, but it was covered up by the groans of the prisoner on the floor.

"We haven't much time." The cloaked man pushed past her and pulled out the key. Moments later, Henry stumbled out and embraced his sister.

"This is where I leave you," the shadow man said, turning his attention back to his charge.

"You can't leave us!" Charlotte said, and then winced at the echo. She tensed, hoping that her outburst hadn't put them all in jeopardy.

As the shadow man prepared to load up the prisoner again, he said over his shoulder, "The contract was for one, not three. You have nothing to offer." With the body on his back, he suddenly stopped, head cocked toward the hallway. "We have lingered too long. Guards are coming."

"Let us help you," Charlotte insisted. If she and Henry could prove their worth, then maybe the stranger would return the favor.

"We need to move now. You may follow me, but be prepared if you outlive your usefulness." He didn't need to clarify the sentence for Charlotte to understand what he meant. His 'contract' would be completed with or without Charlotte and Henry. With those final words, he extinguished the last torch and plunged the room into darkness.

Charlotte grabbed her brother's hand and dragged

him behind her through the main door, listening for the quiet groans of the prisoner to lead her the right way. None of the torches along the hallways were lit, leading Charlotte to suspect the shadow man had many contingencies in place to ensure his success. *It's a good thing the shadow man has a passenger,* Charlotte thought, as she stumbled over yet another broken flagstone. Without his pained breathing to follow, they would have been left behind in the maze of blackened tunnels. She had no idea where they were or how far they had gone.

The stranger moved like a ghost. If he wasn't weighed down by the burden across his back, Charlotte knew that he would have been outside of the castle already, the siblings a regrettable casualty in his wake.

Charlotte didn't realize how comforting the darkness had become until she was blinded by a bright light at the far end of a hallway. The shadow man froze, and Charlotte followed suit. She watched as two guards descended from a staircase, ale mugs in hand, and guessed that this was the same staircase that they needed to ascend in order to escape.

Henry clutched her hand, silently conveying his unease. She squeezed it back, and then dropped her grip, using both hands to tuck her sole weapon back into her braid. *This won't be the moment when we are thrown to the wolves,* she decided, and stepped into the hallway. The shadow man tensed, but didn't stop her, almost as if he approved of her brazen actions.

Charlotte approached the guards with slow, even steps. When they finally looked up from their conversation to realize that a naked woman stood in front of them, the guards gaped at her.

"Where—where did you come from?" one guard asked.

"No matter, Amis," the second guard said. "All that matters is that she's here for us. Our little present." He leered at Charlotte in a way that made her want to cover herself with her hands, but she resisted the urge to show any attempt at modesty. So far her plan was working, and the shock at her appearance had distracted the guards. She had no weapons in hand and nothing to hide, and the guards were too fixated on her to notice the true threat sneaking up on their right, blending in with the shadows.

"Yes, our present," Amis agreed, dropping his mug as he lunged for Charlotte's arm, broken teeth winking through his predatory grin.

Charlotte allowed the hand to close around her bicep, gagging as she breathed in his foul smell. *His breath is worse than the sewer,* she thought. He yanked her closer, and it was all Charlotte could do not to pull back. *Wait, wait,* she told herself.

"You're a plucky little bird, aren't you?" he said. "We'll see how long you last until you scream." Charlotte's free hand moved to touch her hair, not recoiling as the guard expected. "You don't think she's one of those dumb mutes, do you?" Amis turned to ask the other guard.

Charlotte's hand flew around from behind her head and she plunged the hairpin into her captor's hand. He let out a roar and loosened his hold.

"Neither mute nor dumb," she said, and danced away, fresh blood dripping from her weapon. "Just full of surprises."

A black blur launched itself at the second guard,

who had pulled his dagger out in defense of his friend. The struggle was over in seconds, with the guard slumped against the staircase and his dagger thrown out of sight.

Amis, without a thought to his injured hand, reached for his broadsword. He was too slow, and before Charlotte could blink, her would-be rapist was laid out flat, and the shadow man stood over him.

In the abrupt silence that followed, Charlotte whispered, "Are they dead?"

"Unconscious." He dragged the bodies so they were sitting next to each other, propped up against the wall. "Find their mugs," he instructed her.

She did as she was told, and the shadow man placed the cups in their laps.

"Is it safe to come out?" Henry asked, from far down the hallway.

"They will be unconscious for an hour at least," the shadow man said. "That should give us enough time."

"Why didn't you kill them?" The question blurted out of Charlotte's mouth before she could stop it.

"Dead bodies draw more attention than drunken guards," he answered. "It will be even longer before anyone discovers the prisoner is gone." He turned toward the hallway, watching Henry stumble toward them while trying to hold the old man up. "Prisoners," he corrected himself. With a few long strides, the cloaked man was upon them, relieving Henry of his burden.

"Quickly. Up the stairs behind me," he ordered the siblings.

Charlotte didn't need to be told twice. *Apparently I proved my worth*, she thought, relieved, as she tucked her pin back in its hiding place.

They followed the endlessly winding staircase up until the cloaked stranger opened a door that led into the main castle. The floor was silent and unoccupied but for the light of the moon sneaking in through the slats of the window shutters. Charlotte was utterly lost, having never been to this part of the castle before. *This certainly isn't the kitchen*, she thought as she tried to orient herself.

In her futile attempts to gain her bearings, Charlotte almost lost the shadow man, and only the sound of his cloak whisking around a curved hallway hinted at his direction. She picked up her pace, Henry stumbling loudly behind her.

"Be quiet," she snapped at her brother, but they caught up to the stranger. He was peering out of an open window, one with a grappling hook caught on the bottom ledge. Charlotte realized that they were in one of the turrets, and though she had no idea what level they were on, the ground looked to be a dizzying distance away.

The cloaked man wasted no time. With calculated efficiency, he found the free end of the rope that was curled at his feet in looped piles. He then tied a complicated harness around the old man, who still looked incapable of coherent thought, and even less capable of rappelling down a castle wall. Holding up the old man with ease, the stranger watched out the window and waited for the right moment.

Charlotte peered around his broad frame to see a pair of guards strolling through the gardens. Once they were out of sight, the cloaked stranger sat the old man up onto the ledge.

Charlotte finally spoke. "You can't be serious."

"We have exactly four minutes until the guards reappear. Make your choice by then," he said, and began to lower the old man rather steadily to the ground, only bashing him into the stone wall twice. Once his charge lay at the bottom of the tower, the cloaked stranger double-checked the grappling hook and perched on the sill. Hanging onto the rope with both hands, he walked his feet backward and disappeared over the edge.

How long has it been already? Charlotte wondered. *One minute? Two minutes?* She turned to her brother. "Can you make it?" she asked him.

He looked paler than usual in the moonlight. "It's either this, or torture and death. I pick this." He tripped while approaching the window, and for a sick second Charlotte thought he was going to fall out, but he bravely grabbed the rope and inched his way down.

My turn, Charlotte thought. Part of her was amazed she had even made it this far, and she wanted to pinch herself to make sure it was real. She leaned over the edge to check her brother's progress, and the sight made her vision blur and her stomach churn. She would have braved another sewer trip rather than risk breaking her neck in a fall.

The relief she felt when Henry's feet hit the ground brought her back to the moment. It was now or never, and she had already trusted the dark stranger to bring her this far. Flashes of the never-ending night flicked through her mind. As if crawling through the earth, freeing her brother, and fighting off a rapist weren't enough, she was still expected to confront her worst fear.

Clutching the rope for all she was worth, Charlotte felt her shoulders screaming their protest. Her body trembled with exhaustion and fear as she forced it inch by inch down the turret. Dangling almost halfway down the rope, she hit her breaking point. "I can't…I can't…I can't…" she whispered. Her body refused to move any further. *But it was all worth it,* she rationalized. *Henry is free. Nothing else really matters.*

"Let go and grab onto my back." The voice broke through Charlotte's morbid acceptance of her fate. She wrenched open her eyes that had been clenched tight with fear. The shadow man hung just below her.

"I'll fall."

"No, you will not. Hurry."

Charlotte's hands slid down slightly. Her legs found the heavy cloak first, and she wrapped them around a solid waist, anchoring herself to him. Her arms locked around his neck one at a time, and then he was flying down the rope. When his feet touched solid ground, Charlotte immediately let go and fell onto the dirt with a thump. She lay still, trying to catch her breath.

Henry peered at her with concern. "Are you all right?"

Charlotte sighed, grateful for the firm earth beneath her. *Never again,* she thought. "We made it," she said, avoiding his real question.

"Not just yet," the shadow man said sharply. Voices floated from around the turret, a banter that surged Charlotte's adrenaline yet again.

The stranger picked up the old man and pulled him behind a nearby tree. The siblings followed close behind, hardly daring to breathe as they stood and waited for the guards to patrol past them.

Once the conversation faded, Charlotte turned to Henry. "Head for the stables. Steal a horse and whatever else you need to get away from here."

"Aren't you coming with me? Duke Belaq will know it was you! He'll know you helped me, and then you will be the one in prison!"

"Henry, someone has to be here to look after Mother. I won't abandon her, and we can't make her travel far. If we do, she'll die," Charlotte reminded him. "Do you really think the duke will suspect that a woman freed you?"

"The blame will be mine," the shadow man said to Henry. "The duke will suspect I took both prisoners. The girl won't be suspect."

Henry looked as though he was going to argue, so Charlotte used her older-sister tone and ordered, "Go! Before it's too late." He hesitated a moment, then kissed his sister's cheek. "Thank you," Henry said. He turned and ran, slipping through the shadows and staying out of the bright moonlight.

Charlotte tried not to cry as she watched him go, but a tear escaped and made a clean track down a dirty cheek. She wiped it away, refusing to dwell on how it might be the last time she ever saw him. *I gave him a future,* she thought. *A future on the lam, to be sure, but it was better than certain death.*

The young woman shivered and prepared to sneak home to the village. Before she could take a step, a warm weight settled around her shoulders. The black cloak hung past her feet, enveloping her completely in a protective cocoon. Charlotte whipped around in surprise, but the stranger had his back to her, already walking away with the old man slung over his shoulders.

She meant to say 'thank you,' but instead she asked, "What is your name?"

"It is not important," he said. Then he stopped, as if debating internally over something, and turned ever so slightly. "But what is your name?"

She caught a glimpse of a strong jaw with a long, thick scar running from temple to neck. It was unlike anything she had ever seen, and how anyone could survive the wound, she didn't know. "Charlotte T-Tanner," she managed to stutter out.

And then he was gone.

Chapter Two

How long do I have to keep acting like everything is normal? Charlotte wondered as she trudged the dirt road up to the castle. She had been waiting for a week for any repercussions or questions regarding the whereabouts of her brother, but so far there was eerie familiarity in her routine. A few of the other scullery maids commented that Charlotte had been jumpier than usual lately, but with the arrest of her brother and the stress of caring for her ailing mother, they expected her nerves to be a bit frayed. Other than that, life remained the same.

As Charlotte mulled over the events from the past few days, she grew more unsettled. Why hadn't the town been alerted to look out for Henry? Why weren't guards storming the streets of the village? How had such blatant defiance of the duke gone unpunished? It was like no one knew about the escaped prisoners.

Lost in thought, she didn't realize that she had crossed the threshold and into kitchens, and almost collided with the head cook.

"Child! Watch where you are going!"

Charlotte mumbled an apology and went to grab her apron. "Not today," the cook said. "I've got a serving girl who got herself into trouble, and I need someone to serve the council breakfast."

No, no, no, Charlotte thought, panicked. He would

see it, the guilt that was written all over her face. She would be found out immediately.

The cook mistook her wide-eyed terror as nervousness, and said to her, "The duke will be with the council. You won't be alone with him. Just help serve the fish and biscuits and keep quiet. They won't even know you're there. Follow the lead of the other girls, and be invisible."

As the cook prepared the silver platters and the staff lined up to receive them, Charlotte tugged nervously at the sleeves of her dress. Underneath her clothing, she was still one giant scab. Her scrapes had begun to heal, but she couldn't afford any more questions. Her awkward excuse for the bloody mess of her hands the day after the dungeon escapade had been suspicious enough. *I cut them on pottery shards,* she explained to curious servants. *Mother had another episode in the house.* But there was no explanation ready for the cuts that crisscrossed the rest of her body, waiting to turn into a silvery web of scars.

As she reached for the heavy platter stacked with biscuits, Charlotte tried not to wince at the weight added to her battered body. Head held high and arms shaking with effort, Charlotte fell into the back of the line and the serving girls paraded to the Grand Hall.

Duke Belaq lounged at the head of the long table, his council of six leaning toward him eagerly in their chairs, but only succeeding as far as their protruding stomachs would allow. They talked over one another, seeing who could cluck the loudest to capture their lord's attention. *Like chickens at feeding time, pushing each other out of the way to get the best scraps,* Charlotte thought. Lean and deadly, the duke was a fox in the chicken coop, and the birds were too distracted to realize the danger they were in. Charlotte sensed it, unable to keep her eyes off of him as she watched his impassive expression darken to irritation.

"Enough," he said. No yelling, no hint of exasperation. With only that quiet word, the advisers' mouths snapped shut. "I have decided not to report it to the king."

One brave member spoke up. "But Your Grace, it has been happening all over—"

"No. Not in my holdings. I will not show any weakness. We will handle it internally and quietly. I will not have it get back to the king that we have failed in any way."

Invisible, be invisible, Charlotte told herself, as she tried to stop her hands from trembling. His pride finally gave her a reason as to why the news of her brother's escape had not spread like wildfire. She could feel hot rage seeping off of the duke in such close proximity, though he tried to hide it under a cool exterior.

Charlotte glanced over at the other servants, each studiously focused on serving the food, lacking the context to understand what the duke had just revealed. But Charlotte knew, and thanks to the council member, she had also discovered that her shadow man had visited more than one castle recently. The duke wouldn't be able to keep the outlaw's existence a secret for long, though. It was only a matter of time before rumors from surrounding villages reached Belaq's lands.

Charlotte ached to know more about the shadow man, and silently willed the council to give her another crumb of information, but their attention turned to their plates. Trying not to gag as the men sucked loudly on their fish bones, her eyes flitted to the duke once more.

He didn't touch his food, redirecting his focus to what looked like a letter off to the side of his plate. Even if Charlotte could risk getting close enough to his side to see it, she wouldn't have been able to read it anyway. *But what if it contains information about my dark stranger?* Her careful control slipped, and Charlotte let out a frustrated sigh.

The duke's dark eyes snapped over to her, and Charlotte froze. After a beat, she gathered her wits about her enough to cast her gaze to her feet. Her neck bowed completely forward and she flushed with horror. She didn't dare look up again until the order came to clear the meal. She could still feel a dangerous gaze on her as she exited with the other girls, sending a shiver up her spine.

Charlotte had grown up surrounded by gossip about Duke Belaq. She remembered the stories she was told as a young girl, just starting out her work in the kitchens. "Stay away from him if you can," the older girls cautioned her. "Don't catch his attention." She had successfully followed this advice for ten years.

She had been working in the kitchens since she was nine, and pointedly shown no initiative in order to rise beyond the station of a scullery maid and become a serving girl. It seemed to be a cruel twist of fate that the cook had decided to promote her at exactly the wrong time. Now, the duke's new-found interest in her directly coincided with the escape of her brother, and it was all her fault. Serve the food and get out—that was all she needed to do. *How could I have muddled it up?* Charlotte groaned.

Worst case scenarios wove their way through her brain as she ferociously scrubbed the kitchen floors, desperate for a distraction. Her prayers were answered when the head cook interrupted her cleaning. "I need chickens for supper. Go and fetch them."

Suddenly frantic for fresh air to clear her head, Charlotte jumped at the chance. She savored her walk to the coop, glad to be out of the confines of the castle. Once she was no longer in the same building as the duke, some of the tension eased behind her neck. Any thoughts of further relaxation fled, though, when she stumbled upon a group of stable boys talking.

"They're calling him the Cloaked Shadow," said a boy who couldn't have been older than twelve.

"And nobody knows who he is?" his friend asked, breathless.

"No. But he's been in and out of dungeons all over the kingdom, freeing prisoners."

"All the prisoners?"

"No. Only some. But a lot of those from wealthy families, I guess." The twelve-year-old clearly enjoyed all of the attention from his audience and gave them a conspiratorial grin. "They say that the duke's castle is the only one he hasn't broken into yet."

So I'm right then, Charlotte thought, *Duke Belaq is determined to cover up the escape of his prisoners. And Henry wasn't supposed to be freed after all. He would have been left there to rot if I hadn't been there to muck up the Cloaked Shadow's plans.*

Her dark stranger was a professional, well on his way to infamy within the kingdom. *And I'm the only person who has probably seen his face*, she realized with a jolt. Part of his face, anyway. As rumors of his prowess spread, he would become the most wanted man in the land. What would he do to her, though, if he thought she would recognize him? He didn't seem like a bad man, but that was before Charlotte was a risk to his identity.

"Does he kill people?" she blurted out, and four pairs of eyes turned to her, surprised.

"Not usually," the boy said. "Guards get taken out, but usually nobody dies. People think he is some kind of ghost, able to get in and out without being seen and without killing. My brother says that everyone they questioned after the break outs all said the same thing— a tall, cloaked shadow attacked them, and then they woke up hours later."

Charlotte thought about what the stranger had said to her—"Dead bodies draw more attention." Just how long had he been operating? Years, maybe, without drawing suspicion. But lately, hushed talk of spies and the state of the kingdom traveled through the countryside. Rumors abounded about rebel forces growing in number. Belaq had promised the king that he would root them out. In the past year, arrests became even more frequent, and not even money or a title could keep a suspect safe.

"What, have you heard something about him?" the boy asked, shaking Charlotte from her thoughts.

"Um, no, nothing," she stuttered.

"I'd like to take him on!" one of the other boys exclaimed. "I bet I could catch him."

The three others began to push him around. "I'd like to see you try!" Their rowdy behavior escalated, and Charlotte was forgotten as she scurried toward the hen house. "You'd be knocked on your bum before you even saw him!"

Her dark stranger was making waves throughout the Kingdom of Algonia. Though he was an outlaw whose very existence was shrouded in mystery and exaggeration, Charlotte felt like she knew him. A little thrill went through her every time she remembered how he had helped her.

And she still had the cloak. *The duke would probably love to get his hands on the one piece of evidence that proves the Cloaked Shadow really exists,* she thought. It was safely stashed inside her mattress, carefully folded within the hay. Every night, she was tempted to sleep within the warm embrace of the fabric, but she didn't dare bring the cloak out from its hiding place. Plus, it didn't feel like it was hers to do with as she pleased. It was simply a loan, and Charlotte had an ever-increasing feeling that it needed to be returned to its rightful owner soon.

Charlotte returned to the kitchen, flapping poultry in hand.

"You will fulfill your regular duties here this afternoon," the cook told her as she took the chickens. "Some of the council has already departed, and we have enough wait staff to attend to the rest. Hurry up, get back to the floors."

Overcome with relief, Charlotte finished her routine. She had been petrified of seeing the duke again and had almost considered hiding from the head cook until the end of the day. However, Charlotte couldn't risk displeasing her employer when she was so close to receiving her monthly wages. Her mother's medicine was running low, and it was the only thing that kept her calm during the day while Charlotte and Henry were gone.

Once dismissed, Charlotte bolted from the castle. The sun began to set, casting a warm orange glow across the village down below that didn't match the brisk temperature. Hugging her threadbare shawl across her shoulders, the young woman made her way through the familiar muddy paths. She was almost home when she halted in the middle of the street. A tingle at the back of her neck warned her she was being watched.

As discreetly as possible, Charlotte inclined her head left, and then right. There was nothing out of the ordinary she could see in her peripheries, so she picked up her pace. Seizing an opening, she darted into a narrow alleyway and through to the other side. She tried to make herself invisible, blending into a crowd of vendors hawking the remainder of their wares.

I can't go home yet, she reasoned. *I can't lead whoever this is to Mother.* But it seemed that no matter which way she went, she could feel eyes on her. Whoever it was, they were relentless in their pursuit, and Charlotte's thoughts turned erratic. *The duke. It's because of the duke. He figured it out, and he knows what I did. He's coming for me.*

As she circled the streets and alleys around her home, Charlotte felt her stalker disappear as suddenly as he had appeared. Eyes no longer tracked her every move, but to be safe, she crouched behind a shop stall, waiting for her heartbeat to slow to a regular rhythm. Only then did Charlotte felt secure enough to venture inside her home.

There, wrapped up in a blanket by an unlit hearth, sat her mother. The sight made Charlotte's gut clench. She reached out gently to touch a wrinkled cheek. "I'm sorry I was delayed, Mother. I'll make us some supper and get the fire started right away."

"Marguerite! Papa told us hours ago to bring in the cows. What have you done with the cows, dear sister?"

Charlotte sighed, committing herself to her mother's delusion. "That's where I was. I was out with the cows. Just as Papa asked."

Content with the answer, Charlotte's mother started quietly humming while her daughter prepared their scant food. In her mother's bowl, Charlotte sprinkled the dried herbs that would lull her into a peaceful sleep by the end of the meal. She hated constantly sedating her mother, but with Henry gone, she couldn't risk her mother wandering outside in the middle of the night. Before Henry left, they could take turns watching over her, but it was all up to Charlotte now.

She did it without complaint, though her mother's condition was so severe by this point she hardly recognized her own daughter. Some days, though, Charlotte thought that the confusion was a blessing in disguise. It allowed her mother to live in a simpler time, before the many tragic events that defined her past. If believing she was an eight-year-old gave her reprieve from the memory of her husband dying in the Great War, along with the nights of near starvation while she relentlessly scavenged for food to feed two tiny mouths, her daughter could only be grateful.

However, Charlotte still braced herself for the rare occasions when her mother would break through the fog. Those instances had recently been fewer and further between, and Charlotte had yet to tell her mother about Henry. But what good was telling the truth and putting her mother through the pain when she would just forget all about it hours later?

While she cooked, Charlotte's thoughts wandered to the whereabouts of her brother, just as they had during every other spare moment for the last week. She hoped that he had found refuge somewhere far away, and maybe even made it out of Algonia altogether. She knew the odds were against him, and that it was more than likely he had already become a victim of highway robbery or a savage animal. Her little brother was all alone, outside of the village for the first time in his life, and did not possess the skills of a mastermind spy, as much as Duke Belaq wanted to believe. Had Charlotte only helped Henry exchange one death for another? She doubted she would ever find out. But at least without knowing the truth of what happened, she could hold onto hope and imagine him healthy and well.

She wanted to crawl into her mother's arms, and feel the soothing embrace take away all of the fears that swirled in her brain since the day Henry had been arrested. It would be a relief to unburden herself for just a few moments, to allow herself a second of rest. Glancing at her mother with quiet envy, she wished she was eight years old again.

Against the dying daylight, Charlotte finished preparing their meal and stoked the fire to a roaring heat. The warmth and the meal overpowered her preoccupations, and the young woman closed her eyes for a moment.

****

She awoke with a start in the pitch darkness. Frantically, she groped around until her hands found the sleeping body of her mother. Relieved that the herbs had worked and her mother was safely resting, it took

Charlotte a moment to wonder why she had woken up in such a fright.

It was that feeling again, the feeling of being watched. Even through the night's thick blackness, there was no mistaking the tingle.

Hardly daring to breathe, Charlotte crawled over to the hearth and tried to silently grab the iron poker. Just as her fingers found the cold metal, a hand closed around her wrist. Shock at the touch expelled all the air from her lungs, and before Charlotte could draw another breath to scream, another hand closed over her mouth.

"I would not do that if I were you."

Charlotte let out a whimper, muffled by her captor's grip. Though still disoriented from sleep, she could never forget that voice.

"I believe you have something of mine."

Chapter Three

The Cloaked Shadow loosened his hold on Charlotte. Was she dreaming? How could he actually be here, in her house? But she swallowed back her questions and said, "Let me light the candle. I'll get your cloak."

As she stood up, the lump of wax was pressed into her hand, as he already anticipated her needs. Truthfully, she could find the cloak in the dark through touch alone, but the opportunity to try and catch another glimpse of the Cloaked Shadow was too tempting to ignore.

A spark followed a sharp tap, and she held out the candle with both hands, like an innocent child asking for more food. The flint in her visitor's hands hit the mark the second time, and Charlotte was momentarily blinded by the sudden light as the spark caught the wick.

So much for trying to sneak a peek, she thought. Blinking helplessly, she turned around to the direction of her bed. She placed the candle on the dirt floor beside her and reached into the hay.

The entire time she searched for it, Charlotte felt the Cloaked Shadow's eyes on her back, but she didn't dare turn around and try to look at him. Her curiosity grew so sharp it was almost painful, but for some odd reason, boldly turning around to confront him in the light would feel like a betrayal. He had already entrusted his infamous cloak with her for over a week, and had also trusted her not to raise the alarm when he broke into her house.

Charlotte decided that if she saw him by accident, however, it would be a different situation. Or if he chose to reveal himself to her, but she wasn't counting on that. After he helped save her brother, the least she could do was to respect his privacy.

Charlotte pulled out half of her mattress stuffing before her hands closed over soft fabric. She stood up, shaking out the hay-covered cloak. "Sorry about this," she whispered, brushing off the fabric as best she could. The breeze she created knocked out the candle, and they were plunged back into darkness. She turned to him, blind again, with the cloak laying over her outstretched arms.

The weight of the fabric disappeared in an instant, seeming to jump from her arms to its rightful owner effortlessly. She felt a pang of sadness instead of relief as the last piece of evidence tying her to Henry's escape left her possession; the single object linking her to the Cloaked Shadow. The cloak had been solid proof that he wasn't just a spirit or a memory, but an actual living, breathing man.

Charlotte expected the stranger to vanish from her life yet again with hardly a word, so she nearly fell over when she heard him speak. "You kept it safe. Thank you."

Shocked, she blurted out, "Why wouldn't I?"

She felt rather than saw him hesitate. "You were very brave to keep this," he finally said. "This cloak has…significance to me. I will not forget it."

While she gaped at his statement, Charlotte heard the front door open and the night air whisked her stranger away. They had almost had an actual conversation. He'd *thanked* her, even. Lending the cloak to Charlotte had been much more important than a simple act of chivalry.

Without bothering to stuff the hay back into her mattress, Charlotte lay down, her head spinning. *It's over now,* she told herself. *That was the last I'll see of him.* Sleep evaded her as she tossed and turned, imagining all the different faces he could wear underneath the cloak. Nothing her mind could come up with seemed to match his voice. It was just before sunrise before she drifted off, finally accepting that it was a mystery she would never solve.

****

Pounding at the door woke Charlotte from her brief slumber. She tried to sit up, but her muscles felt limp and her eyes refused to open more than halfway. Rubbing her face, she looked over by the hearth to see her mother, still wrapped up in blankets. Relief whooshed through her when she realized that this early morning house call had nothing to do with an elderly woman wandering around the village.

This feeling was short lived, however, and quickly turned to gut-clenching fear when she heard, "Open up, in the name of Duke Belaq."

All traces of fatigue disappeared and Charlotte shot out of bed, throwing a blanket over herself for modesty before remembering that she was still dressed in her clothes from the day before. There was no point in pretending she wasn't home, but maybe it was just a mistake, and the guards were breaking down the wrong house.

"What is that awful noise!" her mother yelled. "Don't you know there's babies sleeping in here?"

The young woman cracked open the door, only to find herself nose-to-nose with a man in full armor. "Can I help you?" she asked.

"Charlotte Tanner?"

It wasn't the wrong house after all. "Yes?"

"And Isobel Tanner?"

They were asking about her mother? Charlotte's pulse quickened, and she looked past the first guard to see five others standing behind him.

"I'm one of Duke Belaq's kitchen maids, up at the castle," she said, trying to stall. "Whatever the problem is, I'm sure it can be sorted out when I tend to my duties this morning."

"We're here to escort you to the castle. And you won't be going to the kitchens," he said, completely emotionless.

"What's this about?" her mother's voice asked from behind Charlotte.

"Go back inside, Mother. Nothing to worry about."

"She is to come, too," the guard said.

"Wait. No. Please. She's frail and confused. You can't drag her out of here." Charlotte's voice rose, panicked at the thought of her mother struggling up the path to the castle, surrounded by unnecessary guards. "What is this about, really?" she asked.

A hand came out of nowhere and backhanded her across the face. "Let's go," he said. Two other guards pushed the door open all the way and grabbed Charlotte's arms to tow her out into the street.

"Why are you doing this?" she asked, trying to

sound indignant, but her shrill tone exposed her fear. Charlotte's breath exhaled rapidly in puffy clouds over their heads. The orange sun peeked over the horizon, casting long shadows behind them as it illuminated the hard, unsympathetic faces of her captors. She saw curious eyes peeking out through windows in the surrounding houses. Neighbors she had known her whole life remained silent as they witnessed the ruckus in the street.

"Help me," she begged them. "Don't let them take my mother." She knew she didn't stand a chance taking on the guards by herself, but she still thrashed against their hold as she watched another pair of armored thugs drag her mother outside.

"Marguerite?" Charlotte's mother asked her, bewildered. Her expression held the purity of a child's, out of place within the wrinkles of her face. She turned to her daughter as if Charlotte was able to provide an answer for her unreasonable predicament.

Rage at the indignity boiled up inside Charlotte. Duke Belaq had already taken her brother from her, and now another innocent member of her family was being dragged through the village for no other reason than to instill fear in the rest of the people. *But it is your fault your mother is here,* an internal voice whispered to Charlotte. You *were the one who helped your brother escape.* You *caught the duke's attention yesterday.*

The captain stepped in front of the restrained pair and gave them a satisfied smile. To the four other guards, he said, "Now, proceed."

Charlotte bucked harder against the immovable walls of armor. Her mother watched the display with narrowed eyebrows, her meek confusion about to erupt into a full-blown episode. She began to copy her daughter's violence and added in some blood-curdling shrieks for good measure.

The captain whipped around and strode toward the old woman. He laid a slap on her as he had done with Charlotte, and said, "Silence."

Only instead of another display of defiance, the old woman's body sagged, held up entirely by the two men on either side of her. Her head hung limply, shocks of wild white hair hiding her face. A red stain began to blossom from her temple, its sharp color contrast visible. Time slowed as Charlotte watched the captain grab her mother's bloody hair and yank her head up.

"Bugger," he muttered. "Duke will have my head for this."

"What do you want us to do with her?" the tallest guard asked.

"Just dump her here. She's of no use now."

That was when Charlotte saw the truth behind her mother's completely blank stare, eyes still open in surprise from the blow to her head. Her jaw hung slack, the sticky blood from her wound ran from her temple down into her mouth. There was no look of peace on Mother's face, no dignity in death after suffering for years from her illness.

A roaring filled Charlotte's ears as she fought to remain conscious. Her eyes locked on her mother's body, unable to tear her gaze away from the horrific sight but wanting to hide from it at the same time. It had happened so fast—one second she was there, and the next she was gone. It didn't seem possible. Watching her once-brilliant mother descend into madness had been a slow agony, but it was nothing compared to the searing pain in Charlotte's soul at such an instantaneous and unexpected demise.

Was it inevitable that a member of Charlotte's family had to die by the duke's hand no matter what? In playing with the fates and rescuing Henry, had Charlotte directly set up the events that led to her innocent mother's death? In that moment, Charlotte had never felt so utterly alone and helpless in the world. With her mother and brother gone, she saw no reason to keep struggling anymore in the face of a futile situation. Charlotte's legs gave out. "*No,*" she moaned.

The captain didn't spare her a glance, and instead pointed to the alley where his guards could leave Isobel's body. "Drag her over there," he ordered. The pair hauled the old woman behind a building while Charlotte still watched, unable to accept that this was the last memory she would ever have of her mother.

"Now, are you going to behave, or are you going to end up like the old bat?" The captain sneered, stepping into Charlotte's line of sight.

She didn't say anything. She didn't look at him. Tears pooled in her eyes, but Charlotte wouldn't give him the satisfaction of showing him just how deeply he had destroyed her.

"I believe that's a yes," he said, chuckling. "Martin, Thomas!" he yelled. The captain looked over his shoulder for the guards who hadn't reappeared from behind the building. There was no answer. "Go see what's taking them so long," he ordered the guards responsible for Charlotte.

"With her?" one of them asked.

"What, does she weigh too much for you to handle?"

"No sir."

Charlotte's feet skimmed across the mud as they dragged her over to her mother's final resting spot. None of the early morning sun slipped into the narrow alley, but Charlotte couldn't feel the damp chill of the air anyway. She was numb, her thoughts refusing to become more than fleeting emotions in order to protect herself from further trauma. She wouldn't fight her captors anymore.

Charlotte wasn't even aware that her eyes had adjusted to the dim light until she saw the prone bodies of Martin and Thomas beside her mother. "What—" the guard on her left started to say, as he loosened his grip on her arm.

Like a bird of prey, a black figure dropped down on top of him. In a swirl of dark material, the guard joined his fellow men in the mud. The guard on the right let go of Charlotte completely and reached for his dagger. As he strode forward to intercept the attacker, Charlotte broke through her fog, and without thinking, shot her foot out to trip him.

Admiring her handiwork as the fourth guard sprawled on the ground, she plucked the dagger from his hand and clocked him over the head with the heavy hilt. Then Charlotte turned to face her savior.

It was him. The Cloaked Shadow, yet again, his timing eerily precise. Even beneath his hood, in the gray light of the alley, Charlotte could feel his eyes on her, assessing everything from her fierce posture to the dagger she held at the ready.

"Martin, Thomas!" The impatient voice of the captain reached them from across the street.

After what seemed like an eternity, the Cloaked

35

Shadow seemed to finally make his decision. "Keep up, and follow closely." With dancer-like grace, her rescuer vaulted up onto the roof behind them.

Considerably clumsier, the young woman followed him, clambering on top of a feed bin and then hoisting a leg up onto the thatched surface. From her vantage point above the streets, Charlotte saw the people emerging from their houses to start their day. The sun was almost above the horizon, and the black cloak that blended in so well at night was all-too-obvious against a bright sky. Charlotte prayed that no one would look up as they crouched down to scurry over the rooftops.

The Cloaked Shadow jumped the distance between the roofs with relative ease as he led Charlotte toward the outskirts of the village. Every time Charlotte hesitated before taking a leap of faith between buildings, she looked over at the duke's castle in the distance, a sharp reminder that she had no choice. *Don't think about the height*, she warned herself, and chose instead to focus all of her attention on the black figure leaping ahead of her.

She got into a rhythm of sorts, until her thoughts flashed to her mother's last moments and the image of the captain's smirk. Fear gripped her mind, and her foot slipped. For a sick moment, the roof she stood on sagged with a groan as Charlotte's body leaned back over the edge. Time slowed, and as Charlotte waved her arms in circles to regain her balance, she somehow managed to turn her heel around so she fell backward against the incline of the roof instead of pitching into thin air.

Adrenaline surged through her bloodstream as she cursed her carelessness. *I could have broken my neck,* she thought. It was sheer, dumb luck that saved her. She knew her innate instincts and quick reflexes were good, but they weren't that good.

Charlotte crawled up to her hands and knees and frantically searched the surrounding rooftops for the Cloaked Shadow. He was nowhere to be found, but the edge of the village was close. *I might actually make it,* she thought, hope spurring her on to navigate the roofs on her own. The forest beyond the last building beckoned her with promises of safety in its depths, and she slid off the edge of the final roof and sprinted for the trees.

Profound silence greeted her as she slowed to walk among the mossy giants. No animals made their presence known as they silently watched the intruder, judging their unwelcome guest.

This wasn't Charlotte's first time in the forest. The lure of the Cursed Forest was just too strong for young, imaginative children to ignore. As a rite of passage, childhood friends egged each other on to see who was brave enough to walk the furthest into the forest, but no one had ever gone so far as to disappear out of sight of the village. Once the thrill of the dare had worn off, everyone always came running back to the safety of the open sky.

Charlotte hadn't been inside the forest since she was fifteen, after Henry had taunted her with bets that she wouldn't go further in than he did. Of course, she proved him wrong, but never told him about the nightmares she experienced for weeks afterward.

As she progressed farther into the shadows, the forest looked the same as it had four years ago, and the same goosebumps pricked her arms. "Hello?" Charlotte whispered, and it sounded like a shout. Still, as creepy as the forest was, it was infinitely better than the chaos she left behind.

And in that chaos lay her mother. How could she have left her mother like that? Overcome with guilt, Charlotte stopped walking and sank to the ground. She wanted to turn around, to sneak back into the village to lay her mother to rest properly, but her legs wouldn't cooperate. Laying her hands on the earth and trying not to cry, vibrations through the dirt caught her attention.

The vibrations grew stronger, turning into the sound of a thunderous gallop as a black horse shot through the trees. It bore down on Charlotte, forcing her to her feet. The Cloaked Shadow reached down from his seat, scooping her up before Charlotte remembered to be afraid. Hanging onto the mane in front of her for dear life, Charlotte closed her eyes as the forest became a dark green blur.

By the time the heaving horse finally came to a stop, Charlotte's legs were numb. They had ridden deeper and deeper into the forest for hours, far off of any path and miles from any sort of civilization. As a small comfort, there was no way that even the duke's best trackers would be able to follow them this distance into the wild.

She felt the Cloaked Shadow slide to the ground behind her, landing noiselessly on the spongy earth. Hoping her legs wouldn't fail her, Charlotte followed. After steadying herself on their faithful steed, she turned to look at her rescuer. An involuntary gasp escaped her throat when she saw that his hood had been blown back.

Of all the ways Charlotte had imagined her dark

stranger looking, this was never one of the possibilities. Charlotte had known that the Cloaked Shadow was tall and broad—his disguise couldn't hide that—but the rest of him didn't match any of the aristocratic, graceful variations she had constructed in her mind.

His hair was trimmed short and unevenly around his head, golden tufts of it sticking up wildly in the back as if he had cut it himself. A tanned face with the beginnings of crow's feet encircled intense blue eyes that stared back at her as she appraised him. The square jawline she had caught a glimpse of during their first meeting was the same, but the thick scar that ran from his temple down to his neck and disappeared under the cloak looked even angrier up close. It was at least the width of her thumb, a puckered pink that hadn't faded to white. To round out his hardened appearance was a nose that must have been long and straight at one point, but had been broken at least once.

Charlotte spoke first. "Hello again."

"Hello, Charlotte." His face remained impassive, letting her set the tone of their meeting. Serious eyes stared her down until she needed to say something to break the silence.

"Who are you?" she blurted out, then immediately regretted it. It dawned on Charlotte that she was alone with him, and she had no idea what he was capable of, especially now that she had seen his face. How far would he go to keep the identity of the Cloaked Shadow hidden? She reached for her braid, only to realize the pin she kept hidden there was long gone, thanks to her horrific morning. Charlotte settled for taking a few cautious steps away from him.

Her emotions must have been written all over her

face, because he said, "None of that. I am still deciding what to do with you." Sighing, he combed his fingers through his hair, forcing Charlotte to reassess her assumption of his age. She originally guessed he was in his late twenties, but seeing the tired mask drop over his face as he regarded her, she realized he was probably in his mid-thirties.

"Well, you wouldn't have come back for me if you were just going to kill me," Charlotte said, with more certainty than she felt. She swore she saw his mouth twitch upward in the semblance of a smile before settling back down into a ponderous line. "And that makes twice you've saved my life," she pointed out.

"You just...remind me of someone," he said quietly. He continued to think out loud. "I could take you over the border. You will be safe from Duke Belaq there, and the rest of the Algonian forces. You will never be able to return here, of course."

"How do you know I won't go telling everyone who you are?" Charlotte asked, genuinely curious after hearing that he wanted to help her escape. He narrowed his gaze at her, and Charlotte realized that her question could be misconstrued as a blackmail threat. She tried to back up. "Not that I'm not grateful for everything. I just don't understand why you've gone through all the trouble."

"You risked your life to save your brother, and you kept my cloak safe," he said, as if that was all that was needed to show Charlotte's true character.

"And so you'll trust me with your name?" she pressed. "If we will be together for some time, I need to call you something other than the Cloaked Shadow."

He waited a beat, deciding whether or not to reveal

another part of himself. "You may call me Fawkes."

Chapter Four

With the sound of his name hanging heavy in the air between them, Fawkes turned his back to Charlotte and walked over to a nearby tree. After crouching down between the exposed roots, he stood back up with a bulging burlap bag. He offered no explanation for the surprise, so Charlotte assumed he had stashed his possessions there before going into the village. How he brought them back to the exact spot within the maze-like Cursed Forest remained a mystery, but Charlotte wasn't going to complain with the promise of food and fire in her future.

In the small clearing, he began to set up camp with the seemingly endless supplies he pulled from the sack. With practiced, methodical movements, Fawkes remained engrossed in his task until Charlotte interrupted. "How can I help?" she asked, and saw his hands falter. *He isn't used to anyone else being here,* she realized.

"Gather some firewood," he said, "but take care not to stray too far."

Charlotte did as requested, thankful for the distraction to keep her thoughts from wandering to her mother. And her brother. And the fact that she could never go home again. Tears pricked her eyes as she swallowed her emotions. There would be time to mourn later, when she wasn't running for her life. After getting herself under control, Charlotte returned to find a sparse campsite already set up, with a bedroll and basic foodstuffs set out.

Fawkes took the wood from her without a word, setting up the pile but leaving it unlit. "Stay here," he ordered. From the sheath on his hip, he pulled out a deadly-looking dagger and melted into the trees.

Under the oppressive canopy, while wrapped in dim light and shadows, Charlotte began to drift off. Exhaustion almost claimed her but released its hold abruptly when Fawkes returned carrying two rabbits.

He made quick work skinning his kills, then skewered them onto a thin branch. By the time twilight whispered into their campsite, a merry fire crackled and browned the rabbit meat.

Charlotte nibbled on a piece of hardtack while she watched Fawkes prepare their dinner. At least, she hoped he was going to share. She had pried only a few sentences from him all day, but she got the distinct impression he was a man with a deeply ingrained sense of fairness. He seemed to have a moral code all his own, but his actions so far indicated that Charlotte fell on the right side of his internal justice system.

A roasted rabbit was unceremoniously dumped onto a tin plate and shoved into her lap. "Thank you," she said, and got a grunt in response. She tried again. "Won't the duke's men see the fire?"

He gave what almost sounded like a laugh. "Duke Belaq's men, in the Cursed Forest, at night?" With that, Fawkes seemed to be done talking for the night, but spoke once more when he ordered her to take the bedroll once their meal was finished.

"But where will you sleep?"

He gestured to the cloak that wrapped around his large frame. Leaving more than enough space between them, he lay down with his back to Charlotte, hood snug over his head.

****

When she woke the next morning, Charlotte sat up in her bedroll. She wondered if she had overslept for her scullery duties and tried to remember if she had given her mother her nightly sedatives. As she frantically looked around for the elderly woman, a bewildered Charlotte remembered where she was, and events that had transpired the day before came back in a flood.

Fawkes was already up and saddling the horse. The rest of the campsite was already packed and free of any human evidence, minus Charlotte in her bedroll, still on the ground.

"Was about to wake you," Fawkes said, walking over to shove a piece of jerky into her hand. He ignored the sadness that lingered from her memories and got straight to the point. "The border remains a week's ride from here, slower with two. Duke Belaq doesn't take kindly to insults. He will have all the men he can spare out looking for us today."

Charlotte put on a brave face as she processed his words. She still wasn't safe, and Fawkes was taking a considerable risk by continuing to aid her. She remembered what he said in the dungeons, about getting in the way of his contract. Any mishaps on her part could cause him to abandon her, and right now, the Cloaked Shadow was the only friend she had in the world. She gritted her teeth and met his gaze. "I'm ready."

With the long trek to the border ahead of them, the pair switched off riding and walking to give the black horse, whom Fawkes called Ghost, respite. The farther away they got from Charlotte's village, the more relaxed Fawkes appeared. The tension in his shoulders lessened until Charlotte thought he was almost enjoying his stroll through the Cursed Forest.

But as their first full day of travel got underway, Charlotte could not escape her worried thoughts. She had nothing and no one, so how was she supposed to start her life in a foreign country? Granted, the neighboring country of Croantis was similar to Algonia, even speaking a dialect of the same language, but would her life be filled with more of the same? The thought of finding work as a scullery maid depressed her. *A future where I trudge through my days, an orphan far from home...but maybe I'll meet a man and*—no! Charlotte thought, panicked.

One glance at her traveling companion, so free and dangerous and wild, struck a chord within Charlotte that yearned for more. Maybe something good could come out of all the tragedy. Everything that tied her to Algonia and her village was gone. There were other ways to start a new life, and to live it on her terms. There was just the small matter of convincing the tall renegade who walked beside her.

It took miles more before Charlotte plucked up the courage to talk to him. "Do you have business at the border?" she asked, trying to discern how much time she had left with Fawkes.

"In a trading village a bit before the border," he said, seeming surprised that she asked. "Lands owned by Earl Hawthorne."

So it wasn't out of the goodness of his heart that he offered to escort me, Charlotte realized, a bit dismayed. *He was heading there anyway.*

"How long will you be there for?"

"As long as I need to be," he answered.

"And then where?"

"Yet to be determined."

He was capable of deflecting her questions all day, so she'd better get to the heart of the matter. Charlotte took a deep breath. "Take me with you, wherever you go next," she said, feeling like she had nothing left to lose.

"No."

That was it. No excuses, no reasons, just 'no.'

"Just for a little while," Charlotte begged. "I can be useful. Don't make me go back to my old life, not after everything."

"I have no need of an apprentice," he said, voice tinged with annoyance.

"I can get information for you, talk to people in the villages," Charlotte said, scrambling. "I can take care of your horse. I can follow your directions while you...conduct business," she put delicately.

That stopped him short. "What is it, exactly, that you think I do?" He faced her with such seriousness that Charlotte flinched.

"From what I gather, you...help people who are imprisoned? For profit? You talked about contracts back at the dungeon." He said nothing, and his blue eyes bored into her soul, as if seeking her true intentions. Finally, he looked away, but Charlotte couldn't let the conversation drop.

"I'm already a fugitive, and I have nothing left to

lose." Her plea was approaching a level of desperation she wasn't comfortable with, but she needed some sort of an answer.

"You could not endure my way of living."

"I rescued my brother from Duke Belaq's dungeon! He's alive because of me!"

"No, he is alive because of me. To stay alive, you would do well away from me. I will not be held responsible for you."

It was like talking to a stone wall. *I still have a week to convince him though, that he's wrong about me.* Her skills could come in handy in his line of work; she just had to prove it to him.

****

Charlotte began to regret begging Fawkes to become her mentor, as the request had widened the distance between the two of them. He pulled away from her, avoiding speaking to her unless asked a direct question that he felt like answering. Whatever burgeoning friendship, or at least a mutual appreciation, that existed after they eluded the duke's men disappeared.

By the time they reached the edge of the Cursed Forest, Charlotte was so frustrated she couldn't even enjoy the feeling of unobstructed sunshine on her face for the first time in days. Begrudgingly, she marveled at Fawkes' navigational skills, but also chastised herself for believing that the Cursed Forest was actually cursed. They hadn't come across anything remotely dangerous, not even a large predator. When Charlotte commented on this, Fawkes just shook his head and said there were great dangers lurking, but they were protected. Whatever that meant.

It was Charlotte's turn to ride Ghost, so she was the first to spot the thatched roofs and smoke in the distance. "There!" She pointed. "Is that where we need to go?"

"Yes. We will be there by nightfall. I have some business to sort out, and then I will take you to the border."

Charlotte's stomach clenched, but she pretended to be unperturbed by his general disregard for her. She dismounted, and the three of them trudged toward civilization.

Just before the village, Fawkes shrugged off his cloak and carefully folded it into a saddlebag. Since the night she had given it back to him, Charlotte hadn't seen him take off the cloak again. To see it stripped from him now felt like seeing him naked. She blushed and averted her eyes, though he was fully clothed underneath. Without it, he looked vulnerable, exposed. Ordinary. The man who was the Cloaked Shadow seemed to lose a piece of himself that was larger than life whenever he took it off. Again, Charlotte wondered why he had loaned it to her the night of Henry's escape.

The question of the old man's identity in the other cell turned in her mind, always on the tip of her tongue—why had the duke imprisoned him, and what happened to him after that night?

This pondering kept Charlotte occupied until she realized just how noisy everything was when they reached the marketplace. She had forgotten what it felt like to be surrounded by other breathing, moving, talking bodies. During their time in the forest, Fawkes moved so quietly that unless Charlotte had her eyes on him, it was hard to remember he was even there. This new chaos assaulted all of her senses, and Charlotte fought the urge to turn and run back the way they came. The smell of unwashed people, sewage, and animals made her want to vomit. A headache began to creep its way forward, and she steadied herself against Ghost. Among the milieu of the crowd, no one spared them a second glance. Fawkes kept his head down and his eyes on the mud in front of him while Charlotte tried to do the same.

"We will journey to the inn and wait until nightfall," he murmured to her.

Fawkes navigated through the streets, confirming his comfortable familiarity with the town. It was bigger than Charlotte's village, and she soon lost all bearing. If she got separated from Fawkes now, she would have no idea how to find him again.

The inn he stopped in front of was a rough, two-story building. Though it was the middle of the day, raucous laughter poured out through the open windows. Used to a parade of nameless and faceless travelers passing through, the trading town wouldn't notice the addition of Fawkes and Charlotte, especially at a less-than-reputable inn.

"Take Ghost to the stables," Fawkes ordered her. "But fetch my bag before you return inside. I will secure us a room."

She led Ghost around back without argument, hoping to prove how convenient a travel companion could be, especially an accommodating one. Walking into the barn, the musty scent of hay, manure, and animals triggered an onslaught of memories of Henry that hit Charlotte with such force she almost doubled over.

He was one of the duke's best stable boys. Since the time he could walk, Henry had been fascinated with horses. While Charlotte drudged through her scullery maid duties at the castle, Henry found his calling working with the gentle creatures. They trusted him completely, and even the most ornery stallion turned docile as a foal under his touch. Charlotte remembered him whispering into their ears and stroking their long noses, and wondered if the duke's animals missed him.

How Henry suddenly went from trusted stable boy to wanted criminal still eluded Charlotte. All she knew now was how badly she missed him, and how alone she felt in this strange village, in a barn that didn't have her brother in it.

Shaking off her dark thoughts, she focused on making sure Ghost was settled in comfortably for the evening before grabbing their supplies and heading back to the inn. Fawkes paced just inside the front door, and grabbed the bag—which contained his precious cloak—from her as soon as she approached. He turned and headed upstairs without a word, leaving Charlotte to follow quickly behind.

Their room was the last one on the left, at the end of a long, dark hallway. Fawkes opened the door with a rusty key and a shove. "Do not wander about without me," he cautioned. "There are many unsavory folk that you should not want to come across unaccompanied."

"Will I be accompanying you tonight?" she asked.

"No. I have official business."

Now that she knew she had no chance of going with him anyway, she couldn't resist goading him a little further. "Official business as the Cloaked Shadow? Or just as Fawkes?"

His stormy glare answered her. "I need to sleep," he said, flopping down on the only bed.

Charlotte sighed and looked over at the only other piece of furniture in the room—a rickety wooden chair that promised to fall apart any minute. She crossed her fingers and carefully sat down. *Nighty night,* she thought darkly. She glared at Fawkes, who sprawled out on the mattress.

In the end, sheer boredom overcame her discomfort and she actually fell asleep. When she awoke, moonlight was streaming in through the window and onto a distinctly man-shaped depression in the mattress. Fawkes was gone, and a quick search in his bag told her that the cloak was with him.

With a sinking heart, and already guessing the outcome, she tugged on the door. Locked. Pacing the room liked a caged animal, Charlotte tried to formulate her plan.

Above all, Charlotte needed to make herself indispensable to Fawkes so he wouldn't just abandon her in Croantis, but so far she had failed. He hadn't even trusted her enough to say where he was going or how long he'd be gone. Noises from the pub below drifted up through the floor, and Charlotte realized one way she could be useful.

Inside Fawkes' bag lay a coil of rope, which Charlotte pulled out with trembling hands. *This is such a bad idea,* she told herself, as she wound one end around the bed frame. When Fawkes got back, he was either going to be furious with her, or simply leave her behind in the town while he rode off. She didn't know which response she feared more.

Next, she crept to the open window and looked out

at the ground below. It wasn't as high up as she had originally thought, and definitely not as high up as she had been when rescuing Henry. This time, though, she was determined not to let fear get the best of her.

Throwing the other end of the rope out the window, Charlotte repeated the same rappelling technique she used down the castle wall. Though her heart felt like it was going to pound out of her chest, she made it to the ground without freezing up once.

Ha, she thought, triumphant. *Can't endure his world, huh?*

The rope still dangled from their room, just begging for a thief to climb up it. Charlotte found a rock and tied it to the end, tossing it back through their window on her fifth attempt, thankful there were no witnesses to her four other tries.

Wiping her hands on her skirt, she slunk around the inn and entered through the front door. The pub was rowdier now that night had fallen, and no one noticed as Charlotte bolted for an out-of-the-way corner to watch the festivities.

Copious amounts of ale flowed into mugs that never seemed to fully empty. Bar maids scurried through the crowd, trying to avoid the onslaught of pinches, gropes, and vulgar suggestions thrown their way as they satisfied customer orders. Every woman inside seemed to be working, whether it was on their feet with heavy trays or on the laps of drunkards. In other words, it was the perfect place for Charlotte to try and gather information.

From her secluded vantage point, Charlotte's gaze darted to the only other person who looked as out of place there as she did, but for entirely different reasons.

The man was obviously wealthy and had done a poor job of hiding it from the commoners. The working girls must have thought so, too, because he entertained four of them at his table. His loud bragging carried all the way over to Charlotte, who perked up her ears to listen.

"So I told the duke that he'd better respect me, seeing as I *am* Earl Hawthorne's official *li-ai-son*," he said, drawing out the word for the benefit of his audience and puffing out his chest.

"Then what happened?" One of the prostitutes leaned forward expectantly, as if she knew what the word 'liaison' meant. *Yes, then what happened?* Charlotte thought.

"I told him that if he really wanted the Cloaked Shadow alive and delivered to him, we needed more gold. Earl Hawthorne's plan will work, *guar-an-teed,* but the duke doesn't know that." He winked at his enraptured companions. "Made it seem like we were taking too big of a risk for him, and we needed to be, ah, *compensated* more appropriately."

"You really think you can catch him?" the blonde in his lap asked.

"He might have been able to pull one over on Duke Belaq, but the Cloaked Shadow'll be getting more than he bargained for in Earl Hawthorne's dungeons."

Charlotte stopped breathing. Did Fawkes have a contract in Earl Hawthorne's dungeons? Had he walked blindly into a trap tonight? She never would have guessed that Duke Belaq would work so willingly with another noble. Rumor had it that the duke was only loyal to King Otan, and only interested in furthering his own agenda and family name. He would consider it beneath him to negotiate with an earl, especially because it meant admitting that the Cloaked Shadow had bested him, a secret the duke had seemed so intent on keeping. *What has changed in such a short time?*

She kicked herself for not going with Fawkes. But instead of giving into her feelings of despair, Charlotte maneuvered herself closer to the liaison. *Come on,* she begged. *Give me something, anything, that will lead me to him.*

In trying to eavesdrop, she stumbled over an extended boot and fell to the floor. A meaty hand grabbed her arm and hoisted her upright, and Charlotte found herself choking on heavy alcohol fumes filling her lungs.

"Care to join us?" the man asked her, slurring. "You don't want to be around the likes of him." He gestured over to Earl Hawthorne's man and his gaggle of women. "We'll take care of you. Honorable-like."

"T-that's very kind of you," Charlotte stammered. "But I was just looking for something to eat before going back to my room."

Maintaining his grip on her arm, Charlotte's overly-friendly new acquaintance tried to steer her back to his table, where three other men sat. "No need to be afraid," he said, "we won't hurt you. Some female company would be nice for the evening."

"No, really," Charlotte insisted. "I'm waiting here for my friend. I mean, husband."

"Your husband? He left you in a place like this, alone?"

"We can treat you better, girl," one of the men at the table grunted at her.

She was stuck, unable to try to wrench her way out of the man's grasp without causing a scene. Charlotte had no doubt she could put up a substantial fight and show the men that she was more trouble than she was worth, but then she would sacrifice the opportunity for any other information she could glean from the liaison. With warring emotions, Charlotte sat down at the crowded table. She would find a way to excuse herself as soon as she could, especially once the ale sent the men to sleep.

The man responsible for her current predicament turned to look back at the earl's employee with a disdainful glare. "Poofter," he muttered.

Charlotte saw her chance. "Do you really think what he said was true?"

"What was true?" he asked, oblivious. Apparently, she had been the only one listening.

"About being Earl Hawthorne's liaison," Charlotte clarified.

"Lemme tell you something, girlie. Earl Hawthorne is going to need better men than that ponce if he's going to quash the rebels. He's too coward to face them, and I don't blame him if he's got gits like that in his employ." He took a big swig out of his mug, leaving the foam to drip off his mustache and into his beard. "Enough. We didn't bring you over here to talk about that." He pushed the mug at her. "Drink up."

As she tried to come up with a polite way to refuse, a hand fell onto her shoulder. "And just what is it, pray tell, do you think you're doing?"

Charlotte's heart leaped, and she whipped around to stare up into familiar blue eyes— eyes that held her own with such barely-contained ferocity that she shrank back into her seat. Her initial excitement at witnessing Fawkes alive and well dissipated as she watched him try to rein in his temper.

Charlotte's bearded new acquaintance spoke up. "This your husband, huh? Now, it's not what it looks like. Your woman here just looked all on her lonesome, needin' a spot of company. We were just happy to oblige her. No need to get worked up."

Charlotte gave an imperceptible shake of her head, letting Fawkes know that it was not how it happened.

"I told you to stay upstairs," he said, voice so low into her ear that only she could hear it. "You defied a direct order from me. We will talk about this in the room. Now go."

Charlotte slid out from her seat and scurried up the stairs. Her cheeks and ears burned. She felt like a chastised child, unable to tell her side of the story and unfairly punished. Fawkes wasn't far behind her, having smoothed over the situation downstairs. The less of an impression they made upon the local populace, the better. They couldn't afford to draw any attention, or people might remember their presence.

Charlotte waited at the door of their room for Fawkes to unlock it. She caught a glimpse of familiar black fabric as he withdrew the key from a small satchel hanging by his side, before he opened the door and pushed her in unceremoniously.

Fawkes opened his mouth to speak, but Charlotte cut him off. "I have information for you," she told him. "Everything else can wait." It certainly wasn't what he was expecting, so he remained silent and allowed her to continue. "Wherever you went tonight, whatever business you have with Earl Hawthorne, it's a trap. Duke Belaq is behind it, and they are going to capture you whenever you try to enter the earl's dungeon."

"And how did you discover this?"

"One of the men downstairs. He was bragging about being 'liaison' between the duke and the earl. He said they were going to capture you. When you disappeared tonight, I thought..." Charlotte couldn't finish her sentence.

Much of the anger disappeared off of Fawkes' face, and he turned thoughtful. "Well, then, Earl Hawthorne has lowered himself to a greater level of treachery than that which I thought him capable. Duke Belaq, yes, but Hawthorne...to condemn an innocent..." Fawkes paced around their small room. Seeing Charlotte's confused face, Fawkes seemed to remember he had an audience. He stopped pacing and sat on the bed. Charlotte stood up straighter and tried to look competent enough to be worthy of any more information he wanted to share.

Fawkes motioned for her to come closer. "What I'm about to tell you cannot be repeated, do you understand?"

Charlotte nodded.

"I met with the head of the Lindsor family tonight." Fawkes sighed as he settled in to tell his tale. "They are a wealthy family who began as traders and are now rich enough to be nobles but lack the title. They are within Earl Hawthorne's jurisdiction, but he has always looked the other way while the Lindsors conduct their business across the borders. As long as the earl receives his taxes, he does not interfere, no matter which kingdom codes are violated."

"So why did you have to go to the Lindsor estate tonight?"

"They still owed me gold," Fawkes said, "from a previous contract a few months ago. When I arrived to collect the rest of my payment, the household was in an uproar. Earl Hawthorne's men had taken the Lindsor niece two days prior. Arrested her on charges of witchcraft."

This must have really rattled him, because Charlotte had never heard Fawkes share so much of his internal dialogue at one time.

"Let me guess—the Lindsors want another contract. They want you to rescue her."

"Yes."

"And you believe she is innocent of the charges?"

"Completely. Earl Hawthorne knew exactly who to arrest if he wanted to draw me from the shadows. If what you tell me is true, then both Earl Hawthorne and Duke Belaq know where I am and are attempting to use the Lindsor family to entice me to take another contract."

Charlotte shook her head to clear her confusion. "But why would Earl Hawthorne turn on the Lindsors?"

"Threats, blackmail, bribes—it is impossible to say what lengths the duke went through to get the earl to cooperate."

Charlotte shuddered, imagining what terrors could have possibly been conveyed through the liaison that forced Hawthorne to cooperate without even meeting the duke face to face. "Was it really worth it?" she asked.

"Worth it?" Fawkes repeated.

"I mean, crossing Duke Belaq in the first place," Charlotte clarified. "Now he will stop at nothing until he captures you. Was your contract in his dungeon really worth all of this? What happened to that old man you rescued, anyway?"

He pointedly ignored the first part of her question. "He was returned to his family. They have since fled the country."

They sat in silence for a while, until Charlotte asked, "So now what do we do?"

"We?" Fawkes quirked an eyebrow. "*We* go to the border. Then I send *you* on your merry way and *I* find a new contract to take. One that will not result in my capture."

"But I helped you!" Charlotte exploded. "You would have walked right into that trap if I hadn't found out the truth." She took a deep breath. "Teach me how to be like you. I can help. Now with Duke Belaq on your tail, any contract you take might be false. He is hell-bent on your capture, and he can reach anyone across the kingdom. You need a second-in-command. That way if things go really wrong, I can get you out."

Fawkes scratched his stubble, and Charlotte could tell she was wearing him down. His chosen career was much more dangerous for him from this point onward, now that the nobles were willing to work together to catch him. "Gather your things. There are a few hours before dawn, and I hope to be far away from here by then," he said. Charlotte tried not to be disappointed by his response. It wasn't a yes, but it wasn't a no, either. Fawkes stood and began to pack.

A wave of sadness fell over Charlotte when she heard the purse on Fawkes' waist clink with the sound of coins. "Are you just going to leave the Lindsor niece to hang?"

"Cannot save everyone," Fawkes answered, his back to her. A lump formed in Charlotte's throat when she thought about how the poor girl must be feeling.

Terrified, she was sure. Her breath hitched at the unfairness of it all.

Fawkes turned around to face Charlotte, gesturing to the heavy purse. "This is the gold that was already owed to me," he said, gentler than she would have expected. "I did not take any advance payment for her."

Hoping to distract Fawkes so he wouldn't see the tears in her eyes, Charlotte focused on variables within her control. "We're not leaving down the rope, right?" she asked.

He strode over and untied the length from the bedpost. "No, we can be civilized and leave through the door." Picking up his satchel, he looked around the room one last time. "Get the supply bag."

****

It was a relief to be outside in the fresh air, away from the stink of the inn. Fawkes kept watch outside of the stable while Charlotte darted in to get Ghost ready for their journey. Off to her left, she heard Ghost's familiar snort of recognition at her scent. Finding his stall, she grabbed the bridle and the saddle from their hooks, then she clucked for him to follow. Ghost trailed after her obediently but started to trot as soon as he saw his master waiting outside.

Charlotte picked up her pace to reach them, and once Fawkes had mounted, he helped pull her up onto the massive animal. She settled in behind him, arms around his waist, and they left the village without a trace.

Chapter Five

Fawkes wanted to avoid the main roads, so they stuck to the wilderness trails and relied on his memory to take them in the right direction. They had to be doubly careful now that both Duke Belaq and Earl Hawthorne had men hunting them, but Fawkes seemed relatively unperturbed.

"When I met with the Lindsors last night, I told them that, should we agree on a contract, it would take a few days to survey the castle and figure out the best plan of approach," he explained to Charlotte. "That leaves us time to put enough distance between us and Earl Hawthorne's lands. A head start."

The trees thinned out over the miles, turning into tall grass plains, and soon Charlotte found herself wishing for the cool damp of the Cursed Forest again. It was an unseasonably warm day for fall in Algonia, and Charlotte had never been this far east before. The sun beat down on them. Rivulets of sweat dripped out of her hair, down her neck, and under her arms, soaking the now-ragged clothes she wore on the day she left her home behind.

Fawkes seemed to feel the harsh effects of the heat as well, and had dismounted a while back to walk within the small amount of shade beside the horse. Charlotte was grateful; the last thing she needed was another sweaty body increasing her temperature. With

Fawkes on the ground, at least he wasn't blocking the scant breeze.

She held up her hair. "I don't think I've ever been this hot," she complained. Fawkes just handed her the flask of water in response. "How much further today?"

"There is still plenty of daylight left."

Charlotte swallowed a bit of water. *At least you aren't dead,* she reminded herself. *And the people who want to kill you will be following soon enough. The more distance, the better.*

Fawkes suddenly halted, Ghost followed suit, and Charlotte almost tipped out of the saddle. "Stay here," he said, and pulled out his dagger.

Charlotte watched his back as he stealthily moved through the tall grasses, like a cat stalking a mouse. Looking at his graceful form, Charlotte didn't envy the mouse, or whatever it was that caught his attention.

From her vantage point on top of Ghost, she tried to see what had suddenly turned Fawkes into his Cloaked Shadow persona. *You forgot your cloak,* she wanted to yell at him, certain that he was overreacting. They hadn't seen a single soul since leaving the trading village, and they were on a little-used back road. The armies that pursued them were behind them, not ahead. Fawkes had told her that they wouldn't come across any more villages this close to the border. Years of warring in the past had turned it into a dead zone. Citizens from both countries feared that the ground was either cursed or haunted, and no one dared to live there anymore.

Fawkes shrank in the distance, and Charlotte saw he had reached a dark lump, which lay off to the side of the path. A rustle to her left caught Charlotte's attention. Ghost's ears pulled back flat against his head, and he snorted nervously. However, his four feet remained flat on the ground, as if not willing to move a muscle unless explicitly told.

"Wait," Charlotte told him, and slid off his back to investigate the noise. *It's probably a deer*, she thought. It sounded bigger than a rabbit. From the depths of the dense grasses, a blur launched itself toward Charlotte. She let out a scream and stumbled backward to avoid the animal's attack.

Except it wasn't an animal. Though covered in blood and dirt, the creature that lunged again for her was most decidedly a wiry and, despite his numerous injuries, agile man.

Ghost reared up, deadly hooves slashing the air and coming down inches from the feral stranger. Dodging the horse distracted the man just enough for Charlotte to get her bearings. She braced her stance, and when he ran for her again, she shoved her fist into his face.

A sickening crunch filled her ears as her hand collided with his nose. The added momentum of his forward attack, and his unfortunate assumption that his victim didn't know how to land a punch, knocked him out cold. He fell straight backward onto the ground with a thud.

At the same time, Charlotte let out a howl, cradling a hand that felt like it was on fire. Her vision tunneled from the pain, and her legs nearly gave out while she held onto consciousness. Charlotte was so focused on her own agony that she barely heard the shouts from up the road. Raising watery eyes, she saw Fawkes sprinting toward them.

Charlotte swore she saw relief replace terror on his

face as he immediately analyzed the situation. He was over to her side in a flash, gently prying her injured hand from where she cradled it against her chest. With a feather light touch, he examined it thoroughly. Still, Charlotte couldn't help the wincing at the contact. "Bruised," he pronounced.

"Not broken?" she gasped.

"No. Though I'm surprised, considering our friend's condition, here." He kicked the man in disgust.

Charlotte regained her breath. "Who is he?" she managed to ask.

"Highway robber, I would wager. There is an overturned carriage up the road. All the travelers are dead, but they put up a good fight. A good number of robbers are lying next to them. If I had had any idea there were more, I would not have left you here..." He looked at her, frowning, regret written on his face.

"I handled it." She managed to stand up straight to face Fawkes. "Maybe next time, you should just take me with you."

"Next time?" He almost cracked a smile at her, but then busied himself with the body on the ground. "He still breathes," he observed, "but we cannot leave any witnesses behind."

"I thought you didn't kill people?"

"I don't kill people when it isn't necessary. This is necessary."

Charlotte didn't argue with him. She knew it would have been stupid to leave the man alive. After all, he attacked her and would have stolen Ghost. His desperation and injuries made for a deadly combination, and she was lucky to have escaped without a scratch, minus a swollen hand. It could have been so much worse, a possibility Fawkes must have recognized, considering how fast he ran back to her.

"Take Ghost up the road. I will follow behind in a moment," Fawkes told her.

Charlotte and Ghost were almost to the carriage crash site when Fawkes appeared beside her. She noticed the blood on his hands and his tunic but said nothing more about it. She wondered how many men he had killed, and if this one was just another number to add to his count. Did he remember everyone he killed? Was that why he only did it when it was necessary? Charlotte wondered if Fawkes had cut the man's throat, and if the robber had woken up once he felt the cool blade of the dagger on his skin. Did Fawkes look him in the eyes as he killed him? She gave an involuntary shudder and decided maybe she didn't want answers to her questions after all.

Still, she couldn't squelch her morbid curiosity as she walked by the splintered carriage and examined the disaster. Bodies littered the site, the differences between the robbers and the wealthy riders immediately apparent. The robbers were skin and bones, their clothes in tatters, hanging off of their filthy bodies. The finery of the wealthy victims was a stark contrast, each vest or shoe or corset worth more than a month's worth of food for the robbers.

A lump formed in Charlotte's throat. *What a waste,* she thought, *so much needless death.*

Fawkes strode over to one of the bodies. He began to strip the modest but clean apparel off a slender young man. He wasn't a wealthy member of the family, nor was he a dirty robber. *The driver, or servant perhaps?* Charlotte wondered. Whoever he was, he at least deserved some dignity in death. "Stop! Why are you doing that?"

Fawkes ignored her, taking the britches off the boy, followed by his tunic. "You need clothes. This boy no longer does."

"Well—you can't just—" Charlotte tried to come up with an excuse and failed. She couldn't voice how much she did *not* want to wear a dead man's clothes. Fawkes would scoff at her if she said it made her squeamish. The words he had said to her still rang in her ears—*You could not endure my world.* This was the reality of his world, and she needed to face it.

His next words, though, made her forget all about the origin of her new outfit. "You can't very well train in that dress, can you?" He said it so casually that Charlotte had to clarify.

"You'll train me?" she asked, stunned.

"We will see how you do in the coming days. If we get to the border and I am not convinced of your skills, then we will part ways." He paused, as if hesitating to continue his thoughts. "You have good instincts," he told her. "And courage."

At his words, Charlotte's heart swelled with pride. She couldn't keep the grin off of her face when she asked, "When do we start?"

"Tomorrow. The swelling in your hand needs to go down, and we need to put more distance between us and the highway robbery. This road is no longer secure."

"What's our new course?"

"Around the valley, instead of through it. It will add additional time to our journey, but I do not want any more surprises."

An extra few days? Darn, Charlotte thought with a grin. Her good mood almost made up for the fact that her injured hand emitted its own heat source. The throbbing, swollen limb pulsed in time with her own heartbeat, but at that moment, the punch was completely worth it.

****

After Fawkes redirected them onto a new trajectory, they finally came across a shallow stream, just as afternoon turned into evening. "That's far enough. We will camp here for the night."

Charlotte went to the stream in a flash, plunging her hands into the cool water and splashing her face. The sweat from her skin tingled on her lips as she licked the salt off. She resisted the urge to walk all the way in and submerge herself under the surface.

Fawkes, understanding the desperation in her actions, reached into a saddlebag and threw the new clothes at her. "Bathe and change," he instructed. "I will hunt for dinner." He headed upstream and out of sight.

Charlotte waited a few minutes until she was sure Fawkes wasn't going to return, and stripped out of her dress. A pang of regret hit her as she watched the last reminder of her old life crumple to the ground. A sensation of absolute bliss replaced that feeling as she entered the water. A groan escaped her lips as the water lapped up her sore feet and calves. She waded in until the water touched the top of her thighs, at the deepest point of the creek.

She took a deep breath, crouched down, and felt the water envelop her completely. Bubbles streamed from her mouth and nose, but Charlotte stayed under for as long as her burning lungs would allow. When she finally broke the surface, clean for the first time since leaving her home, she felt as though her soul had been scrubbed as well as her body. The old Charlotte, along with her past and sadness, washed away downstream. She lingered a few moments longer, relaxing in the current, thinking about Fawkes and the circumstances that brought her to this exact moment in time. Her new life might not have been what she expected, but she embraced it now. She had been given a second chance.

Charlotte stood up and made her way to the bank. Still dripping as she put on the dry clothes, she gave silent thanks that they didn't have any blood on them from the previous owner. Fawkes had been very careful not to soil them.

After tending to Ghost and setting up the rest of their camp, Charlotte was just beginning to wonder where Fawkes had disappeared to when he popped out in front of her.

Charlotte yelped. "How do you do that?"

"Do what?" He innocently held out two fish.

"Sneak up on people like that. Move without any noise."

"Practice."

"Will you teach me?"

"That comes later." Fawkes chopped the heads off of their dinner. "No fire tonight," he said. "We are too exposed." He tossed the fish to Charlotte. "Finish gutting these; we can eat them raw. I'm going for a wash."

Charlotte realized that he was just as sweaty and uncomfortable as she had been but had pushed it aside to make sure she didn't need to eat jerky again for dinner. "Thank you," she said, as he walked downstream.

He kept his pace, so she didn't think he heard her, until he said, "The britches suit you better than the dress ever did."

The next morning, Charlotte awoke to a repetitive, grinding sound. The scraping of rocks on rocks was incessant, and she sat up in irritation. Her swollen hand kept her awake long after she had gone to bed, and now the sun had not even crested the horizon, yet she was being forced from her slumber.

"What are you doing?" She suppressed a yawn to keep her tone sharp.

"Come here," Fawkes said. He sat wrapped up in his cloak, the wetness on his boots testified that he had been up and about in the pre-dawn morning for some time. In between his legs sat a flat stone, and on it was a kind of greenish sludge. Fawkes worked the material back and forth with a stream-rounded stone, grinding it to a smooth paste.

She made her way over to him, wiping sleep out of her eyes and shivering in the gray chill. Parts of her old dress, now torn into strips, lay beside him. The fabric was damp, as though it had been recently washed.

Fawkes used his fingers to scoop the poultice onto one of the strips, spreading it out evenly. "Hold out your hand." She felt immediate bliss as the cold compress wrapped around her skin and a groan escaped her lips. Working quickly, Fawkes bound the injury from her second knuckles down to her wrist, rendering it immobile as he secured the trailing edge of the bandage.

"Better?" he asked.

"You couldn't have done that last night?"

"I stumbled upon the materials this morning. Usually crestwood refuses grow this far east."

Reprieved from pain, Charlotte didn't question him further. Obviously, he knew what he was doing, but Fawkes' extensive knowledge of medicinal plants surprised her. She sniffed at the bandage. Charlotte had used crestwood in the past, but she had a suspicion that it wasn't just crestwood in the poultice. There was something else added to the mix, but Fawkes wasn't willing to let her in on the secret.

Interrupting her thoughts, Fawkes said, "Go find us something to eat."

Charlotte's eyebrows shot up. "But I've never hunted before. Or fished." She held up her wrapped hand. "Plus, I've only got one good arm."

"You said you wanted me to train you. Be my apprentice. Well, here is the first lesson. Go catch us some breakfast." He tossed his dagger at her feet. "Gut and scale them before you come back."

She bent down to pick up the deadly blade, the same blade that had killed a man just the day before. Wondering if that even bothered him, she shoved the dagger into her belt and headed upstream.

The icy water had felt so refreshing the day before, but now it felt like needles pricking her tender skin. Maneuvering slowly so she wouldn't scare her potential prey, she waded in up to her knees. At first, she couldn't see anything. The sun had just started to peek over the horizon, casting shadows and sending shimmering sparkles across the water.

Frustrated, she turned her back to the light and stared down at the bottom of the stream. *There's nothing here*, she thought. Just as she was about to search for more promising territory, she caught a flash of movement out of the corner of her eye. The small fish camouflaged in with the rocks below, their movements matching the graceful ripple of the current.

Charlotte lowered her uninjured hand down to the surface of the water before pausing. Crouching, she waited until one of the bigger fish drifted directly underneath her ready palm. "Got you!" she exclaimed, her triumph creating a massive splash that soaked her pants up to her rear. Her excitement disappeared when she came up empty handed. "Bugger."

Again she waited, muscles tensed to spring. Waiting for the right moment tried her patience, and she came up short when another opportunity presented itself. *I'm just too slow*, she thought, discouraged. Again and again she missed, until her body was soaking wet and her teeth were chattering.

In her final attempt, she reached down to grab the biggest fish she had seen yet, only to have Fawkes' hand hold her wrist steady. "Watch," he told her. Somehow he had managed to sneak up behind her from the bank without her noticing. Charlotte winced. Obliviousness was not a good way to start an apprenticeship.

With his other hand, Fawkes dangled his fingers lazily through the water, looking like delicious bait. Curious fish nibbled on the tips, but still he waited to make his move. It wasn't until the largest fish was within his grasp did he strike.

The flapping fish was hauled out of the water, spraying the pair and trying in vain to wiggle free. Fawkes held onto the tail, gaze boring into Charlotte's with a look of nonchalance. *Wonderful,* she thought. *At least we get to eat.*

Fawkes bent down, and with a gentle motion that gave no reminder of his initial yank, set the fish free. At her disbelieving stare, he raised an eyebrow. "You took too long. No time to prepare it."

When they got back to Ghost, Fawkes reached into the saddlebag and pulled out two pieces of jerky. He tossed her one, and bit into the other. "There are many miles to walk today. We are already late."

As they set into their familiar patterns of travel, Fawkes finally spoke. "What did you learn?"

At least it wasn't a lecture on how she was a total failure. The grumbling of her stomach was enough of a reminder for Charlotte. "That I'm slow? I lack patience?"

"Do not guess, think about it."

Charlotte took a moment to compare all of her attempts with Fawkes' singular success. He pushed her to analyze, and go deeper. "I need to draw them in, not just wait for them to move," she said. He grunted in approval, so she continued. "I have to wait for the biggest fish, and not worry about the small ones. I need to wait until the perfect moment to strike, because once it's gone, it wastes too much time to orchestrate another attack."

"Good."

Her cheeks reddened with pleasure. "But the most important part," Fawkes said, "is that the water can affect your vision. It distorts from the surface and makes underneath unclear, so when you think you are grabbing the fish, you have already missed it. Remember, you are an intruder in your prey's environment. You have to play by his rules."

"Until you get the fish to the surface," Charlotte pointed out.

"And he's gasping for breath," Fawkes agreed. "When you hold his fate in your hands."

They continued their journey parallel to the stream, following as it meandered. "Fill up all the bladders," Fawkes told Charlotte when they had stopped for the night. "Tomorrow we break from the stream and arc wide around the valley."

"Do you think the duke's men are still looking for us?" Charlotte asked.

"They will have realized by now that I do not intend to rescue the Lindsor niece from Earl Hawthorne's dungeons. I expect they are gearing up for pursuit, dawn at the earliest. They can travel lighter and more quickly and have many men to spread out their search. We need to reach the border soon."

Adrenaline rushed into Charlotte's small frame, chasing away exhaustion from the day's travel. "If we are to come across any of the duke's men, a few more training lessons wouldn't hurt," she suggested, ducking her head to hide a smile.

"Show me you have learned something from this morning, and I will consider it," Fawkes told her, after a long and thoughtful pause. He turned to care for Ghost while Charlotte eagerly kicked off her shoes and jumped into the water. *Calm and slow,* she reminded herself. *Follow his rules.*

It only took three tries this time, and with a cry of triumph, she flipped the first fish up onto the bank. Fawkes, having approached to observe her, quickly thumped the flapping creature over the head and got to work with his dagger. Two more tries and Charlotte tossed her own dinner up to him. She thought she caught a glimpse of pride in his gaze as he watched her, but his attention was diverted by the task at hand.

Splashing her way to the bank, Charlotte didn't even feel the cold water as it soaked through her clothes. She realized her bandage had come off at some point during her excursion, and flexed her hand experimentally.

"Why, it doesn't hurt anymore!" she told Fawkes. Throughout the day, the throbbing had ceased, but she had chalked it up to a numbing component in Fawkes' poultice. She had never expected that the medicine would have worked so completely, mending an injury that should have taken weeks to heal in only twelve hours. There was still some faint discoloration molting the skin, but her fingers moved with easy dexterity.

Charlotte held out her hand for him to examine. Fawkes took her smaller hand in between his large, calloused ones and lightly traced each finger. The touch sent shivers up Charlotte's spine, and she thought he held onto her for a beat longer than necessary. Then, as if realizing what he had done, he dropped it like a hot poker, declaring her healed.

Seeming like he needed an immediate distraction from their uncomfortable closeness, Fawkes said, "You learn quickly. It might actually be within my power to teach you a few techniques to use in case we run into trouble."

"I'm ready to start right now," Charlotte said, jutting her chin out in what she hoped was a confident gesture toward her mentor. Internally, her stomach was doing flips. She was both nervous and excited at the prospect of learning real material. Not that catching fish didn't have its uses, but it wasn't as helpful as, say, throwing a punch without almost breaking her hand. Wet and tired, she pushed all discomfort aside and planted her feet in front of Fawkes.

All of the walking and riding during the past few weeks had honed her muscles enough for her to feel a marked difference in her body. Years of scullery cleaning duties had resulted in an upper body that was stronger than the typical woman, defying the definition of what was deemed 'attractive' in society. Charlotte had accepted long ago that she would never possess the soft, supple curves and delicate ivory skin of the noble women. It used to bother her to see how the boys she fancied lusted after these shining examples of demure femininity, until she realized she would rather be able to hold her own and defend herself. Though she had a petite frame, she could put up enough of a fight to be too much trouble for an attacker, who would move on to easier prey.

Physical strength had also carried over to create a strong mind. Charlotte was willful, determined, and knew how to push past bodily discomfort. But in order to rival Fawkes' skills, she knew there would be a great deal of training to come. Now that her hand was healed, there was nothing to hold her back.

Still, she did not expect the blow that crashed into her stomach, knocking the air out of her lungs. Gasping for breath, she tried not to vomit, and came up flailing with a punch of her own, which Fawkes easily deflected. Angered, she launched into an erratic series of punches and kicks, all of which he dodged.

"You have the fire," he said, "but before you can

channel it, you need to learn to wait for your opening. I am stronger and faster, but you can use your size to your advantage. Refuse to make it easy for me to get to you. You lack the body mass to match me punch for punch. Become a small target. Let your attacker tire himself out, then use his moves against him. This will keep you alive."

During Fawkes' speech Charlotte's ineffective blows had slowed considerably, until she had to stop, arm and core muscles burning from the workout. Wiping the sweat from her brow, she glared at Fawkes, who wasn't even winded. He remained completely unperturbed by her furious physical exertions.

"Gather your breath, and we will go again."

No matter how hard Charlotte tried to find her opening, Fawkes always knew a split second ahead of time where her ineffectual fists would try to land. "Your face betrays you," he said. "Put a wall up between it and your emotions. Remain a mask."

Her heart pounded in her chest, beating against gasping lungs. Her arms dropped to her sides, and she said, "Enough. I can't do anymore."

"You wanted this," he reminded her, stepping closer. He forced her chin up to look at him, before grabbing both her shoulders. "But this does not have to be the life for you—" He was cut off when Charlotte rammed a punch into his side.

"How's that for masking my emotions?" she asked.

Hot anger flashed in his eyes before the emotional barrier slammed down between them. Fawkes refused to let her see his thoughts. He ignored her question, and said, "Seeing as you still have more than enough energy left, you can do some muscle exercises until sundown."

He backed away from Charlotte and dropped down to the ground, balancing on his hands and toes. With his shoulders centered directly above his wrists, Fawkes bent his elbows until his chest touched the dirt, and then straightened back up.

After pausing a moment in the 'up' position, he stood up, brushing his hands on his pants. "Your turn. Keep going until I tell you to stop."

If Fawkes thought that she would back away from the challenge, he had underestimated Charlotte's hatred of failure. She nodded at her mentor and started the exercise. The dip in her elbows grew shallower with each repetition, until her entire body shook with effort. Sweat beaded and dripped into her eyes, the stinging doing little to distract from her screaming muscles. The punches had worn her out more than she wanted to let on, but she was still determined not to concede.

"How much longer will you go?" Fawkes goaded her.

"Have you ordered me to stop?" she grunted, red-faced.

"You can quit at any time."

She didn't have the breath to answer him, and instead bent her arms a fraction of an inch. The movement was too much, and her arms buckled and gave out, and she greeted the dirt with her face.

Fawkes sighed. "Stop."

Gritting her teeth and maneuvering her hands back underneath her chest, Charlotte ignored him and gathered all of her remaining strength. So slowly it was almost imperceptible, she began to push back up. When her arms locked out straight, she held the position for a beat more, just to prove that she could. Only then did she step her feet underneath her and rise to face Fawkes. "Now I'll stop," she said, "until tomorrow."

Charlotte meandered off downstream, and once she was out of sight of the camp, collapsed in agony. She lay spread-eagle on the bank, wondering if she would ever be able to use her arms again. Closing her eyes for just a moment, Charlotte rested.

When she awoke the next morning, she discovered that somehow she was back at the camp, tucked into her bedroll. The last thing she remembered was lying down and… *Wonderful,* she thought. *Just as I try to prove to Fawkes how tough I can be, I go and fall asleep, and have to be carried to bed like a child.* Now he would know how much the training had exhausted her. She felt she had taken a giant step backward in gaining his respect.

Rolling over, she spotted the familiar black lump that was Fawkes wrapped in his cloak. It was so early that the man still slumbered, the steady rise and fall of the dark material indicating that he was resting peacefully.

She couldn't recall ever seeing him so vulnerable. Calm and quiet, yes, but always alert, muscles tensed like a cat. Watching him sleep, curled up tightly in the fetal position, gave Charlotte a glimpse of the man he hid from the world. This figure couldn't put up walls or present the persona of the Cloaked Shadow. *Is this the real Fawkes?* she wondered. *What does he dream about? A life before this one, maybe?*

His back was to her as she pondered him, and she saw his shoulders tense. *He can sense I'm staring!* she thought, panicked. Her head dropped back down, and she tried to feign sleep.

"And what, may I ask, is so very interesting about watching me sleep?" Fawkes' low voice traveled over to her. His question rumbled through the ground, and Charlotte could feel vibrations on her cheek. Instead of answering him, she let her mouth drop open slightly.

"That will not work on me, Charlotte. I know you are awake. Get up and go tend to Ghost."

Her eyes popped open. "How can you tell?" she asked, genuinely curious. She was alert, having slept more soundly than she had in weeks. Though her body protested every movement and her soreness begged for her to keep still, the exercise had done her mind wonders. It was at least an hour before dawn, but she felt as spirited as if it were midday.

"You were not drooling like you usually do."

Charlotte slapped a hand to her mouth and furiously wiped. "I don't drool!"

"I am pleased you woke up early today. We have a lot of ground to cover. Hurry and prepare. Am I right in assuming you want to walk instead of ride first?" Fawkes cocked an eyebrow at her.

The thought of getting up in the saddle made Charlotte wince. "I'll walk," she said.

He chuckled, revealing a much better mood than he was in last night. "This part of the journey will be difficult, as we must trek along the mountain pass instead of through the valley. The elevation will slow us considerably, but we cannot risk being trapped by Duke Belaq on the main road."

Charlotte gulped. Heights. Not her favorite thing. "Will we be able to see our enemy from the mountain road?" she asked, trying to distract herself.

"I might be able to get a good location on the

scouts if they have traveled more quickly than anticipated, but I predict that they are still a day or two behind us. However, due to our extended route, they may have traveled too close for my comfort and might already be on the valley road. Regardless, our course should only take another three days."

The memory of Duke Belaq's cold, calculating stare flashed in Charlotte's mind. "What makes you think the duke will just give up hunting us if we cross into Croantis? I hardly think breaching diplomacy will matter much to him." Duke Belaq was a savage hound on a blood trail. He would not give up until he had Fawkes in his jaws.

"The duke does not dare pursue over the border because he knows he would be outnumbered," Fawkes answered her, as they started on the trail. Charlotte wondered if it was just her imagination, or if the ground was already starting to slope upward. The crest of the mountain still looked impossibly far away. *Three days?* She groaned internally. At a leisurely, realistic pace, the journey would take a week at least. How she was supposed to cover all those miles and still have energy to train at the end of the day? Logically, she knew it had to be done in order for the two of them to safely escape. Emotionally, however, she felt that maybe Fawkes was doing it on purpose in light of last night's session.

As if reading her thoughts, Fawkes spoke again. "How are you feeling today?"

"Achy," she confessed. *And not ready to climb a mountain,* she refrained from saying.

Their footsteps trudged in synchronicity. "To maintain the edge over your enemy, you must be willing to sacrifice everything in pursuit of your mission, including physical comfort. I believe Duke Belaq has this passion, but his men do not. This is why he still trails behind, instead of on top of us. His knights hold him back, but he knows that he cannot defeat me alone, otherwise he would have left them behind. I imagine this causes him great frustration." Charlotte's mouth turned up into a small smile at the thought of a vexed duke, but it quickly disappeared when her next thought was how he might relieve his frustration on her and Fawkes, and she was very glad of the distance between them now.

"This single-minded ferocity is rare, and only those people who can push all other thoughts out of their minds except completing their goal will triumph," Fawkes continued. His steps never faltered, his pace never slowed. Placing one foot in front of the other, he kept his gaze on the horizon as he spoke. Charlotte mimicked his actions, focusing on leveling her pace in spite of her soreness. She realized that this was her training lesson for the day, and she embraced it wholly.

"I can do it," she told Fawkes.

He gave what sounded like a snort of disbelief. "And just what will happen when we reach the top of the pass?" So her mentor hadn't forgotten Charlotte's fear of heights. Her face burned with embarrassment when he summed up her last experience.

"Clutching that rope…you had done admirably in releasing your brother, yet you were willing to fail your mission because you became lost in your fear. Do you think your brother would have abandoned you? No, he would have stayed and tried to help you, only succeeding in getting both of you caught and executed.

You were willing to send both yourself and your brother to death, all because you refused to slide down the rope. You do not possess the mental strength, even if I can teach you to fight hard enough to stay alive."

Bile rose in Charlotte's throat, cutting off a biting response to his accusations. He didn't know her, not truly, and he severely underestimated what she was capable of. Her fists shook in anger as she tried to think of the right words to say to Fawkes that would shame him.

One foot in front of the other. She forced herself to breathe. Had he really said all of that to break her down? Was it a way to test her? To find out how far she was willing to push herself? Charlotte risked a glance in his direction. His face remained neutral, as though he had just finished talking about the weather, unaware of how his statements crushed her.

As much as Charlotte wanted to deny it, there was truth in his words. She would have been caught that night if it hadn't been for Fawkes. She would not have made it down the tower, and all would have been lost. But to have her deepest fears and flaws thrown into her face so casually wounded her pride. They had been having such a pleasant morning, even bantering back and forth a bit before heading out. *How can Fawkes be so nice to me one minute, and then switch into a brutally blunt arse the next?*

A burst of understanding hit her. *Because right now you're talking to the Cloaked Shadow, not to Fawkes*, a voice in her head piped up. Charlotte thought back to her previous training sessions, and realized that the switch had happened then, too. She wondered if Fawkes even realized who he channeled when showing her techniques and lecturing her, or if the transformation was subconscious and automatic. The line in her mind that separated Fawkes and the Cloaked Shadow had blurred over their journey together, and she had starting thinking of them as the same person. Their recent interaction, however, reminded her of the stark distinctions in her mentor's personalities.

You're mad at the Cloaked Shadow, not Fawkes, Charlotte told herself. The mentor instead of the man. But it didn't help that both sides were able to stare into the depths of her soul with piercing blue eyes that demanded the truth. She couldn't hide anything from them.

Charlotte resolved to prove the Cloaked Shadow wrong when the time came. For now, the miles stretched out in front of them.

****

"Your turn to ride Ghost," Fawkes reminded her once the sun hit midday. He had just dismounted from the sweating steed.

Looks like the Cloaked Shadow has turned back into Fawkes, Charlotte noticed. She wouldn't give into his courteous offer, though. Her pride still stung from his earlier remarks. "I'll walk," she told him. He let the matter drop, and they didn't speak again until stopping for the night.

Charlotte sat down on a small boulder and peeled off her shoes, hissing in pain. Calluses that had slowly formed during the days on the road had been ripped off in one afternoon due to her impetuous march. Her feet were raw and bloody, but she felt like she had restored some of her dignity. Fawkes said nothing about her injuries, and she refused to bring attention to them.

The climb had deposited the weary travelers above the foothills to rest for the evening. Fawkes seemed pleased with their progress, going so far as to pull a special treat from his bag for their dinner. "Apple?" he asked, before taking a bite out of the juicy fruit, and tossing the rest to Charlotte.

Sweetness exploded in Charlotte's mouth, chasing away her negativity. Happily, she took another bite. "Where did you get this?" she asked, through a dribbling mouthful.

"I took it from outside the inn. Been waiting for the right time to eat it."

Companionably, they passed the fruit back and forth until only the stem was left. Charlotte decided it was an acceptable peace offering, and finally asked the question she had been mulling over all day. "What did you mean when you said that the duke would be outnumbered if he crossed the border?"

Fawkes' eyebrows narrowed thoughtfully. "Do you know what has been happening in the kingdom these past few years?"

Charlotte nodded. "King Otan is paranoid that there will be an uprising. That the Great War will happen all over again and destroy everything."

"Yes," Fawkes said. "But the uprising is already happening. There is already a war going on."

Charlotte scoffed. "The country would know if we were at war!"

"The rebels have organized, striking out with small attacks throughout the kingdom. The king can't fight an enemy that disappears before the smoke clears, nor can he declare all-out war without causing mass panic. The war is being fought underground right now."

"Are…are you one of the rebels?" Charlotte asked, feeling stupid. *Of course he is,* she thought, *why else would he break people out of prison?*

His eyes hardened. "I care not for any ideology or political side. I get paid for my services. Nothing more. And I do not ask questions."

"But you work for them, mostly," she pressed.

"In recent years, yes. They seem to find themselves imprisoned quite frequently. Their gold is good, so—" Fawkes shrugged.

"You don't care what they're doing?" Charlotte asked, incredulous. "After the death toll and the famine that the Great War caused, and these people want to start it up all over again!" Another thought dawned on her. "The rebels have made the king and the duke so paranoid that they've begun arresting innocent people. They are the reason that *Henry* almost died for no reason!"

"Citizens have been falsely accused and imprisoned within the kingdom for centuries. This is nothing new. Just because it was not happening right in front of your face does not mean it hasn't been going on in the shadows." Fawkes almost looked disappointed, as though he expected more analysis and critical thinking from her. "Open your eyes, girl. There is never peace. We will never have true peace. We can only take moments of serenity as they come and do what is best for ourselves."

"You don't really believe that, do you?" Charlotte snapped. "If you did, I wouldn't be standing here. What was best for you was to abandon me the soonest chance you got."

"Best does not always mean logical," Fawkes

murmured.

Chapter Six

Little droplets pattered onto Charlotte's face like tiny kisses, cool and refreshing on her weathered skin. Her tongue reached out to lick her lips while her mind tried to hold onto a deep sleep. As she snuggled into her bedroll, snippets of an argument from the night before drifted to the forefront of her consciousness. Her frustration with her mentor never seemed to cease, and she suspected he felt the same way about her.

The memory of her last words to Fawkes crystallized, and she sat up in horror. Her frantic gaze swept the camp, but she caught no sight of Fawkes or Ghost. It appeared he had taken her words to heart, and Charlotte's own sank. All trace of him was gone, save for the bedroll that Charlotte occupied. *He left me nothing,* she realized. *No food or water.*

As she was cursing herself for not waiting until *after* Fawkes got her safely over the border before pissing him off, she heard the familiar sound of Ghost's upbeat trot. Rider and animal emerged from around a stone outcropping farther up the trail, and Charlotte choked back a sob.

Fawkes dismounted and said, "Roll up your bedding and load it. The storm is closer than I thought—" He was cut off as Charlotte jumped up and flung her arms around him.

"You didn't leave me!"

He staggered under the unexpected affection. "I packed Ghost up early to avoid the rain. I rode him up to observe the storm…" He trailed off, bewilderment in his tone. "You were tired, so I let you sleep. You assumed I left?"

Charlotte nodded, her head pressed against the folds of his cloak. Fawkes patted her shoulder awkwardly. She sighed and let go. "Quickly," he said. "We need to crest the mountain pass today. The downward slope is easy to traverse. We could be in Croantis by nightfall."

As if feeling the same sense of urgency, the rain started to fall frantically as the trio headed up the trail. The sky rolled like the sea, shades of gray shifting and crashing against each other with every gust of wind. The dirt under their feet disintegrated into slick mud. Ghost dug his hooves into the thick paste, but each step he took ended with a slide backward. Their progress seemed glacial to Charlotte, but it was impossible to tell the time of day while the sun stayed hidden behind thunderous clouds. Charlotte guessed she had been pushing upward for hours, but time felt like it stood still. She tried not to think about the increasing steepness of the trail and kept on the inside between Ghost and the stone wall the mountain provided.

However, morbid curiosity finally compelled her to peek over her shoulder to see how far they had climbed. Ghost continued his plod behind Fawkes, leaving Charlotte rooted in place as she took in a view that made her stomach flip. As the comforting bulk of the horse deserted her, an unobstructed view of the valley stretched out below her. All thoughts of proving Fawkes wrong about her phobia flew right out of her head. In fact, the very ability to form actual thoughts deserted her at that moment.

She didn't notice that Fawkes had doubled back until he was standing in front of her, slapping her cheek. "Charlotte! Look at me."

She tore her gaze away from the tiny blue river snaking through the valley and latched onto the blue eyes of her mentor. Her throat closed and her tongue dried up, rendering her unable to speak.

"It is not safe to stop here." Fawkes' voice was miles away as it struggled to reach her ears. He gripped Charlotte's arm with both of his hands, as if to tow her paralyzed body back to Ghost.

At her first step, Charlotte felt the earth drop out from underneath her feet as blood rushed to her head. Her senses betrayed her as the vertigo took hold. Her vision clouded, confused as to why her feet remained planted while the path had slanted vertically. Overwhelmed, she slid down to sit in the mud, and started screaming. "I can't! I can't! Make it stop!"

"Stand *up*," Fawkes ordered her, any patience for her condition washing away the longer he stood immobile in the pouring rain.

Charlotte remained on the ground and squeezed her eyes shut, trying to right her equilibrium in a world flipped upside down. *Nothing is working,* she thought. *I'm going to die up here.*

Strong hands grabbed her underneath her armpits and hoisted her upward. Next, she felt soft, velvety fur before entangling her fingers in a long mane. With a death-grip secure around Ghost, Charlotte felt his muscles twitch with the added weight, and he snorted his displeasure.

Each slide of Ghost's hooves sent a jolt through his unwilling passenger. Charlotte was certain he was going to send them both careening off the mountain, but in her current state, there was nothing she could do about it. Her nerves screamed at her to run, to get off the mountain, to get away from the certain death that awaited her just a few lengths to her right. Charlotte remained trapped in her own personal hell, and the only way out was through.

At least with her last height-induced panic attack, the ride down the rope put her onto flat ground within a few moments. The journey now was not close to completion, and she had to sit astride the horse, humiliated as the animal showed more courage than she possessed, for many hours more. Charlotte could not bear to lift her head, so she only surmised what Fawkes was thinking about her.

Finally, Charlotte couldn't bear it anymore and said, with eyes still closed, "Fawkes?"

He remained silent, letting her stew in her doubt and misery for a while, before speaking. "We crested the top. We have been descending for a while now."

Relief flooded through Charlotte, but the tone of his answer stopped her from asking anything more. He seemed, what? Resigned? That felt infinitely worse than disappointment, or even anger. She mulled over his words and switched her focus to Ghost. *How could I have missed the obvious changes in slope and elevation?* Her internal voice answered for her. *Because you were too worried about yourself.*

In failing to overcome her fear, she had endangered not only herself, but Ghost and, most importantly, Fawkes as well. The mission. She had almost cost them the mission.

****

Charlotte rode face-down on Ghost until the weary, muddy travelers reached the foothills on the other side. She slid off without looking at either of them, and Fawkes said nothing to her. *Thank you for saving me. Again. For getting me off the mountain, and not abandoning me.* The apology remained lodged in her throat.

Ashamed, she risked a glance over to Fawkes. The light was fading fast, but she could still see him. Barely. His usually-magnificent cloak was covered in mud, enabling him to blend in perfectly with their surroundings. Charlotte was so used to his silence that she jumped when Fawkes finally spoke. "Come. I know where we can find shelter."

"Are we across the border?"

"Not yet. But Ghost cannot go much further this night."

Charlotte laid a gentle hand on the horse's trembling flank. "I'm sorry," she whispered to the animal. Fawkes opened one of the saddle bags and pulled out their foodstuffs, slinging the sack across his back, lightening Ghost's load. As tired as she was, Charlotte followed suit and loaded her arms with as many supplies as she could carry. She hoped it would be enough to make it up to the horse, while vowing to take extra good care of him once they were somewhere safe and dry.

Instead of leading them toward the border crossing, which should have been a half day's journey straight ahead from the mountains, Fawkes turned left. Hugging the curve of the mountain, he seemed to be looking intently for something hidden within the rocky crags. There was no marked path, but Fawkes' agitation hinted that they were getting close.

Darkness was already upon them when he finally halted. Charlotte wondered if he was lost, as there was no sign of a village or cottage anywhere. *We should have tried to reach the border tonight,* she thought grumpily. It would have been idiotic to risk the road at night, in the rain, while they were being hunted like animals, but at least they would be closer to their destination. She did not relish the thought of spending the night exposed and soaking wet.

Fawkes crept toward a large crack in the mountain, a gaping maw that looked like it would swallow him whole. Cupping his hands around his mouth and leaning into the pitch black, he said, "Desmund." Just once.

After a few moments, during which Charlotte seriously questioned her mentor's sanity, a warm glow spread from the gash in the mountain, growing brighter and brighter. A lit torch clutched by a withered hand shot out from a hiding place within the rocks. The orange light bathed Fawkes' face as his usually serious face broke out into a grin.

"Are you trying to frighten a man to death?" a reedy voice grumbled.

"I expected you to be long-dead already, old man," Fawkes said.

Charlotte couldn't tear her eyes away from Fawkes' face. He looked ten years younger and even boyishly charming. She was shocked even further when he reached out and pulled the white-haired man from the shadows to embrace him.

The ancient figure pulled back first to hold Fawkes by his shoulders, examining him. "Aren't here because you've gotten yourself into another spot of trouble, have ye?"

"Do you always regard your visitors with such suspicion?"

"When it is you, always."

Charlotte couldn't help but laugh at the old man's brazenness. The torch turned her direction, and suddenly she stood in the spotlight. "And you haven't come alone," Desmund said. He appraised her with dark, clear eyes.

"I'm Charlotte. His apprentice," she added bravely. It heartened her that Fawkes did not immediately contradict her statement.

"You are a young'n, aren't ye? Come. All three of you, inside. This weather'll be the death of me."

She feared that Ghost wouldn't fit, but when Fawkes removed the saddlebags, the horse was able to squeeze through with minimal prodding. Charlotte followed last in the line as Desmund led them through a short, winding passageway and into a cozy cave within.

Fire crackled merrily in a hearth built into the mountain. A small table, barely big enough for two, sat in front of it. In the recesses near the back of the cave, Charlotte could make out what looked like a bed. Satisfied with the basics, she was soon distracted by what filled up the rest of the cave.

Books. Piles and piles of books. Thick ones, thin ones, some that looked to be her own height. They teetered, precariously stacked, filling every possible space with no rhyme or reason that Charlotte could discern.

Desmund scurried around, clearing a path while he mumbled to himself. Fawkes walked Ghost through to the back of the cave and began tending to him. Transfixed by leather-bound spines, Charlotte reached out to touch one, and knocked over the tower with a crash that echoed through the cave.

"Sorry! Sorry!" she stammered, and started stacking them again. Desmund tottered over and touched her shoulder.

"No need to fret, child. You must have quite the interest in *The Magick of Herbs* to feel such a strong pull to it. Have you studied it yet?"

Charlotte's cheeks burned, and not because she was finally starting to warm up. "I don't know how to read," she whispered.

He pursed his lips. "Well now, isn't that a shame."

Fawkes wove his way around the books to interrupt their conversation. "Thank you, again, for your hospitality, Desmund."

"I didn't have a choice, did I?" The old man snorted. "Appear at my door for the first time in two years, with this poor girl in tow. She's the only reason I let you in, I'll have you know."

Charlotte turned her attention back to the rest of the books while they bantered. The two men obviously had a history together, but she could only guess how they were connected, because they couldn't be more opposite. Fawkes roamed the world, free, reckless, and strong. Desmund appeared to live most of his life in a makeshift cave, alone, reading books. Was he hiding from someone? Or was he hiding from the rest of the world? Why was Fawkes privy to such an isolated life?

Soon they all sat around the wobbly table,

Charlotte and Fawkes enjoying their first hot meal in days.

Their host spoke. "Now tell me, what kind of trouble have ye brought to my hearth this time 'round?"

Fawkes lowered the bowl of soup from his mouth and sighed. "Hardly trouble. Just a duke eager to show how big his sword is. Wants to prove to the king that he is stronger than his father was and make a new reputation for his family."

"Not Duke Belaq?" Desmund asked.

"The very same."

"I've heard wind of him in recent years. He is ruthless, that's what they say. Some wonder if he is even truly his father's son."

"He is determined," Fawkes admitted. "No evidence of his father's cowardice in him as far as I could tell."

"Until you get him alone with a woman," Charlotte muttered.

The two men turned to her with questioning eyes. "Don't tell me you haven't heard?" she asked. "All the servants have been talking for years. But then again, everyone is too afraid of him to speak very loudly." Charlotte tried to sound nonchalant. In reality, the rumors that swirled around the duke's desires terrified her to the core during her time of employment. Charlotte considered herself lucky that she had started her scullery duties early in life and had kept her head down since. Girls who came looking for employment at the castle, the more attractive ones at least, were often assigned to the duke's personal serving staff. The games he was rumored to play with them appeared on their flesh months later.

"It takes a certain kind of man to torment women for the sake of tormenting them," she told her audience.

"Rape?" Fawkes asked, face stony.

She sighed. "None that I ever heard of," Charlotte confessed. "Not with his...you know...One girl swore he tried, many times, but always had to resort to other various methods instead. But no matter what, he never let them go unless they screamed themselves hoarse first. I believe him to be a coward, for no truly brave man would behave that way. He can act as high and mighty as he wants, but there is a sickness in him. Not that it makes him any less terrifying."

"He only recently received his title, correct?" Desmund asked.

"His father died seven years ago," Fawkes said. "Until called back to claim his title, he was away, traveling the country, competing in tournaments and the like. His violent exploits must have been few and far between in his youth, too rare for anyone to construct a pattern. Now, as a full-fledged duke, he feels himself to be unstoppable."

"And he will stop at nothing to see the former glory of his family name restored, all memory of his father's retreat erased. Instead, he wants the Belaq name replaced with fear and awe," Desmund said. "I've seen it time and time again throughout the years. Read about it in many of my books, see. Families always fighting, always feuding, struggling for the power that wasn't theirs to begin with. It will end badly for him. Belaq is not fighting for the kingdom; he is fighting for himself."

"It will end badly for *us* if he catches us," Charlotte said, stating the obvious.

Desmund peered at her. "And what road, might I ask, has led you down the treacherous path to my dear friend here? It seems you have traded one dangerous man for another, with an equally uncertain fate."

"Fawkes has helped me. More times than I can count," Charlotte said, coming to his defense. "I can't believe you would place him in the same category as Belaq—"

"Well, Fawkes," Desmund cut her off. "It seems that the Cloaked Shadow is not such a frightening enigma after all. This little girl doesn't seem the slightest bit afraid of you."

"I'm not a little—wait, you know who he is?"

"Desmund," Fawkes said in a warning tone.

"Of course, I know who he is. You think he survived that gash on his head all alone? No. Bloody near tripped over him one morning, I did. Outside of my cave. Wrapped in that damned cloak and all but invisible against the rocks. How he crossed the mountain pass, I have no idea, only that he ended up on my doorstep more dead than alive. I thought for certain he was dead, so covered in blood, until I accidentally kicked him."

"She doesn't need to hear this," Fawkes said.

"She is your apprentice, is she not? Shouldn't she know the origin story of her mentor?"

"Charlotte is not my apprentice," he growled. "I'm getting her across the border tomorrow."

"Could have fooled me." Desmund smirked. "You seem to have quite the instinct when it comes to her. In mere hours I've seen how you track her movements—"

"Enough!" Fawkes roared. He whirled around and stalked toward the exit. "I'm going to check the perimeter. Not another word to her."

Charlotte watched the exchange with wide eyes, not daring to interrupt. She was dying to know more about Fawkes' injury and his connection with Desmund. But what exactly did the old man mean when he talked about Fawkes' instinct?

The second he was gone, Charlotte turned to Desmund. "Now where were we?" she asked, sweetly.

That earned her a chuckle of appreciation. "You really aren't afraid, are you? Let's see. Fawkes was delirious with fever when I found him. I thought that the infection might do him in if the blood loss hadn't already. Still, I couldn't leave him there, could I? Dragged him inside, stitched him up as best I could, then all I could do was wait. He has an insatiable will to live, that boy. Most others would have been done in."

"I've seen him fight," Charlotte said. "His power and precision—it is beyond compare. He isn't afraid of death."

"That's because of the anger deep inside, and that is a feeling not even fear of death can overpower."

"Anger?" Charlotte asked. *Is that searing anger inside of Fawkes all the time, even when he is with me?*

"That's what made him fight to live. I believe that only those who are at peace can let go. Fawkes will never have peace. Never."

"Why not?" The thought that Fawkes could never be truly happy disturbed the young woman.

"He blames himself, you see. His wife—" Ghost nickered, interrupting Desmund and sending Charlotte's thoughts reeling. *His wife? Fawkes is married?* She blinked and Fawkes was back in the cave, dripping wet from the rain.

"I couldn't see much through the storm, but I found no sign of Duke Belaq and his men. This weather is showing no sign of improvement."

"You can stay as long as ye like," Desmund offered graciously. With the subject of their discussion back inside, Charlotte knew she would not get any more answers out of their host.

****

As tired as she was, sleep evaded Charlotte. Every time she closed her eyes, she flashed back to earlier that day, frozen on top of the mountain. Her heart raced and her body was slick with sweat, the stench of fear refusing to let her fall into an uneasy rest. Adding to her fire was her shock at discovering that Fawkes was married. *Married.* Her daydreams of being such a unique woman that she caught the attention of the notorious Cloaked Shadow now seemed silly and embarrassing. Of course he was eager to get rid of her at the border, and had only entertained her desire to be his apprentice to appease her before getting back to his wife.

She told herself it wasn't jealousy and that she didn't want to be his wife anyway. *But you want the Cloaked Shadow's attention, and his instruction,* the voice in her head whispered to her as she tossed and turned. *Admit it. You want Fawkes all to yourself.* He was all that Charlotte had left in the world. She trusted him completely, no matter his past, and survival instinct made her want to hang on to him with all her might. He held the key to transforming her, to training her into the person she had always wanted to be. But he wasn't hers. Fawkes belonged to his wife.

With every muscle humming for action, Charlotte

gave up on sleep and slipped quietly into the passageway between the cave and the storm outside. She shivered in the whistling breeze, evaporating the sweat from the stifling interior of Desmund's home. She dropped to her plank position and started her exercises.

One…two…three… Soon there was only the rhythm of the exercise, cleansing both her body and her mind. *Inhale, exhale. Keep going. Don't stop.*

Charlotte reached thirty before a tingling on the back of her neck told her she was being watched. She sprung to her feet and whirled around to face her unexpected visitor.

Fawkes stared back at her through the shadows, the light from Desmund's hearth flickering across his features. Feet rooted in place, Charlotte waited for him to come to her. He seemed to know what she was waiting for, and closed the space between them in a moment, quiet as a cat. His fist shot out in an attempt to greet her face, but she ducked just in time. She didn't try to hit him back, but focused all of her energies on avoiding his attacks. With so little room to maneuver in the narrow passageway, Fawkes' strikes were not at full force.

Charlotte ducked and dived, using her small frame to her advantage. Every once in a while, she was too late, a well-aimed kick or punch grazed her body, but it wasn't enough to slow her down. Running high on the adrenaline of the fight, the two of them spoke no words. Their breathing fell in tandem as they danced.

She knew he was holding out on her, that this attack was not at his full effort. But it wasn't about who won or lost the spar, it was about being suspended in that dance together. For Charlotte, it was an apology and a promise, and for Fawkes, it represented acceptance and forgiveness. Whether or not their journey together ended tomorrow didn't cross Charlotte's mind. It was all about this singular moment in time as she held her own against the Cloaked Shadow.

Fawkes' attack pressed Charlotte backward, and soon they were outside. As Charlotte's feet slipped in the mud, she realized she had lost her size advantage. Lightning cracked across the sky, illuminating her surroundings long enough to blind her, and she failed to anticipate the next punch. It landed hard on her right shoulder and spun her around.

Before she could steady herself to counter, her arm was wrenched behind her back. Fawkes had a grip on it with one hand, the other around her throat. She stood flush against him, feeling his harsh breath and pounding heart as it beat against her back. They stood like statues, neither one of them wanting to be the first to break the spell.

The roar of thunder made her jump and brought them back to reality. "I've gotten better, haven't I?" Charlotte couldn't help asking. She'd meant it as a quip, but it came out too hopeful.

She felt Fawkes sigh, tensing his hold on her before dropping his grip. With her back still to him, she waited for his answer. Instead, his hand brushed wet hair back from her face before a finger traveled down and traced her jawline. Charlotte leaned into the touch, but then it was gone. She turned to see only darkness, and then a flash of lightning showed his tall frame heading back to the cave.

Though she was more confused than ever, her physical exhaustion finally overpowered her restless mind, and Charlotte dragged herself back inside. She slept before her head hit the blanket.

Chapter Seven

Charlotte awoke to the sounds of a whispered conversation already in progress. "...and you're just going to leave the poor girl alone in Croantis?"

"What would you have me do?" Fawkes snapped. "Take her with me on the next contract? She will be safe in Croantis." He paused. "Though I might stay a day or two while I finalize new business," he conceded. "The increasing rebel activity and escalating conflict mean that my services are in greater demand than ever. If I am fortunate, there will be multiple families with a relative in some trouble. I might have to raise my price."

"Very convenient," Desmund said. "It's all about the contracts, isn't it, Fawkes? Not the fact that you're scared this girl is making you focus on something other than your 'contracts'? This life you've chosen, how long will it last? It's already been five years. Things need to change—"

"Things are already changing. This war is only going to get worse, and I intend to profit from it."

"It is only a matter of time before your secret is revealed, Fawkes. You've lived and worked in the shadows, but now your exploits are becoming legendary. Your anonymity will disappear sooner than you are ready."

"Earl Hawthorne attempted to capture me," Fawkes

admitted. "I will just have to be more careful about which contracts I accept in the future, now that nobles are sharing information and working together." Charlotte heard the scrape of a chair as he stood up. "We're leaving now, Charlotte," he said, already knowing she was awake and eavesdropping. "The rain has stopped. The valley will have flooded, which will set Belaq back even further behind. We will cross the border today."

With a heavy heart, Charlotte got ready, trying to move as slowly as possible while avoiding rebuke. Desmund appeared to see her despair and tried to bring a smile to her face. "Here, child," he said, pressing the same book she knocked over the night before into her hands. "This is for you. To practice your reading, and maybe learn a thing or two."

"I couldn't!" Charlotte protested. A book like that was probably worth a fortune.

"You can return it when our paths cross again," Desmund said, and gave her a wink.

"You're so certain they will?" she asked. She hugged the book to her chest, covering the title.

He rolled his eyes over in Fawkes' direction. "Yours will with him, and thus by extension, to me. So keep it safe for me."

She shook her head. "Fawkes is leaving me at the border."

"Maybe." Desmund shrugged. "But everything is temporary. You never know with that boy." He embraced her hard, then approached Fawkes. "You'd better not turn up half-dead or on the run next visit," he warned the younger man.

That earned Desmund a small smile from Fawkes,

whose distracted thoughts were already beyond the confines of the cave and focused on the outside world. "I can't promise that," he said, and stooped to hug Desmund. "But I can promise that this is not goodbye." He let go and grabbed Ghost's bridle, heading for the exit.

Charlotte followed, but turned around at the entrance to wave at their host one last time. A pang hit her heart to see how small and old and alone he was, hidden away from the world. She thought once more of her own mother, and how the world turned against her in the end, becoming an overwhelming and unforgiving place. Aching for a hug from her mother, she settled for patting Ghost affectionately as they walked away.

"I'm worried about him," Charlotte confessed, as Desmund became a black dot in the distance behind them. Charlotte wished they could have stayed longer. The corner of her new book peeked out of Ghost's saddlebag. One of the only possessions she had, and she couldn't even use it properly. Desmund could have taught her how to read and unlock the book's secrets. *Maybe I should have stayed with him instead of following Fawkes to the border.* But watching Fawkes ride off without her would have been more than she could bear.

"Desmund?" Fawkes asked. "He can take care of himself. There are a few others who know of him and will check on him." He sighed, looking a bit guilty. "He is a survivor," he said, almost to reassure himself. Suddenly, he swung his leg up and over Ghost. Looking down at her from the horse, he offered Charlotte his hand. "Come," he said, with a dare in his eyes.

She grabbed his arm, and he heaved her up in front

of him. Ghost danced with anticipation. Fawkes wrapped his arms around Charlotte and secured her back against his chest. "This journey deserves a memorable end." His voice reverberated through her body as she tensed, ready for what was to come. He leaned forward and said, "Go."

Ghost was off, galloping at a speed that left Charlotte breathless. He hadn't been let loose like that since the forest. This time, though, Charlotte embraced it instead of feeling terrified. With the wind on her skin and the sun on her face, racing at an unrivaled pace, she laughed with pure joy. Belaq, her family, the destination ahead—none of it could touch her. She was flying.

Mentally, she urged Ghost on. *Faster, faster!* She swore she heard Fawkes laughing along with her, but it was hard to hear anything over the pounding of hooves.

The weight of her worries had lifted off of her small shoulders by the time Ghost started to slow. Charlotte had no idea how far they had gone, or how long they had been running, only that it seemed like an eternity and an instant all at once. Ghost's pace slowed to a walk, his sides heaving underneath her legs. Sweat soaked his dark coat, but the horse seemed to be in good spirits. He pulled at his bridle as if to ask for more, which Charlotte heartily agreed with. Instead, Fawkes kept them at a controlled pace.

"King's road ahead," he said, by way of explanation.

Charlotte squinted at the colorful banners in the distance. Just behind the guard tents, she saw a walled city that stretched on forever. It was ten times bigger than any of the villages in Algonia, and she wondered just how different life would be on the inside.

"Right now we are in the neutral land between countries. The soldiers up ahead are part of the Croantis forces. They monitor the road into their city." Fawkes halted Ghost and dismounted. He took off his trademark cloak and tucked it safely away in the empty saddlebag opposite to Charlotte's book. Next, he drew out his heavy purse, silver clinking as three coins tumbled into his hand. He stared at the pile for a moment, then pulled out one more coin. Gold glinted in the sunlight as he handed it to her.

Charlotte was about to refuse, but he pressed it into her palm with a stern glare. "Put it in your belt pouch. Just in case." Fingers trembling, she did as she was told. It was more money than she had ever possessed in her life. She could feel the warmth of the metal burning into her hip, reminding her that this was supposed to be her new start.

Fawkes mounted again and they merged onto the main road. It was still muddy from the rain, and other travelers were few and far between. Charlotte and Fawkes stood out against the poor peasants and farmers who braved the trek, and she wished for a bustling crowd to blend into as they neared the guards.

"Halt!" a guard ordered them. "From where do you hail?"

"We come from Algonia," Fawkes answered. Charlotte was a little shocked at his honesty, until he continued. "I am delivering my niece to relatives inside the city."

Charlotte tried to keep her face blank, but her heart thudded in her chest so hard she was sure the guard could see it. *What if Duke Belaq somehow got ahead of us? He might have already alerted the soldiers, warning them to look out for a man traveling alone with a young woman!* Charlotte didn't understand how Fawkes could remain so calm, as she was certain he was a wanted man in Croantis as well. Dungeons in Croantis were probably just the same as in Algonia, and as long as Fawkes had a paying contract, borders meant nothing to him.

If Fawkes had been alone, Charlotte knew he would have simply sneaked into the city after dark. However, this was the fastest way into the city and out of the reach of Belaq, whose forces were most likely mere hours behind them, slogging through the valley. If they could just get to safety before the duke could launch an overt attack, they might be able to disappear into the city.

The guard gave them a once-over. "Toll is one silver piece," he said, while staring hard at Charlotte's face. "And these relatives you are visiting," he said to her, "they don't mind a woman who dresses like a man?"

Charlotte stared at him with wide eyes, uncertain how to answer. How could she be so stupid? She should have changed her clothes. What guard would believe she was from a respectable family? So she took a gamble.

"I'm here to study, in fact," she said, in her haughtiest tone. Fawkes tensed behind her, but didn't contradict her as she veered from the original plan of 'don't draw attention'. *Well, maybe we would have thought about this if you saw me as an actual woman,* she thought. *But because I appear sexless to you, we overlooked the most obvious problem.* It was up to her to fix it.

"A woman scholar?" The guard snorted.

"My father had no sons, and assigned me to learn the healing arts with distant family members in Croantis. He's quite progressive, you know." Charlotte cocked an eyebrow. "But if I am to be in a man's world, I might as well dress like one."

The guard shook his head. "Never heard anything like that in my life."

"Check the right saddlebag if you are uncertain," Charlotte offered.

He eyeballed her skeptically, then reached in to pull out Desmund's book. Behind her, Fawkes let out a hiss when he saw the cover.

Charlotte doubted that the guard could read anyway, and watched as he thumbed through the book, stopping to look at the illustrations. "This is about medicine? Herbs and the like?" he guessed.

"Of course," Charlotte said. "I told you, I'm here to study."

"Woman scholar." The guard shook his head again, but carefully put the book back. He looked at the pair of them with a glint in his eye. "Such a respectable profession must make you very wealthy."

Fawkes sighed and held out two more silver pieces. "For your assistance and professionalism. And discretion," he said, as he tossed the coins to the guard.

"Be on your way." He nodded them past, and soon the city wall stretched high in front of them.

Before they entered through the gate, Fawkes' angry whisper tickled Charlotte's ear. "Why did Desmund give you that book? What did he say to you?"

She craned her neck to try to look at him. "He said

I must have been drawn to it. I knocked it over when we first got there. Why, is it important?" she asked, confused.

His blue gaze locked on hers with a steely strength, his face inches from her own. Fawkes' teeth ground together as he clenched his jaw, chewing on his words while he decided what to say. "That was my wife's book."

Charlotte's mouth formed an 'o' of understanding. Blushing deeply, she leaned away from him. *His wife's book.* "Does she want it back?"

Fawkes let out a harsh laugh. "Desmund failed to tell you the most important part then, did he? My wife is dead. Josephine died years ago. A fire. There was nothing left of her when I got home."

Horrified for him, Charlotte's eyes filled with tears. *I've been jealous of a dead woman.* Desmund's insight to Fawkes echoed in her memory. *Of course, he is angry. His life has been stripped from him, and nothing he does will ever get Josephine back.* That was why Fawkes wasn't afraid to die. Josephine's death had been the catalyst to create the Cloaked Shadow.

Charlotte pictured Fawkes returning to a home ravaged by fire. She saw him digging through the rubble, burning his hands on the still-smoldering remnants, searching in vain for his wife. Screaming her name. *I'm sorry* didn't seem enough, so Charlotte settled on, "She must have been brilliant, your wife."

This seemed to catch Fawkes off guard, because he said, "Why do you think that?"

"The book was hers. All about the art of healing and such. To be able to read and study and help people... I imagine she was very special."

His eyes softened, and he stared past Charlotte, reliving a memory. "She was extraordinary. People came from far and wide to seek treatment from her. She had many gifts, but her ability to perceive the truth about others was her greatest talent. It allowed her to heal her patients, but also mend their hearts and their minds. You couldn't hide anything from her—or yourself—in her presence."

"She possessed a second sight?" Charlotte asked, awed.

Her question snapped Fawkes out of his reverie. "It didn't save her."

Charlotte laid her hand on top of his white knuckles that gripped the reins. He didn't jerk away, so she allowed her fingers to comfort him by moving in languid circles. His skin was brown as leather, chapped and scarred until there was no part left unmarked. They were hands that were forced to keep busy, moving and fighting and never resting, lest their idleness allowed their master to remember things he worked hard to forget. As Charlotte used gentle contact to chase his dark thoughts away, she also remembered how carefully those hands had tended to her injuries, and how strong they felt when they picked her up effortlessly. A gentleness lay in them that contradicted their appearance. His tension eased underneath her touch, and then traveled up his arms, and finally to his body, where Fawkes slumped in his seat with a sigh.

As they crossed the threshold into the city, however, Fawkes straightened up to his watchful state again. Charlotte tried to copy his movements but was quickly overwhelmed by the bustle of her surroundings. Vendors hawked their wares, selling food Charlotte couldn't identify. Snippets of conversation in a foreign tongue reached her ears, harsh and grating. Women in bright and colorful clothing leaned out of doorways and beckoned to them.

How can I even begin to fit in here? But as Ghost continued his plod deeper into the city, Charlotte began to see a greater blend between Algonian and Croantian cultures. Neighborhoods emerged that were clearly occupied by immigrants, who combined the familiar comforts of home with the vibrant flair of their new country.

"Is it all so wild?" Charlotte asked Fawkes.

"Croantis citizens act with freedom and abandon. Some consider it savage, which is why 'uncivilized' Croantians are not welcome in Algonia," Fawkes said. "Fortunately for the Algonian defectors, this attitude does not prevail in Croantis. They are free to act as they wish, as long as they don't harm anyone within the borders."

"The king knows the rebels fled here after the Great War?"

"Yes, but to send in his armies to capture the traitors would mean offending a much more powerful neighbor. King Otan must settle for capturing his targets when they travel back to Algonia instead."

"Except innocent people are getting caught up in the mess," Charlotte pointed out. A thought struck her. "Do you think this is where Henry might have fled?" she asked him hopefully.

"Possibly," Fawkes admitted. "Though you would be searching a very long time in this city to find him." Charlotte could tell he held back from adding, *If he is still alive.* "Many change their names and identities when coming here. It is a good place to disappear. A good place for you."

Charlotte's heart sank. "Where are we going?" she asked, unable to keep her dark mood out of her question.

"I have to make an appointment first, then we shall find an inn to rest at for the night." *We. He said 'we'!* Relieved beyond measure that Fawkes wasn't leaving her just yet, Charlotte cracked a smile and tried to enjoy the city. For the first time since leaving home, she didn't feel Duke Belaq breathing down her neck.

Fawkes directed Ghost down a narrow alley in a neighborhood with a distinctly Algonian flavor. On the side of a decrepit shack, Fawkes used a stray piece of charcoal to draw a symbol. Charlotte tried to get a better look at the finished product, but they were back out on the main street a moment later.

"Why did you do that?"

"I set up a meeting for tonight."

"For us?"

"For me. These are not the people you want to get involved with."

His contracts. He is going to meet with rebels tonight. As irrational as it was, Charlotte couldn't help but hold them partly responsible for the imprisonment of her brother, and, by extension, the death of her mother. Without them, none of it would have happened. But then she would have never met Fawkes, either. Could Charlotte stand by Fawkes if the new contract helped the rebels? Would she be able to separate the emotion from the mission? If she wanted to live as Fawkes did, to truly be his apprentice, she needed to let go of the blame and refuse to take sides.

"I'm coming with you tonight," she told him.

"This has nothing to do with you." His voice hardened. "Our time together is nearing its end."

"You'll still be here, in the city, for a while longer. You told me you would train me until you had to leave me. Lock me in a room all you want, but I'll escape and come find you. I can help."

"Are you threatening me?" Fawkes asked, tone deadly.

"More like promising."

****

Their rendezvous point was in the cellar of a less-than-respectable pub in the middle of the Algonian district. She repeated Fawkes' instructions in her head as they navigated the sewer-filled streets— *Don't make a sound, keep your head fully covered, and stay by my side.*

Though her shabby cloak was no match for Fawkes' trademark disguise, it fell to her feet and the bulk hid her feminine body. As long as she kept to the shadows and her hood stayed put, she could probably pass for a teenage boy.

It had been weeks since she had seen the Cloaked Shadow fully emerge and take over Fawkes completely. Their casual sparring and training on the journey hadn't done enough to remind her just how spectacular he could be as he padded silently through the night. Charlotte felt him slip away from her like liquid, and struggled to keep up, her own movements a poor imitation of her mentor's skills.

No one spared a glance their way as they passed the pub's raucous entrance and headed for the side of the building. Two young men flanked heavy wooden doors inlaid into the ground next to the wall. They stiffened as Fawkes approached, giving him a respectful nod of their heads before pulling the iron handles. The doors opened like a butterfly's wings, exposing a steep staircase lit by torchlight.

"Sir," one guard whispered to Fawkes. "They've been waiting for you." Fawkes nodded and started down the stairs. "Sir, not the other one. Only you are allowed."

"The boy is with me," Fawkes growled, his voice so deep it was almost unrecognizable to Charlotte's ears. "He comes, or there is no meeting."

The guards, exchanging a quick glance, decided it would be prudent to let the dangerous man have his way. Charlotte tailed immediately behind Fawkes as they descended, trying not to slip on the slime covered stones. She risked a peek forward over Fawkes' shoulder.

Charlotte counted ten men standing directly in front of them, and guessed that even more guarded the perimeter of the cellar. Swollen casks of wine and ale loomed over the dirt floor in the flickering light. Tension thickened the air as the rebels waited for Fawkes to speak first. He was, after all, the one who called the meeting.

"Good evening." Fawkes' voice rumbled throughout the cavern. Charlotte noticed with smug satisfaction that some of the men jumped in surprise. *So, they aren't the big, bad rebels they might see themselves as. Besides, anybody with a lick of sense should treat the Cloaked Shadow with caution.*

The tallest rebel stepped forward. Bean pole thin and with fiery red hair, he was the last person Charlotte would have expected to be in charge. "Your timing is fortuitous, Cloaked Shadow," he said. "Though we have gotten word that your latest adventures have attracted quite a bit of unwanted attention."

Standing behind Fawkes, Charlotte felt him stiffen. However, his voice remained smooth, without a hint of irritation toward the rebel leader. "Duke Belaq pursued me, yes. Your father is well after his imprisonment, I presume?"

Even in the dim light, the redhead could not hide the blush characteristic of his fair skin. "Yes, he is healing. But it appears you have brought the duke back with you."

"Belaq did not take kindly to his prisoner being taken from him," Fawkes pointed out.

"But you should not have led him directly to our city."

"I had no choice," Fawkes said, but didn't elaborate further.

"You have forced us more deeply into hiding." The redhead's voice raised higher. "Right at the time when our plans are most delicate."

"You wanted him out, Robin," Fawkes said. "These are the consequences. The problems of the rebels are not my problems. I care not for your cause, only for your purse. So, as long as I am here, let us do business. Unless you feel you have no more need of my services." Charlotte could hear the smirk in his voice.

But Robin was not about to gracefully bow out of the argument. "And in trusting you, not only have you led the king's men to our doorstep but brought a stranger into our circle. We are contracted to deal with you, not with this boy. We will not speak further as long as he remains with you."

"As I told your men upstairs," Fawkes said coldly, "the boy is non-negotiable. He is here with me and is in my service. You speak of strangers, and here I see you have brought many more men with you than in the past. I know nothing of them, and yet I stand here in what could very possibly turn into a trap."

"These are all men of the cause," Robin said. "Hardened and vetted."

"You lie. Your numbers have been depleted, and you are desperate for followers." The Cloaked Shadow held up a finger and pointed it to the far right. "You," he said. "Come out from the shadows."

The young man emerged, and Charlotte stifled her gasp. The last person she ever expected to see stood in the middle of the cellar. *Henry.* It was all she could do to remain rooted in place, to prevent herself from flinging her arms around her brother. He was alive and well. But Fawkes had ordered her not to make a sound, not to reveal herself in front of the rebels. So for his sake, she did as she was told, even though all of her sisterly instincts screamed at her to go to him and make sure Henry was in one piece.

"Do you remember me?" Fawkes asked Henry. Charlotte's brother swallowed, then nodded. Fawkes turned to stare at Robin, and continued. "You claim to trust this boy implicitly, yet you have only just met him. He is not a believer of your rebel doctrine. He is a boy with nowhere else to go."

Robin stepped next to Henry to defend him. "His goals align with ours—to bring down the kingdom. He is a part of the brotherhood now. We do not question the loyalty of our brothers." Henry looked at Robin in a way that was both grateful and guilty at the same time. Charlotte wondered just how Henry had gotten involved so deeply in such a dangerous game so quickly.

"You should be suspicious," Fawkes warned him. "Others have tried to betray me. The line between the sides is no longer clear, and we cannot know how far Duke Belaq's reach is."

"I am far more inclined to trust the boy than you. Should I be suspicious of you?" Robin asked.

Fawkes crossed his arms. "It doesn't matter if you are or you aren't. You need me, otherwise your 'brothers' will rot in jail and then be executed. Not before being tortured for information, of course."

Robin began to pace, agitated. The meeting was obviously not going as he had planned it, and he needed the upper hand. He started to close the gap between them, but Fawkes halted him. "That is close enough."

"We will pay you double!" the redhead blurted out.

This seemed to intrigue the Cloaked Shadow. "Double? For what special favor?"

Robin wrung his hands and glanced around the room. He lowered his voice and said, "Assassinations that would further our cause. Only a few. Key figures who stand in the way of our war."

A contract killer? Charlotte's eyebrows shot up. Rescuing people from dungeons was one thing, but to purposefully sneak into a home and kill someone in cold blood? It made Charlotte's own blood freeze, and she held her breath while she waited for Fawkes' response.

"No," Fawkes said. "Let us discuss the usual contract details right now, or I will leave and find work elsewhere."

Charlotte let out a sigh of relief. Whatever arbitrary rules Fawkes set for himself when it came to his morals, assassinations did not fit within them. She did not delude herself of his capabilities, however. She had witnessed Fawkes slit a highwayman's throat, and then use the same knife unflinchingly for supper later that day. But since breaking into the dungeon to free Henry, her own moral code had been corrupted. It was getting harder for her to determine what she would and wouldn't do in terms of absolutes, thanks largely in part to her growing connection with the Cloaked Shadow.

She liked how he made her feel—powerful, capable, and important. She could feel herself changing when she was with him, and it made her feel alive. Learning, training, fighting, struggling—how could she give that up and return to the mundane? Life had placed an extraordinary opportunity in front of her to affect change upon the world, to take action that would have ripple effects across kingdoms. It was an intoxicating pull.

It was like she was being ripped in half in the struggle between wanting to stand by her brother and continuing as an apprentice. Seeing Henry reminded her that she had a duty to fulfill. It brought her back to her old self and reminded her what was important. Her brother needed her help to find his own identity, away from the rebel cause. But however selfish it was, Charlotte craved more for herself.

The seriousness of Fawkes' tone brought her back to the moment. "My prices have gone up regardless. The risk is greater than ever. Now, who am I rescuing and where are they being held? This will also determine how much he is worth to you."

A sheen of sweat glistened on Robin's red face. He appeared to choke back a few key phrases before he finally said, "His name is Stefan. He is being held at Numencaster."

"The king's castle?" Fawkes asked, incredulous. "How long has he been imprisoned?"

"A month."

"A *month?* And you expect him to still be alive by the time I arrive?"

"We've had no word of his execution yet. We hope he has information that is imperative for our operation. We need him back."

"King's castle, rebel spy, Duke Belaq on my arse," Fawkes mused. "Fine. One hundred."

"Impossible," Robin retorted.

"Either you pay me one hundred gold pieces or our business here is done."

One hundred gold pieces? Charlotte thought. That was a fortune, and the risks that Fawkes outlined were enough to make her heart skip. He was being sent into the belly of the beast with the entire Kingdom of Algonia on the hunt for him. It needed to be worth it. With that kind of money, she expected that Fawkes could retire permanently. Not that he ever would, though.

Robin turned back to consult with the other rebels. After they exchanged a few terse whispers, Robin addressed Fawkes again. "Half now, the second half when Stefan is released. There will be an extraction team from our brothers in the north waiting for you in the forest outside the castle. They will also send word directly to us when Stefan is free."

Fawkes bowed his cloaked head in acquiescence. Robin tossed a purse toward them, and it landed in the dirt. Charlotte darted forward to pick it up, and then handed it to her mentor. His quick fingers worked the knot and he glanced at the contents inside. Apparently satisfied, he motioned for Charlotte to follow him as they ascended the steps without a word, leaving the unhappy group inside.

****

Charlotte and Fawkes didn't speak until they were once again in the safe sanctuary of their rented room. She expected him to talk with her about the contract, but one look into his eyes showed her that his barriers were back up. Charlotte searched his face, disappointed.

"You did fine tonight," he reassured her.

"When you go to Numencaster—" she started.

"You will stay here. Against all odds, you have found your brother again. Are you not happy?" he asked her.

"Yes. No. I don't know!" Charlotte exploded. "I am beyond happy that he is alive and well. It was more than I could have hoped for. But this," she motioned back and forth between them, "I don't want to let this go. I thought I was doing better. That I was helping you. You are my mentor. Seeing Henry hasn't changed what I want deep down. I don't feel finished."

The young woman refused to let herself cry, not when she had something so important to prove. She saw Fawkes' mouth soften just a little before he answered. "You have improved. But this contract is not one that I want you to be a part of. It is too risky, and I don't need a liability."

"A liability? That's how you think of me?"

"Your brother needs you. It is time to start a new life here." Seeing that he was making little headway, Fawkes delivered the final punch. "I never asked for an apprentice, anyway."

He was right. She had forced herself on him from the beginning. *But it was his fault, too!* He had saved her, come back to her village a second time even though he should have been miles away. Traveled with her to the border to ensure her survival. The fact that he denied that all of that meant something greater stung the hardest.

"You're just afraid," she shot back. "You could have a partner in this; you don't have to go alone. Yet you choose to, even though I know a part of you wants me to stay. You deny our bond, whether it is mentor and apprentice or," she swallowed hard, and decided to lay it all out on the table. *Nothing left unsaid,* she told herself before continuing. "Even man and woman. But I can't make up your mind for you, and you've made it clear that I am unwanted." She saw him flinch. "I've fought for what I want, and I have no regrets, but fear holds you back."

At that accusation, Fawkes rounded on her and slammed his hands against the wall, holding her captive. The splintered wood cut into her back and she felt Fawkes' muscles tremble, Charlotte's rapid breath the only sound between them. A simple step forward was all that it would take to touch him, but she couldn't move a muscle.

Warring emotions flickered across Fawkes' face as they stared at one another. Deep blue eyes burned with fire as he made up his mind. Soft lips crashed onto Charlotte's mouth, devouring her in hungry desperation. His hands came up to grip her, like he was making sure she was real, as if he was afraid she was going to disappear. Strong hands worked their way over her body, tangling themselves in her hair and protectively cradling her head as he deepened the kiss.

All coherent thought flew out of Charlotte's head and she let her instincts take over. A low moan escaped her throat as his tongue explored every part of her mouth. Her arms went to his waist, wrapping around the steel torso and working her fingers underneath the hem of his shirt. She wanted to feel his skin on hers, and anything less was simply too far away.

The heat she found underneath her fingertips made her want to melt and fly at the same time. After training and sparring together, Charlotte *knew* his body—she could read Fawkes' muscles and predict his movements. So everything she felt as they kissed, she felt it twice, mirrored in both her body and his. Fawkes could read her just as easily, and knew what she craved.

Dragging his mouth away from hers, his lips trailed to the hollow behind her ear and then down her neck. Her hands rose up to grip his head to her, urging him to continue his explorations. The kisses turned so feather light on her collarbone that she lost all control.

Charlotte yanked his head up to kiss him again, hard. His strength matched hers, and he didn't hold back. She shoved him in the direction of the bed and their lips broke apart. Staring at his face—scarred, tanned, and imperfect—Charlotte thought he was the most beautiful person she had ever seen. Somewhere along the way, her fear of him had turned into respect, and respect had turned into something more.

Under her admiring gaze, Fawkes' look of hunger

turned to fear. His body snapped stiff as he realized what he had done. Even though he still stood right in front of her, Charlotte felt him pull away. The part of him that had been raw and vulnerable to her mere seconds before disappeared in an instant.

"Fawkes," she said, raising up a gentle hand to his cheek. Before she could stroke the stubble, Fawkes reeled backward to escape her touch. What had gone wrong? Had she done something?

His panicked gaze shot around the room, as though ashamed to look at her. Both the Cloaked Shadow and Fawkes had been replaced by a stranger, a side of the man that Charlotte didn't recognize. "I—I'm sorry, Charlotte. Goodbye."

Her feet remained glued to the floor as he picked up his cloak off the bed and threw open the door. She waited for him to turn around, to offer her an explanation, or to say when he would be back. The sound of the door slam hit her like a punch in the gut, and left her wondering what she had done to end up alone.

Chapter Eight

After waiting up for most of the night, Charlotte's confusion turned to worry when the dawn brought no sign of Fawkes' return. She started her search at the stables but found Ghost's stall deserted.

When she saw the strip of black fabric dangling from the bridle hook, she knew it was over. He had left her without another word, leaving only a small piece of himself out of guilt, obligation, or whatever else he thought he owed her. She ran the smooth fabric between her fingertips. It felt like a goodbye.

After allowing herself to quietly break down for a few hidden moments, Charlotte picked herself up and brushed the hay off her clothes before tying the fabric into a bow around her hair. There would be time to mourn later, and at that moment, Fawkes needed to be shoved to the back recesses of her mind to be dealt with at a more convenient time. His memory could reside alongside that of her mother, whose death she still hadn't fully processed. She knew that the levee would break soon and the emotions would drown her, but first she needed to find her brother.

Henry remained the only bright spot in her life. She might have failed as an apprentice and as a daughter, but she refused to fail as a sister. If last night was any indication, Henry had lost his way and needed her help. It gave her something to focus on rather than wallowing.

Determined, Charlotte returned to her room, packed up her practical possessions along with one very heavy book, and checked out of the inn. The city's noise and stench engulfed her as she meandered up the winding pathways, searching for anything familiar. The correct Algonian neighborhood wasn't hard to find, but everything looked so different in the daytime, and she couldn't recognize the pub. Fawkes' imaginary voice came through, as clearly as if he were standing right next to her. *Close your eyes and picture the turns. Remember how the stones felt under your feet. Were they slanted? Uphill? Rough? The voices you heard, what were their accents? What did you smell?*

Charlotte's eyes popped open and she prowled in the direction her instincts nudged her toward. Without thinking, her tread took on the same silent and cautious quality that defined Fawkes' movements, effective even in the middle of the day on a crowded street. Charlotte remained so nondescript that no one spared her a second glance as she found her way to her destination.

A brilliant smile broke out on her face when she spotted the cellar door. She turned over her shoulder to share her joy with Fawkes, only to remember too late that he wasn't there. Instead, her eyes met the widened gaze of the red-headed rebel leader.

Though she tried to keep her face carefully blank after the initial shock, the hint of recognition was enough to make his eyebrows narrow. "Do I know you?" Robin asked.

Smoothly dropping into a caricature of a lost young girl, Charlotte let her eyes fill with tears. "I don't know, sir. I don't know anything. I had hoped you were someone I was looking for. It's just... I can't figure where I am and this city is so much bigger than back home and I just want my brother!" Her shoulders shook as she started wailing.

Her performance caught Robin off guard, and he stepped into a gentlemanly role immediately. "There, there," he said, patting her shoulder. "This isn't the neighborhood you want to be in. Especially dressed the way you are." Charlotte felt his eyes rake over her legs, which hid nothing in her slim-fitting trousers. She fought to avoid shivering under his gaze and shrinking back from his touch. His tone might be sympathetic, but his body language revealed another side.

Dragging the back of her hand underneath her nose, Charlotte sniffed and pretended to pull herself together, putting a little more space between their bodies. "I know this is impossible," she said, with a small hiccup. "But I'm looking for my brother. His name is Henry, and I know he came to Croantis and I need to find him."

Robin's talon-grip on Charlotte's shoulder tightened. "You might not have come all this way for nothing," he said, gauging her reaction carefully.

"You know him? Really? Oh, how wonderful!" She beamed at him and clapped her hands together, the very portrait of innocence. "Where is he?"

"I need a few clarifications before I can sort this out." He considered her. "You traveled here from Algonia, by yourself?" She nodded. "And how exactly did you discover the whereabouts of your brother?"

"He—he told me this was where he was going. Before he left."

"Don't lie to me, girl."

"I'm not lying! It's—"

"Charlotte?" Henry's voice asked. She saw him walk out from the pub and over to her like he was in a dream. "Is it really you?"

Charlotte wrenched herself from Robin's hold and launched herself at her brother. "Henry!" Tears, fake earlier, now streamed for real down her face. Henry embraced her hesitatingly as she clung to his neck. "How are you here?" he whispered.

"I came to find you. You know I would never let you go that easily."

"But how?"

Shut up, Charlotte wanted to tell him. Robin was still there, watching their exuberant display and searching for hints during their reunion. The rebel leader probably wondered how exactly Charlotte found their headquarters so easily, and she knew he wanted to interrogate her regarding the coincidental timing of her arrival.

"I'll explain later," Charlotte whispered, and pulled back from Henry. "Let me see you," she ordered. "All in one piece. Good. Your friend over there," she nodded at Robin, "was just about to bring me to you, when you just appeared. We haven't been formally introduced yet."

Henry always needed a gentle nudging from either his sister or his mother when it came to manners, and his cheeks turned pink when he realized his rudeness. "Charlotte, this is Robin. He's been helping me since he found me. Got me a job and everything."

Charlotte dipped her chin and dropped into a miniature curtsey that looked ridiculous with her britches on. "My family is indebted to you, good sir.

Thank you for watching over my brother. I apologize for my emotional outburst earlier."

"Charlotte." Robin said her name slowly. "Henry never mentioned a sister. But before you get reacquainted, I suggest moving inside. We don't want to attract attention."

Robin looked prepared to follow them inside for a bite to eat. Fear gripped Charlotte as she sent thoughts to Henry urging him to keep his mouth shut. He looked so overwhelmed and confused by her sudden arrival, but she needed him to show an ounce of common sense and not speak in front of Robin.

She took a deep breath, mulling over how to answer Robin's inevitable questions. Pure coincidence would not be enough to explain her arrival at the rebel headquarters. Silently, she cursed her dumb luck at running into the rebel leader first. She wondered how long it would be before he started to piece together all of the 'coincidences' in his life to show a larger picture. The Cloaked Shadow's sudden appearance, Duke Belaq at his heels, and now a brand-new recruit's sister showing up unannounced. Just as she was starting to panic, a voice called out from the alleyway.

"Robin!" he said. "You're needed down below."

The redhead sighed. "Can it wait?"

"No, it's urgent."

Robin motioned for the siblings to go inside the pub. "I will discuss these events with you later. I would like to know more about you, Charlotte."

"Of course!" she said brightly. "I'm looking forward to getting to know all of my brother's friends." She steered Henry inside, and then collapsed on a bench near the back. Not wanting to alarm Henry, she started off slowly. "I'm starved. What is good to eat around here?"

He didn't answer but sat down next to her. After an eternity of silence while Charlotte busied herself analyzing the building, looking everywhere but at her brother, he finally spoke. "Charlotte, where's Mother?"

Of all the ways Charlotte had pictured reuniting with her brother, this was not how it was supposed to go. Seeing the hesitation and anguish on his face as he waited for her answer was worse than she could have imagined. She hated being the person to shatter the small fraction of hope he still had left. Her sisterly instincts told her to protect him, so that's what she did.

"Mother died in her sleep," she said, watching as Henry's world came crashing down around him. "Soon after you left."

"No." He shook his head, looking like the six-year-old, petulant child of her memories. "She can't be dead."

"If she wasn't, do you think I could have left her?" Charlotte said gently.

"It's your fault then!" Henry lashed out at her. "You were supposed to take care of her. That's why I had to leave on my own. You have no idea what happened to me by myself." He shuddered. While Charlotte understood his outburst, anger bubbled up within. Hearing her brother blame her, even though she blamed herself for her mother's attack, sparked a fire inside.

"Henry, I'm sorry that Mother is gone. I did all that I could. But you've survived. I'm alive and here with you. This is what Mother would want." She swallowed the lump in her throat. "I know that I put this on you unexpectedly. I know that seeing me is a shock. But you are the only family I have left, and we can start a new life here."

He pulled away from her. "I've been doing just fine on my own. I don't need you to come in here telling me what to do, like you're my mother. You let my mother die. I have a life here already, and Robin and his friends are opening my eyes to the truths in Algonia." He jutted out his chin. "They need me."

Charlotte saw that Henry was just trying to hang on to the stability Robin offered after the trauma of his imprisonment. Still, his words stung. Did he think he was the only one who suffered? Did he not remember what she had done to save him? She gritted her teeth and reminded herself to be patient, even though her hand itched to smack him on his head and knock some sense into him.

Robin and his group of rebels were bad news, but it was going to be harder than she assumed to drag Henry away from them. She closed her hands over her brother's, watching as his lip trembled while trying to be brave.

"You are not a rebel, Henry," she told him.

"What difference did it make when I wasn't one?" he spat, as if embarrassed by his display of grief while desperate to appear strong in front of Charlotte. "I was still imprisoned anyway. Almost tortured. The duke treated me like a rebel, so I had no choice but to become one, didn't I? Robin and his organization want to get back at all of them. At the whole kingdom, for all the wrongs they have committed against the people." He took a deep breath, and continued with his rant, not allowing Charlotte to interrupt him with levelheaded reason. "The Great War didn't end, you know. It just moved underground. But now, Robin says he has a plan to stop it all. For us to finally win."

"Us?" Charlotte questioned. "And what is his 'great plan' exactly?"

"He says it is almost ready. But once it happens, we can go home again," he promised. His eyes shone feverishly with idealism that scared Charlotte.

"What, does Robin expect to rule Algonia?" The man had a certain charisma, yes, but he was also paranoid beyond belief, and Charlotte had witnessed how quickly he lost his temper the night before. Robin was a man molded by revolution and struggle. If that ended, he would lose his identity, and men who thrived in conflict had no idea how to survive in peacetime. "How many people would have to die before Robin got what he wanted?" Charlotte asked.

Henry's brow furrowed, as though he hadn't considered it before. "That isn't the concern. Besides, there are already scores of people dying under King Otan's rule every day. The price would be worth it for a better Algonia."

"And are you paying that price?" she asked her brother.

"I already have. I'm willing to do whatever needs to be done."

Charlotte flashed back to the sight of her mother's body, face down in the mud. There would be no funeral for her; her children would not return to visit her grave. She could not imagine inflicting that type of pain on anyone, stranger or friend, no matter the reason. If Robin wanted to bring the war back up to the surface, she wasn't sure if the deaths would ever stop. "And who are you to make the decision for other people?" she asked, voice deadly calm. "Will you be the one to help families dig the graves when Robin succeeds?"

"Duke Belaq has sentenced hundreds of his own citizens to their deaths. Tortured them, too! Yet you say nothing of him!"

"Duke Belaq is not my brother, and I do not have to wash the blood from his hands," she said. Sighing, Charlotte suddenly understood Fawkes' complete dismissal of politics and his refusal to choose sides. There was no good side. Right now, the only thing that was in her power to do was to protect her family.

Henry grunted in frustration. "I'll arrange to have you come to the meeting tomorrow. Then you'll see. You'll understand what we are trying to do," he explained, as if radical ideas made more sense when spewed in an official capacity.

The last thing Charlotte wanted was to be around Robin again, and witness as Henry became more involved in inciting revolution. However, the meeting would provide the perfect opportunity to gather information about this mysterious rebel plot. *It is to satisfy my own curiosity, not for Fawkes,* she chastised herself when her thoughts immediately jumped to collecting information for the Cloaked Shadow. Weighing the risks of allowing Henry to remain under Robin's spell, she decided that she couldn't walk away just yet.

Chapter Nine

"She's my sister. I can vouch for her," Henry argued with the guard as they stood outside the cellar. Robin had called a secret meeting, and that meant no outsiders.

"No one gets in that Robin hasn't vetted," the guard said. "She can wait out here."

I've already been down there, Charlotte wanted to say. *And believe me, it isn't that special.* Charlotte grabbed her brother's wrist to hold him back. "Henry. It's fine. You go to the meeting and I'll go back to your place. Robin needs more time to accept me, understandably."

Henry ran his fingers through his hair in frustration. "But you need to be there! You need to understand the cause."

"And I'll be there next time," she told him, trying not to sound distracted. She already eyed the building, determining the best way to sneak in and listen once she was left alone. The tricky part was going to be gaining access to the cellar, but she didn't necessarily need to be in the cellar, just close enough to eavesdrop. The building next door looked promising. She suspected that it had a basement as well, and there was a distinct possibility that the two structures connected underground. The rebels had to have ways of sneaking around the city, and Robin's sudden appearance the day prior indicated he could have come out from the neighboring building.

Henry looked from Charlotte to the guard, obviously torn. Though the siblings were still circling each other with caution after their intense reunion, ale and a good night's rest had started to mend their fractured relationship. By the end of the night, they had embraced and shed tears together as they reminisced over their childhoods. Charlotte even got Henry to open up about what he remembered when he was released from Belaq's dungeon.

"You were there," he'd slurred into his mug. "But so was the Cloaked Shadow. Bloody hell, I can't believe I met the man. He is a legend."

"Did you tell anyone I was there?" she pressed. If Robin knew that she had a history with the Cloaked Shadow, Fawkes' arrival and her appearance a day after his would be too suspicious to ignore.

"'Course not," Henry scoffed. "You think I would say anything to get my sister in trouble? I just told them the Cloaked Shadow broke me out. Didn't know him, didn't see his face. I wanted to make sure your name was never tied to my escape. Figured you would be safe in the village."

Relief had turned her limbs wobbly. As long as Henry kept his secret, there was no way for Robin to prove a connection. "I was so hungry though, and weak, sometimes I wonder if it actually happened," Henry confessed. "I don't remember much of that night. But I do remember that you came for me. Did you see who the Cloaked Shadow really was?"

"No," she said quickly. "I was too focused on trying to get us out alive. Besides, the Cloaked Shadow didn't do very much besides show us the way out. We simply followed him through the castle, remember?" *And he actually saved my life when I almost doomed us both,* she wanted to add. But it was safer if she just pretended that Fawkes had hardly noticed them.

"That old man, he's Robin's family, you know," Henry informed her. Charlotte pretended to be surprised, but she had suspected as much from the first meeting in the cellar. "They found me on the road a few days later. Saved my life and brought me back with them." After that, Henry had put his head on the table and fallen asleep.

No wonder Henry feels like he owes them.

****

It was with that sense of duty that Henry now regretfully kissed his sister on the cheek and descended into the cellar. "I won't be long," he promised. "I'll talk to Robin. He'll see that he can trust you, too." His desperation for all of the important people in his life to get along was clear.

Charlotte pretended to return to the dilapidated building that Henry called home, where he occupied one room in a house filled with other aspiring agents against the crown. Most were like her brother—young, lost, eager, and full of grandiose ideas. Boys who lacked the intelligence to ask the more difficult philosophical questions of their leader. To say they were easily manipulated was an understatement.

Once Charlotte got out of the alleyway and back onto the main street, she doubled back. Padding silently through the twisting alleyways and keeping to the shadows, she snuck into the neighboring building through a side door. She found the stairs she was searching for immediately, and descended into the basement. Half-expecting to see guards there as well, she was quite surprised to find it empty.

Almost rolling her eyes at how obvious their 'hidden' entrance was, she pushed aside wooden crates stacked up against the back wall. She exposed a narrow hole, just big enough for one person to enter at a time. Remembering the last time she had been in such a small space, Charlotte shivered. Though it was better than crawling through a sewer drain to break into a dungeon, the consequences of getting caught would probably be the same.

Wondering how in the world she had gotten herself in the same situation for her brother a second time, Charlotte dropped to her hands and knees and started to crawl. She didn't have to go far before voices started filtering through. Holding her breath, she inched her way forward as close as she dared. A few lengths ahead, she made out the silhouette of a pair of legs blocking her exit. *Standing guard,* she presumed, *but not very good at it.* As far as she could tell, the tunnel let out in the far left of the cellar. The guard blocked her view of the room, but the conversation became clearer as voices raised in frustration.

"One month is too soon!"

"We still have not recovered from the last attempt! Our numbers are weaker—"

"We must wait for the Cloaked Shadow to save Stefan. Once the extraction team learns whatever knowledge Stefan was able to glean, they will send us the necessary details. To go ahead with the plan now, while we don't know the specifics—"

"*Enough!*" Robin's voice rang through the melee.

"Stefan's capture was unfortunate and unforeseen. But we cannot delay the time line any further. Duke Belaq is occupied in Croantis. Now is the time to make our move in Algonia against the king while he is weak. To stay and do nothing puts us at risk for Duke Belaq's discovery, which will force us underground again. We must act now or risk the mission failing all together."

The din started up again, some shouting encouragement for Robin's argument while others raised their protest again. "All right, all right! I will give you one accession. We will wait until the last possible moment to leave, in the hopes that Stefan will be delivered to the Numencaster team with all the information we require. The Cloaked Shadow has until the new moon to deliver him to our men, otherwise we assume he failed and instead we continue with the attack as scheduled. Now, we have other business to attend to. What do we hear of Belaq?"

"Still camped outside the city, sir. He is not permitted to enter with his army."

"We need to keep a close watch on him," Robin said. "For it would be easy for him to slip through the gates alone."

The thought that the duke could breach her sanctuary within the walls of the city had not yet occurred to Charlotte. She assumed that once she was inside, she was forever out of his grasp. The duke had come to the city to catch the Cloaked Shadow, but he might settle for the siblings who had been a thorn in his side and an embarrassment to his dukedom.

"We must be more cautious than ever. Our faction here must remain unknown to the duke and the king. All activity must be kept to a minimum over the next few weeks. I don't want to hear about any of you getting into trouble. Do I make myself clear?"

A chorus of "Aye" rang through the cellar. Sensing that the meeting was almost over, Charlotte began to slowly back away. Leading with her rear was a lot harder than moving forward, but Charlotte had to get back to the house before Henry realized she never went home. She intended to be far away from the pub while the rebels staggered back to their respective residences throughout the neighborhood.

Out in the open air again, Charlotte's heart jumped anytime she passed a dark-haired man on the street. She saw the face of Duke Belaq everywhere as she imagined him hunting his adversary, not knowing that the man was long gone. Not even he would expect that the Cloaked Shadow would return so immediately to the country he had just narrowly escaped from. Until Belaq heard of Stefan's rescue, it was unlikely that he would retreat from Croantis.

Charlotte made it back to the house with plenty of time to spare. Twisting the black ribbon in her hair, she paced Henry's small room. She tried to focus on what she heard at the meeting, but her thoughts kept turning to Fawkes. Angrily, she tried to push his face from her mind, but his shocked and regretful expression from their last encounter haunted her.

Choking back a sob of frustration, she pulled out her book from its hiding place under the mattress and threw it across the room. Why had Desmund insisted on gifting her such a painful reminder of Fawkes? And not just a reminder of the man, but of the entire life he had before becoming the Cloaked Shadow. It was his *wife's* book. His deceased wife. The woman he would hold on a pedestal forever, whose death had transformed him.

The book fell open as it hit the door, its words taunting her, full of secrets she could never uncover. A wealth of useful knowledge at her fingertips, and all she could do was flip through the pictures and seethe about the unfairness. Charlotte felt locked out of a world she could never break into, try as she might to become more than a scullery maid. The opportunities of this life fell just beyond her grasp.

Suddenly exhausted and feeling hopeless, she collapsed onto the musty mattress and closed her eyes. Fawkes' face settled in front of her, but she lacked the conviction to push it away again. Allowing herself a moment of weakness, she gave into her dreams.

****

"Who is Fawkes?" Henry's voice roused Charlotte from a deep sleep, pulling her out of a dream she was reluctant to leave. She rubbed her eyes and tried to remember where she was. "What? What do you mean?"

"Who is Fawkes?" Henry repeated. "You kept saying that name while you slept."

"I don't know," she said carefully. "Maybe it is someone I knew from long ago."

Henry looked at her, doubtful. "You were crying, too."

Charlotte's hand shot up to touch a wet cheek. The dream came back to her in pieces. She had been so close to saving him, but Fawkes had slipped away from her, no matter how tightly she clutched him. She remembered screaming his name, telling him to come back. He had been in danger, and needed her help, but she had been too late.

"Do you know where this came from?" he asked,

handing her the book.

Charlotte winced. Not only had she essentially announced Fawkes' secret identity, but she had also forgotten to hide the one object that was sure to incite awkward questioning. Sitting up, she snatched the offending evidence from her brother and inspected it for damage.

"I picked it up on my journey here," she explained.

"From whom?" he pressed.

There was no way she was going to mention Desmund. "I—I found it. It looked useful. I think it is some sort of book about plants and healing."

"Robin will be interested in taking a look," he said, reaching out to graze the book with his fingertips. "This would help us heal our brothers who become injured. If we give it to him, in good faith, he will know that you are on our side—"

"No!" Charlotte shouted.

"But we can't even read it," he pointed out, puzzled. "What does it mean to you?"

"You can't give it to him," she stated. Then she pulled out her biggest bargaining chip. "As your older sister, I am asking you not to."

He hesitated, but seeing the determined set of her expression, dropped his inquiries.

****

If Charlotte had known what Henry was going to do, she would have made him swear on their mother's grave not to reveal the book to anyone. A week later, when Henry mentioned that Robin wished to speak with her, Charlotte immediately checked her hiding spot. It was painfully empty, and she was full of rage.

She whirled around to confront her brother. "What

did you do?"

"Robin is just outside," he said, shushing her. "You just have to trust me."

"Trust you?" Charlotte's voice raised, irate.

"Charlotte, please. I did this for us. He thinks you gave the book to me to pass along to him. I got you on the inside. If he thinks you want it back, or that your gesture of goodwill was unintended, he won't let you in on our mission."

Giving her brother the death stare, Charlotte snapped her mouth shut. *It's too late to get the book back. All I can do now is make sure the sacrifice is not in vain*, she reasoned.

Henry waited a few moments longer until he was sure his sister would not attack Robin, and he opened the door.

The redhead stepped inside. "Henry." Robin nodded at her brother. "And Charlotte. What a pleasure to see you again." Charlotte inclined her head but could not say the same. "I apologize for the late hour, but I have been occupied with some important matters that couldn't wait until now. I wanted to thank you for your generous and valuable contribution to our cause. The knowledge held in that book is incredibly important and will greatly aid us in the war to come."

The rebel leader stared at her expectantly, and Charlotte realized she would have to say something in return. "I'm glad it was of use to you, *sir*. It looked like a big and impressive book, but as I am only a woman, I thought it would be better to be in the hands of a leader such as yourself." Robin didn't appear to hear her dripping sarcasm, and instead regarded her with a smirk.

"Well, you have gifted it to the right place. In return for your help and loyalty, you will be permitted to accompany your brother to our next gathering. I look forward to your presence there. You will be a welcome addition to our cause, amongst all the men."

Charlotte felt torn between the urge to vomit or spit in his face. *Where did you put it? Where did you hide it? Give me my book back! It's* mine.

Robin turned to leave, but before he crossed the threshold, he turned back to her. "Oh, one other thing. I know Henry said that you found the book, but there is the most curious inscription on the inside cover. I wonder if you know anything about it?"

"What does it say?"

"It said something to the effect of— 'My dearest Josie—No gift is enough to equal how you heal me each day, and help me become the man I want to be for you. All my love, your devoted husband, Fawkes.'"

The room spun. Charlotte bit her cheek until it bled to keep her true feelings off of her face. As the coppery taste flooded her mouth, she stared into Robin's sneer. *He knows I'm hiding something.* Henry stood next to her, oblivious to the subtext being exchanged between his sister and Robin.

It was a game to him, seeing how far he could push Charlotte before she revealed a crucial piece of information. *Henry must have told him about my sleep outburst and about shouting Fawkes' name,* she realized. Robin knew there was a connection, and he knew she had been lying. He didn't know it yet, but he held the key to the Cloaked Shadow's true identity, if only he put the pieces together.

She shrugged, refusing to let Robin win the

standoff. "No idea." Inside, the words that Fawkes had written to his wife tore into her. It was strange to imagine the Fawkes that she knew, her Fawkes, saying those beautiful things. No wonder Fawkes had been devastated when he realized Desmund gave Charlotte that particular book. Just how far had he fallen? How much of Fawkes would Charlotte never know, because it had been lost forever years before she even met him? Even though he had kissed her, and possibly had feelings for her, had the romantic died inside of him? Charlotte could not compete with a ghost.

Now Robin had the book, and Charlotte needed to get it back. She decided to play his game for the time being. Flashing a winning smile that wiped the smirk off of Robin's face, Charlotte said, "I'll see you at the next meeting, okay?" Then she reached over and slammed the door in his face.

Henry reached out to her. "Charlotte, I know you're upset—"

"Don't touch me." She gathered herself for a few moments, waiting until Robin had left the building. "I'm going for a walk."

Charlotte stormed her way through the neighborhood, her tunnel vision tainted with red. Steaming, she thought about how satisfying it would be to punch Robin in the nose like she had punched that highway robber. *Crunch.* Only this time, she wouldn't stupidly bruise her hand, because Fawkes had taught her how to punch correctly. Or maybe she would just use Henry's head as her weapon of choice instead. That seemed like a fair punishment for snooping through her stuff and giving away her things.

Except it wasn't her book, not really. It was *his*,

and she was only keeping it safe until he came back. Charlotte soothed her angry thoughts with the possibility of Fawkes' return. She just had to act friendly with the rebels until Fawkes came back to collect the rest of his payment. Charlotte would be there waiting to face him, demanding an explanation. She just had to hold out for a few more weeks.

Unless he ends up in trouble, a sneaky voice in her head whispered. Startled, Charlotte accidentally kicked an uneven paving stone. As she hopped up and down, her throbbing toe served as a reminder that distraction led to misstep.

Guilt and understanding slammed into her. *Of course Fawkes freaked out after our kiss.* He had a contract to fulfill, yet he had kissed her and opened the door to all kinds of emotions and feelings he had been suppressing. It would be enough to put anyone off kilter, and in his line of work, deadly.

For the past few days, Charlotte had operated under the assumption that Fawkes would return to her in one piece, but she suddenly realized that he might not return at all if something happened. If, due to her brashness, her infallible mentor lost focus. At the thought of his demise, the hurt and disappointment she held onto after his blunt departure dissipated. Charlotte prayed he would be all right as tears welled in her eyes. *I can't lose another person I love.*

Her eyes widened. *Do I love Fawkes?* She respected him as a teacher, yes, and felt an attraction, but love... Outside of family, that was a foreign concept to her. She cared for him deeply, she couldn't deny that, but it was complicated beyond words. Charlotte shook her head, trying to rid herself of confusing thoughts.

It was at that moment she felt the cool sharpness of a knife at her throat.

"I've been looking for you," a voice growled in her ear.

Chapter Ten

Charlotte had been in his dungeons, at his table, and under his gaze, but none of those experiences prepared her for the paralyzing terror she felt when Duke Belaq's arms surrounded her. Though she held a sensible fear of his knife pressed against her jugular, it was an unnecessary tool when accompanied by his presence. She choked back her panic, wishing she was anywhere else, even on the top of the mountain pass again. Given the choice, Charlotte would face her phobia a hundred times if it meant that Belaq didn't have his hands on her skin.

He chuckled, as though he was flattered by her physical disgust. "Who would have thought that the Cloaked Shadow's little pet would fall right into my lap? I wanted him, but I'll settle for you." His dangerous tone made her legs give out.

Still holding her captive, the duke pushed her toward a less-crowded side street. *Stay calm, breathe,* she reminded herself, as she tried to formulate an escape. Her surrounding environment was less than ideal, but there were plenty of objects that she could turn into weapons with the right intention.

Duke Belaq walked her up against a wall and whirled her around to face him. He licked his lips, running his knife from Charlotte's throat to her cheek, stroking with gentle caresses. "I didn't think you would have survived this long, but," he leaned in to tell her his secret, "I hoped you would."

"Why, so I can tell you to burn in hell?" Charlotte waited for the cut to come, to feel the blood run down her face, but the knife continued its languid path.

Belaq's forehead rested against Charlotte's, like a lover about to steal a kiss. "Because we never got to have that little chat about your brother. My guards were sent to fetch you. Imagine my delighted surprise when they told me that the girl I wanted to question had run off with the most wanted man in the kingdom? We almost had you in Hawthorne's village, but you both slipped away. Still, I wanted to thank you. For the chase. I haven't had this much fun in years."

The knife nicked a shallow cut near her temple, and Charlotte cried out. Like a serpent, Belaq's tongue darted out to lick the blood with a savory caress. She pulled back in revulsion while he toyed with her, mistaking her trembles of rage for those of fear.

The mention of Duke Belaq's guards, and the day they killed her mother, transformed Charlotte's terror. The emotions those memories evoked were enough to send a burst of adrenaline to her paralyzed muscles. If Belaq thought that she was just a scared little girl, he was sadly mistaken.

Belaq ran his bloody tongue over his lips with a gleam of desire in his gaze, his hand still holding the knife by the side of her head. Before Charlotte could second-guess herself, her hand shot up to grab his arm and slam his wrist down onto her shoulder. The impact sent shock waves through her bones and made her wonder if her collar bone had broken in two, but the jolt was enough to make Belaq lose his grip on the blade.

The knife clattered to the ground behind her, but Charlotte didn't have time to pick it up. She feigned right and bolted left, making use of her opening. She would not have the chance to surprise Belaq again, so she focused on putting as much distance between them as possible.

Light on her feet, Charlotte bounded over strewn debris before launching herself over a wagon that blocked her entrance to the main street. She heard the duke cursing, but she didn't risk a glance over her shoulder. Looking behind her would cost precious seconds she did not have. She was no match for him as a fighter, especially without a weapon, but Charlotte remembered her sparring lessons with Fawkes and concentrated on running away. Sometimes it was better to just avoid getting hit in the first place.

However, the chase was nothing new to Belaq. He panted behind her, never more than a few feet away as they raced up the hill. Her defensive attack hadn't injured him; if anything, it seemed to increase his desire for her. The duke let out a gleeful bellow, reminding Charlotte of hound dogs on the scent during a hunt.

Charlotte understood why the duke was out doing his own dirty work. Here, he was in his element— chasing, toying, and inflicting pain. Nobleman or not, Belaq would have never let his guards have all the fun. The duke that Charlotte faced now was a different duke from the one she knew at the castle. That version of Duke Belaq was restrained, like a dog in a muzzle. Away from his responsibilities and societal constraints, he let the true version of himself escape. His demon was out to play, and it would not be satisfied until Charlotte was at his mercy.

Charlotte's heart pounded, her breath coming in painful gasps as her strides started to falter. Still, she could feel the duke gaining on her, so she took a chance and veered sharply for the pub. If it came to an actual fight, she needed to do it on familiar territory, taking every advantage she could get. She was also depending on the fact that blood lust made Belaq sloppy. His animalistic counterpart was powerful, but it also lacked the precision and cunning that made Duke Belaq so frightening back at the castle.

The heat from his body was so close she could feel him as he honed in on her. As she braced herself for his tackle, suddenly he was gone. Charlotte sprinted for a few more lengths before realizing that no one was in pursuit anymore. Hardly daring to believe it, and half-expecting a trap, she turned around.

Three of the rebels were on top of Belaq. A crowd started to gather, drawn to the violent spectacle of a thrashing, cursing man held down with his face in the dirt. While her burning lungs tried to take in enough air, Charlotte also stared at the snarling duke, not quite willing to believe she had escaped unscathed. *Well, almost unscathed*, she thought, as a trickle of blood streamed down her face.

Realizing how close she had come to disaster, her over-exerted legs gave out and she fell to the ground. The man of her nightmares, the cause of her family's pain, was there in front of her. He had laid his hands on her. Threatened her. And she had bested him.

It wasn't just me, she admitted grudgingly. Charlotte had to admit that the rebels' timing had been most opportune. She had never been so happy to see people she so disliked. A shadow fell over her seated form, and she looked up.

"Had yourself quite the scare," Robin said. "We've been looking for Belaq within the city for three days. Who knew it took a woman to bring out the best in him?"

Charlotte scowled. "You followed me." It wasn't a question.

"It wasn't hard to predict that his history with Henry would extend to you as well. We needed bait to catch the fish." He shrugged.

"He almost killed me!" Charlotte exploded. "Did you happen to see that part?"

Robin ignored her, stepping over her legs as he strode over to Belaq. Charlotte scrambled upright, her fury propelling her forward.

"I don't want any more attention on this—" Robin whispered to his thugs.

The duke laughed as they held him down, his body shaking with mirth. "Somebody quiet him," Robin said, which only made the duke giggle like a madman.

Oh, I got this, Charlotte thought, pulling her foot back with practiced grace. She let it fly, kicking Belaq in the head and knocking him out cold. "You're welcome," she spat at them all.

****

As much as Robin seemed to want the news of Belaq's capture kept quiet, the news spread like wildfire throughout the Algonian neighborhood. Charlotte wondered how long it would take for the story to get back to Belaq's army, and when they would storm into the city to free him. The rebels would realize far too late that they couldn't tame a wild beast, and it wouldn't take long before all hell broke loose.

For the time being, the duke was tied up in the pub cellar while Robin decided on a course of action. The opportunity to kill the right-hand man of the king was within his power, but first the rebels needed information.

Charlotte was surprised to be invited into the inner circle while the two leaders squared off. Henry and only a select few of Robin's most trusted men joined them.

"How fortunate I am," Belaq mused as he faced his captors, "that I should be led straight to the very traitors the king has been searching for. Minus the most important one, however. Still, the Cloaked Shadow led me this far. I should thank him."

Robin's fist came out of nowhere and hit Belaq across the jaw, sending blood and spittle flying onto the walls. The duke just grinned at him with bloody teeth, looking for all the world like he was having the best time.

"You know," Belaq said, "you should have just let me have the girl. Then your whole operation would have stayed hidden. You have no idea what you have unleashed. My men will be combing the city before dawn, looking for me."

The threats earned him two more punches from Robin before the redhead was pulled off the prisoner. "So sad and pathetic," the duke taunted. "Your failed schemes do nothing to the crown but give us prisoners to fill our dungeons with." His eyes flashed to Henry, who unconsciously moved closer to Charlotte for comfort.

He's toying with us, Charlotte realized. *All of us. He thinks that he is buying time by distracting us from asking the real questions.*

He widened his eyes at her. "And you," Belaq address Charlotte. "When will your friend return? We have unfinished business."

Robin turned to look at her. "What is he talking about?"

"I don't know." Charlotte met his accusing glare unwaveringly.

"And here I thought that was why they took you in," Belaq said.

"Charlotte?" Henry asked, looking more confused than Robin.

Belaq sighed. "Unbelievable. It is a shame you have no idea what you've stumbled upon. That girl is all the leverage you need over your employee."

"What employee?" Robin asked.

"The Cloaked Shadow." The duke then burst out laughing. "The only worthy opponent amongst you stumbling buffoons. I had hoped our confrontation would happen sooner, but it appears I will have to wait for another time." Every person in the room turned to stare at Charlotte in disbelief and suspicion.

"Did he teach you those naughty fighting skills?" Belaq asked her, pleased that all of the attention had been diverted from thoughts of torturing him for information. "Because I will need to remember that for next time." He licked his lips and continued. "What else did he teach you? What do you have up your sleeve?"

Charlotte glared at him but refused to answer. Henry leaned over to whisper to her. "I think you should leave for now." She was inclined to agree with her brother. The confrontation needed to end before any further secrets spilled forth. Plus, there was no doubt in her mind that Robin was already considering the implications of the duke's reveal. Silently, she backed her way to the cellar stairs.

"You aren't going anywhere," the rebel leader snapped. "The timing… You were with him, must have traveled here with him. You know the Cloaked Shadow's true identity." His voice had gone breathy with excitement, in a sickening way that made Charlotte wonder just what he had planned for her.

There was no point in denying it anymore. *Wherever you are, Fawkes, please forgive me,* she prayed silently. Now her only course of action was to keep Robin from saying Fawkes' name in front of Belaq. "Don't say anything more," Charlotte warned Robin. Her gaze met his, begging for him to understand what she was asking.

A slow grin spread over the redhead's face. "Yes, I think that is enough talking for now," he agreed. Robin grabbed Charlotte's shoulder and leaned in to whisper in her ear. "When I'm done with the duke, we are going to have a long discussion about *Fawkes*." He savored the name, letting it run slowly through his lips.

Then he turned to address the cluster of rebels waiting for his instructions. "I think I've heard all I need to about our mutual mysterious friend. And until the duke starts giving us answers to our other important questions, we have to do something to fill the time." A boisterous cheer went up in the room.

"Based on recent events, I think it is only right that we allow Henry to go first, right lads?" Robin roared.

An unseen figure nudged Henry forward, pushing him past Charlotte's side. "Go on, son," Robin urged, his face shiny with sweat and sick anticipation. Charlotte watched her brother approach the duke cautiously, stopping within arm's reach of the powerful prisoner before refusing to go any further. He turned around to look for reassurance in his comrades' faces, and instead his gaze found Charlotte's distraught expression. A sense of dread overcame her as she realized what they were all about to do. They wanted her sweet little brother to be the one to start it all.

The duke leered at Henry, challenge in his stance as he readied himself within the chains. "I hoped it would be you," Belaq said. "Do you know what I did to your poor, sweet mother? What my guards did to her as they dragged her, screaming, from your house?" Henry's hands clenched into fists as he tried to process what the duke was telling him.

Charlotte knew then that Belaq had no fear of beatings or torture, not if he could have the upper hand in some form. That intoxicating power was too tempting for common sense and self-preservation to overcome. He prided himself on being one step ahead of everyone else, and loved to pull the puppet strings. He played with Henry, knowing full well the repercussions his words incited. But it would be worth it to him to utterly destroy a man, to watch him disintegrate to his basic urges and lose total control.

"You lie," Henry spat, limbs quivering.

"Do you think I would just let you walk out of my dungeon without punishment?" the duke said, low and deadly. "There is always a price to be paid. Your mother paid it for you with her life."

A small gasp escaped from Charlotte's throat. At the sound, Henry turned around to see if by some miracle the duke was wrong, to reassure himself that his sister had not lied to him. Henry's look of betrayal was enough to send tears pouring down her cheeks. Grief, the same grief that Charlotte had been processing over her long journey, slammed into Henry all at once. Unlike Charlotte, Henry had the very object of blame tied up in front of him, and he unleashed his anger in a frenzy of punches.

Except for a few small grunts, no sound escaped from the duke as Henry struck his flesh. Charlotte, however, started screaming. "Henry! Stop! Please!" she begged. This feral creature in front of her wasn't the brother she knew. She was powerless, forced to witness as the boy she grew up with toss away all semblance of his former self, baptized in violence and blood. Though she herself had fantasized about killing the duke for his crimes, seeing the reality of Henry's transformation deeply disturbed her. Like a mirror, Charlotte could see Belaq's nature taking hold inside Henry and reflecting back upon him.

When she couldn't take it anymore, Charlotte ran forward to pull Henry off while the rebels laughed. He whirled on her while swinging a well-aimed punch at her head. Charlotte ducked just in time, and tackled Henry at his knees. "Enough. Stop!"

Belaq wheezed out a chuckle from his swollen face, already turning black and blue from the assault. He sagged in his bonds, bloody spit bubbling from his mouth and dripping onto the ground.

"Henry!" Charlotte wrestled with her brother. "Listen to me—"

"*You*," Henry gasped. "How could you?"

"I'm sorry I couldn't tell you—"

Henry shoved his sister off of him before she could finish her excuses. Wild-eyed, he stood up and looked around the cellar, taking in Charlotte on the ground, Belaq in his chains, and the rebels grinning at him. He shoved his way to the stairs and out of the cellar.

Charlotte ran up right behind him, and Robin didn't move to stop her. "Henry, wait!" she cried. She needed to make things right with him, but also reassure herself that her brother, and not the stranger that tortured Belaq, still resided in his body. Charlotte heard the door close behind her as they ran into the alley, presumably to continue interrogating Belaq.

As the siblings burst through the door of their temporary home, Henry refused to acknowledge Charlotte. At that moment, something inside of her snapped, and she couldn't take the brunt of his misplaced anger any longer. "I did it to protect you, Henry," she told him. He refused to turn around and acknowledge her, his silence telling her everything she needed to know. "But I can see now you are not a little boy anymore." The sight of his brutal attack flashed in her mind with every blink. "But I've been through hell for you, and I didn't do it so you could become Robin's protégée. I hate Belaq too, but if I ever see you do something like that again, I'm gone. Even if you are my brother, I refuse to stand by and watch while you lose pieces of your humanity."

Like Fawkes has, she thought to herself. *Which is why now he only kills if he has to.* Fawkes might straddle the line between right and wrong, but he never killed out of malice or joy. It was simply part of the job for him. The absolute abandon she witnessed in both the duke and Henry when engaged in violence was directly opposite of the cool, calm, collected manner in which the Cloaked Shadow conducted business. But which was worse? Was one manner less human than the other?

Henry's words broke through her thoughts. "You're going to lecture *me*? After you've been traveling with the most prolific and wanted criminal for weeks now, keeping his identity secret and protecting him? How many people do you think your precious Cloaked Shadow, or should I say *Fawkes*, has killed? Get off your high horse, Charlotte. You are no better than I am. No better than the rebels are. You don't get to tell me when I've gone too far. Not after the secrets you've kept."

Hearing Fawkes' name from Henry's lips left Charlotte momentarily stunned. Her brother had pieced it all together in the cellar, just like Robin. She remained rooted in the doorway while Henry stomped toward their room, leaving her alone with panicked thoughts.

Now that Fawkes' name was out in the open, she suspected it was only a matter of time before Robin used his intelligence network to discover Fawkes' true identity and history. And it was all her fault. Weeks of wishing for Fawkes' return were suddenly replaced with fear at actually seeing him in the flesh. He would never forgive her for giving away the last true part of himself for others to manipulate.

"Don't come back," she whispered. "It isn't safe anymore." Fawkes' memory had given her strength the past few weeks while she handled the rebels, her brother, and trying to start a new life. His lessons taught her the life skills she needed to transform herself. To imagine the look on her mentor's face when he realized she had ultimately betrayed him...it was too much to bear. Maybe it was as much for her as it was for Fawkes that she wished him to stay away.

Robin yearned for power and control. Charlotte knew he would use any means necessary to make Fawkes do what he wanted. Robin had practically begged Fawkes to assassinate people for the cause. What would happen to Fawkes if he could no longer refuse?

****

Charlotte woke up alone in the house the next morning. Henry appeared to be long gone, and she guessed he was already back at the cellar. She refused to think about what the rebels must have put Duke Belaq through during the night. He had harmed many of their loved ones, and she understood their rage. But torturing someone for days…that she could not be a part of, especially if she had to watch Henry do it. The teeny part of her that might have felt that Belaq was getting what he deserved was squashed by nausea.

Her head ached and her throat felt parched beyond belief. Sleep had been a long time coming the night before, as she relived her trauma every time she closed her eyes. The feeling of Belaq's knife on her neck and his hot breath closing in on her would not easily be forgotten. Even in the warm dawn light, the nightmares clung to her.

Desperate for distraction, she flung open the front door and took a cleansing inhale. That was when she saw them. Soldiers, dressed in plainclothes, but soldiers all the same. Their body movements revealed a history of strict discipline as their search progressed up the hill toward her. They carried no swords and wore no armor, but Charlotte was not naïve enough to assume they were unarmed. She counted six of them as they darted in and out of the buildings, stopping to question civilians out on the streets.

They had come for Belaq, just as he said they would.

Chapter Eleven

Robin's ragtag rebel army was no match against the Duke Belaq's soldiers. The rebels thrived in the dark, collecting information, usurping the kingdom from within. A full-on confrontation against trained soldiers would be a bloodbath.

Weighing her options, Charlotte decided to hold off on sprinting to the pub. *There might be hundreds of soldiers combing the streets.*

She shut the door and started to pace, forcing herself to think rationally before careening out the door to warn her brother. *I might stand a chance if it was dark out.* But confronting men twice her size, with no backup, in broad daylight, would be suicide. She was also a known rebel associate. Her usually-friendly neighbors would not think twice to point her out when threatened with bodily harm from Belaq's men.

I'm a sitting duck in this house all alone. Charlotte decided that moving was better than hiding inside and waiting for them to find her. She pulled out one of Henry's threadbare tunics and threw it over her clothes. Next, she scraped at the dirt floor to gather a handful of soil, which she smeared on her face and arms. A scrap of bedding served as a kerchief to hide her hair, and she kicked off her shoes to complete the disguise of a poor beggar child. Her appearance wouldn't hold up to close scrutiny, but she just needed to avoid immediate detection as she navigated the streets.

Once outside, she forced her heart to maintain a steady pace. With eyes cast downward as she hugged the alleys and storefronts, she had almost made it to the pub before she was stopped. "Oi, girl!" one of the soldiers yelled to her.

So close. "Algonian or Croantian?" he asked her. She simply shook her head, eyes wide with confusion. He stepped forward, any evidence of false friendliness gone. "I asked you a question."

Again, Charlotte shook her head, but motioned to her mouth with her hands. She started an elaborate series of hand gestures until he finally sighed. "A dumb mute. Fine. You'll have no information for me." As an afterthought, the soldier reached a hand out and shoved her backward into the mud. Charlotte fell without protest.

Glaring at his retreating back, Charlotte watched as a bystander who had watched the exchange approached the soldier. *Uh oh,* she thought. *Need to leave. Right now.* Using all of the swiftness and grace that Fawkes had taught her, Charlotte was out of sight and down the alley before she could be questioned further.

Through her fear, Charlotte reveled in the adrenaline high. She hadn't felt a thrill like that since her time with Fawkes. Risking her life and sneaking right under the enemy's nose was terrifying, but she had also forgotten how much of a rush it gave her. Feeling so alive yet in control brought Charlotte closer to her true self.

The outside entrance to the cellar was finally within sight. Thankfully, she spotted none of Belaq's men in the immediate vicinity. The two rebels assigned to guard the door sat on wooden crates, looking bored and clueless. Charlotte sprinted up to them. "We need to get inside. Now."

They smirked at each other before one turned to answer. "If you're looking for your baby brother, he's been in there a while, making Robin proud."

It took all of her self-control not to address that statement. Instead, she plowed on to the urgent matter at hand. "Belaq's men are combing the city. They will be here soon. We have to get everyone out."

Both pairs of eyes narrowed. "If you're lying just so you can get in here…"

"Do you want to take responsibility for the death of your 'brothers'? Because if they find all of you together, conveniently crammed in one place, then no one down there is making it out alive. Except for the duke. His men are out for blood. They will tear this city apart until they find him."

That statement straightened the guards right up, and they opened the cellar doors for her. Morning light streamed into the dark room lit only by torches, and squinting faces turned to peer up at her. She walked a few steps down before turning to address the rebel guards still up top. "Hurry. Follow me, and shut the doors behind you."

"What is the meaning of this?" Robin's voice cut through the confused chatter.

For a moment, Charlotte had the wicked thought of just getting Henry out and leaving the rest to their fates. Horrified that she would condemn all these men to death, even in passing thought, Charlotte decided to get right to the point. "Belaq's men are in the city. We have moments to get out and hide."

Robin's eyes widened for a split second, then he dismissed her with a wave of his hand. "They will never find us down here. This is our territory. No one will betray us."

Infuriated by his cavalier attitude, Charlotte saw that he failed to grasp the gravity of the situation. "It only takes one person to flip, Robin," she said. No one else spoke around them, but the tension that formed amongst the men was palpable, permeating the room and building on itself the longer Charlotte and Robin squared off. "Duke Belaq's men are fiercely loyal. You haven't killed him yet, have you? He is our only chance of getting away alive."

Charlotte pushed her way past Robin, to the man still chained up against the wall. She held her breath as she approached the sagging body, sick to see that not an inch of skin remained unmarred. Bruises, swollen flesh, and crooked appendages transformed the sadistic nobleman into someone who hardly looked human. The surface wounds were only the beginning. Torture was always worse when it was inflicted on parts unable to be seen by the human eye.

He would have done worse to Henry if you hadn't gotten him out of prison. And Belaq would have done the same to you. The realization gave her cold comfort as she forced herself to watch the prisoner draw a shaky, shallow inhale.

"Leave him here for his men to find," she instructed the rebels. "We need to get out through the side tunnel and away from the city."

Robin rounded on her. "You dare give my men orders?"

Charlotte met his anger, and they stood almost nose

to nose—she looking up, and Robin towering over her. "Are you not listening? Everyone will die if they find us here with Belaq."

"*I* am in charge. What makes you think I will take the advice of a woman," he spat the word at her, "much less a liar?"

Henry's voice spoke up. "My sister wouldn't lie about this. If she says the duke's men will find us, then we need to trust her." Charlotte felt a rush of affection for her brother, assuaging any doubts that she had done the right thing by coming here again.

Ignoring the siblings, Robin turned his back to them and addressed his men. "Everyone make for the tunnel. I will kill Belaq and leave his men a message for daring to come into our city." A muted cheer went up, and Charlotte jumped in front of Belaq as Robin drew his blade.

"You can't kill him," she said. "If he is alive, his men will rescue him and buy us time to get away. If they find him dead, they will lay waste to the city and everyone in it." She could hardly believe she was defending the life of the duke, but it was the only way her plan would work. Escape was the number one priority, and justice for her family would have to come later. "Please, Robin. Think. It will be weeks before he is healed. His men will wait for his orders to act. This will allow you the opportunity to reorganize elsewhere. If you act rashly now, everything will be thrown into chaos." Then Charlotte pulled out her last card to play. "Algonia will remain under King Otan's rule."

That seemed to snap Robin out of his determination to slit his enemy's throat. The reminder of his ultimate goal was enough to overcome his desire to shed any more of the duke's blood. Charlotte shuddered to think what would happen the next time she faced the duke after this, but that was a nightmare for another day. Belaq would make sure they paid for his capture and torture, she had no doubt.

Robin sheathed his blade, and Charlotte almost thought she heard a sigh of relief come from the unconscious man behind her. "Single file through the tunnel, now," he barked the order at his men. He did not ask Charlotte how she knew about the tunnel, but she suspected another interrogation was coming once they were all safe again.

One by one the men dropped to their knees and crawled through their escape route. Charlotte got in line behind Henry, refusing to let him out of her sight as they all fumbled and cursed their way through the darkness. Robin was last to emerge in the basement of the building next door. He pushed the crates back to block the entrance and said, "We'll head north, to the farms. Our brotherhood faction there will welcome us. Now, everyone up to the surface and split up into groups of four. Take the side streets. You all know where to exit through the wall. Don't draw attention to yourselves, and move quickly. If what Charlotte says is true, Belaq's men will be momentarily occupied when they find the duke. This is our only chance to make a clean getaway. Does everyone understand?"

If Henry and I are going to split from the rebels, now is our chance, Charlotte realized. As tempting as that was, however, they still needed to escape the city in one piece, and she had no idea where to breach the encompassing wall. So when Robin himself insisted that he would accompany them, she raised no objections. He was keeping a close eye on her, just as she was on him.

Robin knew his territory like the back of his hand. He led them safely through the city, and Charlotte's surroundings flashed in a blur as she raced through the maze of streets. At that moment, they were all on the same side—the side of survival. Everything else, including Fawkes, could wait. She was actually grateful for the rebel leader's presence and skill.

When they reached the exit point, Henry balked at diving into the sewage-filled river that led underneath the wall and out to freedom. Robin held the key to the grate that covered the exit, which consisted of iron bars the size of Charlotte's fist that stretched all the way down to the bottom of the riverbed. The redhead dove in first, opened the passageway, and swam through. Charlotte then shoved Henry into the swirling stench before jumping in after him. *It's no worse than the first time I swam through sewage,* she told herself as her head went under. While stretching her hands out in front of her to navigate the water by touch, the fact that she had come full circle did not escape her notice. *At least there is no drain to climb up this time.*

The siblings pulled themselves onto the bank, gasping and gagging, and collapsed as they waited for the other rebels to join them. One by one, dark heads bobbed up out of the sludge and joined the pitiful group on the shore. By midday, everyone was accounted for, save four members.

"Where are Liam, Pierre, John, and Paul?" Robin asked. No one knew for sure where they had gone, but everyone could guess what might have happened. The rebels all looked somberly at the river, as if willing their missing comrades to magically appear. "We will have to trust that they didn't reveal anything. If I know them, they will have gone down swinging their fists, or impaled themselves on a soldier's sword before being captured," Robin said.

Charlotte noticed the worry in his voice, almost as if he spoke aloud to reassure himself that everything would be fine. "They sacrificed themselves for our mission," Robin's pitch raised higher. "We cannot let their sacrifice be in vain. Come, we have to move onward. Our brothers are waiting for us."

Weary, stinking, and disheartened, the group looked less like rebels and more like defeated children. As the Croantian town shrank behind them in the distance, Charlotte felt like she could breathe easier. It felt good to be back in nature, away from the claustrophobic city. If Belaq also lurked there, presumably still alive, then every mile she put between them was a blessing.

However, the enormity of their situation began to blossom as Charlotte's hunger pains grew more insistent. Every rock she stepped on sent shooting pains through her feet, and she regretted her decision to forgo shoes that morning. With no money or food to speak of, she had actually become a poor beggar girl, and her outfit was a costume no more.

She envied the other men who walked ahead of her, all of whom wore sturdy boots and had a weapon or two tucked away in their britches. Charlotte felt as good as naked. The black ribbon still held her hair back proudly though.

To keep her mind from her discomfort, Charlotte's thoughts turned to Fawkes. Had he been successful in breaking Stefan out from under the king's nose? Why hadn't word been sent to the rebels yet of his success? Shouldn't they have heard something by now?

Her heart clenched at the thought of Fawkes returning to the rebel headquarters within the walled city and finding it empty. The rebels still owed Fawkes the other half of his gold, so she had no doubt that if the contract was completed, Fawkes would track Robin down for the rest of his payment. If he saw that Belaq's men had occupied the city and chased out the rebels, then he might be able to guess where Robin would take them to recuperate. Would Fawkes be worried about her? Would he come for her, or just the money?

The small hope that she would see Fawkes again propelled her, mile after mile, with bloody feet and a grumbling belly.

****

Robin led them deeper north into the countryside, and finally to a sparsely wooded area to seek shelter for the night. Charlotte, who expected Belaq's men to come charging up at any moment, couldn't relax even though she was utterly exhausted and beyond hungry. She and Henry hadn't said a word to each other since the cellar, and even Robin avoided asking her further questions. The fact that they had come so close to certain death was weighing on everyone. It was easier to keep the silence than to examine it all too closely.

Careful not to touch him, Charlotte found a spot close to her brother and laid down on the pine needles. A symphony of snores told her that most everyone was fast asleep, trying to recover after their harrowing day. Robin and a few of the others had volunteered to be first watch, but Charlotte still remained on high alert. It wasn't as though she didn't trust them to raise an alarm at the first sign of trouble, but she feared that they would recognize it too late. Her skin prickled, senses alive and telling her that something was coming, something that she could detect but the others could not. This was where she had trained—out in the open. Robin and his followers had let the city dull their senses. Their animal instincts had lain dormant for far too long.

Charlotte couldn't take it anymore and stood up. "Robin," she urged. "Someone is coming. Maybe more than one."

He all but rolled his eyes at her, not dignifying her remark with a response. Her spine straightened as she stared through the trees, waiting for a flash of movement to prove to Robin that she was right. Her ears picked up on the sudden quiet that permeated the camp, as all the nocturnal insects silenced their activities.

Clear moonlight streamed down, creating shadows that tricked her mind as she searched for danger. Robin finally caught on that there really was something there and motioned for the other scouts to follow him. They crept not-so-stealthily through the brush, and Charlotte winced every time she heard a stick crack. She decided to remain in the middle of their pathetic camp, ready to wake Henry and bolt at a moment's sign of trouble.

"Halt," Robin's voice rang through the camp loud and clear. "We have you surrounded." His voice was steady and proud, and it would have convinced Charlotte that he was telling the truth, had she not already known there were only five other men with him. "State your name and your purpose."

"Robin?" a voice asked in disbelief.

"William?"

"Brother, what are you doing here? We are on the way to meet you in the city as we planned."

Robin sighed. "Well, your scout team need go no further. We are all here. What's left of us, anyway."

Charlotte heard the two men approach each other, then their voices dropped to a whisper. Reaching down, she shook Henry awake and waited to see what Robin would do.

The rebel leader walked back to the middle of camp with three strange men trailing behind him. "Everybody up," he barked. Once the men circled around him, he turned their attention to the newcomers. "William has brought word to us from Algonia." Robin nodded at his companion to proceed.

"Revolutionaries of Algonia, I am here to tell you our faction received word that Stefan's rescue was a success." A quiet cheer went up among the crowd, and Charlotte breathed a sigh of relief. Fawkes had done the impossible by swiping an instrumental revolutionary man out from under the king's castle. "As such, Stefan has also provided our men in Numencaster with the necessary information to proceed with our attack. Although I am very sorry to hear of your run in with Duke Belaq, I must urge you to push your discomforts aside. Now is the time for us to act. I, along with our brilliant leader, Robin, will lead you to my farm, where the rest of our forces are waiting. From there, we will journey together to cross the border into Algonia and launch a two-pronged assault."

The men surrounding Charlotte clapped each other on the back, grinning ear to ear. Robin looked both pleased and relieved to see morale lifted, but Charlotte wore a thoughtful frown. Just what sort of attack were they planning? Even if William's forces matched Robin's, they would still be woefully outnumbered by the king's army. Not to mention the wrath of a very pissed off duke once he had healed. Charlotte couldn't think of any actual way that they would be able to emerge victorious, much less unscathed.

Robin stepped in. "Get some rest, men. We leave at first light." As everyone settled back in, Charlotte pretended to walk further into the forest to urinate. Her crashing footsteps halted once she was out of sight of the men, and she doubled back with lithe, silent steps. She concealed herself behind a tree close enough to hear the continuing private conversation between Robin and William.

"And Stefan kept the rest of the powder well hidden?" Robin asked.

"Almost everything is in place," William reassured him. "But there is one small issue. A rumor, really." He hesitated, as if embarrassed to go on. "Stefan was in deplorable condition when he was rescued. Babbling a lot of nonsense. He kept talking about a woman who was brought down to question him from time to time. He claimed...he claimed she has the gift of second sight; that she is the king's seer. Stefan thinks she is why so many of our undercover agents have been captured in the recent years."

"Hallucinations from the trauma, most likely," Robin said, brushing off William's story. "I've never had any other agent report these rumors to me. If she is truly as powerful as Stefan believes, then many others throughout the kingdom would have heard about her by now."

Meanwhile, Charlotte's mind was reeling. She thought back to what Fawkes had mentioned about his beloved wife, Josephine, and her many talents. And although the second sight was a rare gift, Stefan had to be talking about a different woman. It was impossible that Fawkes' wife would still be alive after all these years. *Did Stefan tell Fawkes about the mysterious woman when he was rescued?* Charlotte hoped not. The ramblings would only serve to hurt Fawkes and remind him of his painful history.

William sighed. "We are lucky that Stefan even returned to us at all, with almost all of his mental facilities intact. The ones we need, anyway."

"What did you hear of his rescue?"

"The Cloaked Shadow took an arrow to the shoulder as they fled the castle grounds. He and Stefan got away, but barely. The guards sounded the alarm and were out in full force, rendering the Cloaked Shadow and Stefan late to the rendezvous point. We had almost given up hope that they were coming. The Cloaked Shadow didn't let on that he was in pain, but we could see the broken arrow sticking out of his back when he handed Stefan over to us. Guess that solves the mystery of whether or not the cloak is as strong as armor, eh?"

Charlotte's heart clenched. Fawkes was out there alone and injured. It sounded like he was in no shape to come riding back into her life any time soon. But he was alive, the last time anyone saw him. That would have to be enough for now.

Chapter Twelve

Robin and William rallied the group at dawn, with Charlotte bringing up the rear for another long trudge to the farm. After a few days of promised rest and a resupply of food, horses, and weapons, the rebel army would make for Algonia. The plan was to ultimately meet near Numencaster where Stefan and the other agents would be waiting.

Charlotte wanted to question the men around her and find out all she could about the planned attack, but she couldn't risk drawing Robin's attention again. He seemed to have forgotten about her overnight, and she intended to keep it that way. Also, try as she might, it was hard to have thoughts other than worrying about Fawkes. She was so distracted that she didn't even notice when Henry slowed his march to fall in line next to her.

Out of the corner of her eye, she saw him open his mouth as if to say something, then change his mind as he shut it with a clack. She knew why he was struggling, because she was fighting the same internal battle. Words were on the tip of her tongue; she didn't know whether it was to apologize to him or to lecture him. The boy who walked beside her felt like a stranger. How long would it take before she could reconcile the memory of her feral brother, reveling in blood lust, with the gentle soul she had grown up with?

From Henry's point of view, Charlotte was a liar. Not only had she deceived him with their mother's death, but also denied her relationship with Fawkes. She gave him no reason to trust her of late. The siblings both felt the gap between them, how things had changed, but at the moment, neither one of them was strong enough to reach out and bridge it.

After a few more moments, Henry moved up toward the front of the line, leaving Charlotte behind. The relief she felt when he left frightened her. He was on his own chosen path now, and nothing Charlotte could say would deter him from it.

****

Robin pushed the rebels as far as they could go, but it wasn't enough to reach William's farm by the time twilight fell. It didn't matter to Charlotte though, who almost cried with relief when they had stopped to camp by a small stream. After two days of sewage stink on her skin, Charlotte was beginning to feel more like a rat and less like a person.

William left them with promises that he would be back before dawn and set off for his home on horseback. She expected that he would return under the cover of darkness with more men and a plan for how to proceed. Until another meeting was called, she decided that her presence would not be missed, and sprinted upstream and out of sight.

Humming with delight, she threw caution to the wind and jumped into the water, clothes and all. Once she drenched herself, she disrobed piece by piece and began scrubbing her clothes in the stream. She watched the filth run out of her garments until the water ran clear again. Without leaving the cool delight of the stream, she tossed her newly clean, soggy bundle up onto a boulder on the bank.

Untangling the ribbon from her hair, she rinsed it off tenderly, and then clenched it between her teeth for safekeeping while she scrubbed her hair. Charlotte let the water envelop her completely, and she relaxed into its gentle hold. She didn't mind when she felt the current begin to push her downstream, until her feet hit something solid.

Panicked, she sat up sputtering, yanking the black fabric from her mouth. Wiping her vision clear, she realized she had run smack into the legs of a man who stood at the center of the stream. *One of the rebels followed me!* Charlotte thought and remembered her vulnerable position. Bedrock sliced her palms and heels as she scrambled backward. Charlotte put enough distance between them to look up and see his face.

When her eyes met a blue gaze, she briefly wondered if maybe she had drowned and this was the afterlife. Struck dumb, she simply stared at him, each one waiting for the other to speak first. Charlotte searched her brain frantically for something to say. All those weeks imagining their reunion, and she hadn't prepared for a scenario such as this. Weakly, she held up the hand that still clutched the piece of black cloak. "Did you come all the way back for this?" He looked at it with wide eyes and extended one finger out as if to stroke the fabric. His finger brushed her knuckle instead, sending a jolt through Charlotte's body at the confirmation that he was, in fact, real.

That broke the spell, and Fawkes seemed to finally realize that he had interrupted Charlotte's bath. He immediately averted his gaze and waded toward her pile of clothes. Sloshing back to her, he extended the bundle to her without a word and turned around.

Charlotte yanked her tunic over her head, and then tried not to fall over as she pulled on the britches over her wet legs. The fabric clung to her like a second skin. Tying her hair back once more as a final touch, Charlotte was ready to confront him.

The impulse to yell at him died as she stared at the back of his tall frame. His head was bowed, blond hair dark with sweat on the nape of his neck. His left hand moved to his right arm before falling back to his side, as if he was going to cradle an injury, but the contact would hurt too much.

"You're alive," she said. At her words, Fawkes turned slowly around to face her.

"Did you expect anything less?" He raised an eyebrow.

"I heard it was close." Charlotte struggled to keep her voice level.

Fawkes rotated his right arm and winced. "Still in one piece. Relatively."

"And you came back. You found me."

He didn't answer right away and waded toward shore. Charlotte followed and felt better once she was on solid ground. As the shock of seeing him dissipated, her mind cleared, and she remembered why she was angry at him. "Yes. And I think I need to start charging more for my services," he finally said.

That's it? No mention of leaving without a goodbye, or our kiss, or the fact that my so-called 'new life' in Croantis was a disaster? Charlotte would have been better off staying in Algonia, seeing that a normal life was forever out of her reach. He had come all the way back to collect his precious payment from Robin, not to see her.

But if that is the case, her hopeful internal dialogue whispered, *why did he come to you first?* "Why are you here?" she blurted out.

A look of confusion flashed across his face. "Well, my contract with Robin has been completed—"

"Sod your contract!" Red anger flushed her face as she glared at him, hands on her hips. "Do you have any idea what these past weeks have been like? With the rebels, and Henry, and worrying about you... Why did you do it?"

Fawkes didn't have to ask what she meant. *Why did you leave me without an explanation?* That was the real question. He took a step forward so she was within arm's reach. "I'm sorry," he said, barely above a whisper. Rough fingers reached out to brush a wet tendril of hair off her forehead, and that simple touch broke her.

She flung her arms around his waist, buried her face in his chest, and sobbed. Charlotte finally let herself feel everything she had been repressing since her arrival in Croantis. Fawkes' disappearance, her reunion with Henry, the confrontation with Belaq, Robin's endless suspicions, her deteriorating relationship with her brother, even the memory of her mother—all of it bubbled to the surface.

Fawkes stood there stiffly at first, as if afraid to touch her, but soon comforting hands rubbed circles on her back as he made soothing noises in his chest. Charlotte sniffed and clung to him as her tears subsided, breathing returning to a regular rhythm. A kiss brushed across her forehead, and she felt her strength return. As she stepped back to tell him all that had happened, Fawkes suddenly threw up his hood, becoming the Cloaked Shadow in an instant. Any sign of Fawkes and his vulnerability disappeared. A second later, Henry emerged from the trees.

"Charlotte," he said. "Robin is looking for you." It was then he saw his sister was not alone, and swallowed audibly at the sight of her companion. "I'm sure your presence will be appreciated too, sir," he said, addressing Fawkes' looming form.

Henry's steps jerked awkwardly as he made his way back to camp, not turning around to see if his sister and the Cloaked Shadow were still following him. He entered the small clearing while staring down at his feet and made his way next to Robin. Charlotte looked to Robin's other side and noticed that William had returned during her absence.

"You have done us a great service," Robin said, addressing the Cloaked Shadow. The leader did not seem to be surprised at Fawkes' appearance, nor did he question Charlotte's arrival with him. Seeing the two of them together only solidified whatever suspicions he held from before, and he simply smiled at the pair. Twilight had faded, and now only the silvery light of the moon illuminated their surroundings in an ethereal glow. "The revolution thanks you."

The Cloaked Shadow stepped forward into the center of their circle. "I did not do it for the revolution," he said, voice raspy. "You still owe me fifty gold pieces. And an extra five for injuries incurred."

Robin shifted his weight from side to side, glancing over at William for support. "Since you have found us here instead of in the city, you must have an idea of the unfortunate circumstances that have befallen us." Fawkes crossed his arms and waited for the leader to continue. Robin's voice rose to an uncomfortable pitch. "As it stands, we cannot afford to pay you at the moment."

"Those were not the terms. You either pay me or you will come to regret it immensely." Charlotte didn't know what he meant by 'regret it immensely', and she had no desire to find out. One did not just back out of a deal with the Cloaked Shadow and walk away unscathed. With a predatory slink, he took three steps toward Robin.

Pure panic overtook Robin's face. "I know who you are!" he shrieked.

That stopped the Cloaked Shadow dead in his tracks. "I know who you are," Robin said again, this time at a lower register. Charlotte saw William's head whip back and forth between the two of them, presumably wondering why his partner had kept such an enormous secret from him.

Robin's next word was so quiet that Charlotte could barely hear it whispered. "Fawkes," he said.

The Cloaked Shadow remained rooted in place. William looked confused. "Fawkes?" he echoed. "Stefan said the woman from the castle often screamed that name. But I never said—"

Everything crashed into place for Charlotte. It was Josephine. The woman in the king's castle was Josie. In that split second, any hope for a future with Fawkes was ripped from her.

"No!" she screamed, just as Fawkes was about to leap onto Robin. Fawkes didn't know what William was talking about, but he knew that Robin had just

revealed his true name in front of everyone. Only Charlotte had all the information to put the pieces together in that instant, and realize what it meant.

Her outburst stalled Fawkes' attack, and every pair of eyes in the camp turned to her. She would have to be the one to tell him that the love of his life was still alive. She took a deep breath and prepared to lose him. She loved him too much not to tell him, even though it would destroy her.

Charlotte grabbed Fawkes' wrist with both her hands. "I have to tell you something," she said. "Come with me, now."

Fawkes jerked his arm from her grasp. "I have business here," he told her. "Stay out of this." His tone was icy. Charlotte realized that he thought she gave away his identity. There was no one else who could have told Robin, because she was the only one who knew his real name.

"I didn't do it," she begged him to listen. "I never told. It was an accident they found out, but—" Charlotte dropped to a whisper. "Josephine is alive."

That stopped Fawkes in his tracks, and he turned back to Charlotte. His fingers gripped her shoulders, squeezing until she felt her bones would break. "What did you say?" His voice was deadly calm; all traces of the heated emotions from moments ago were gone.

"It's true," she whispered, solidifying her fate with Fawkes as the words tumbled from her lips. "Leave them alone for now; don't let them find out. Come with me, and I'll tell you what I know." Charlotte held her breath, afraid that he wouldn't believe her. The truth seemed outrageous, even to her. But whatever irrational hope her words had stirred in him, Fawkes' hood bobbed once in acquiescence. Through his haze of anger, he still listened to her.

The black cloak swirled magnificently as Fawkes rounded on Robin again. "Two weeks," he warned. "I will collect my payment in two weeks. Otherwise, I needn't remind you that the Cloaked Shadow is not the only wanted man in Algonia with a price on his head. I will get my gold one way or another. You choose." Even in the moonlight, Charlotte could see the blush creep over Robin's face. His plan to blackmail Fawkes had gone over as well as could be expected. To make an enemy of the Cloaked Shadow was to spend the rest of your life looking over your shoulder, waiting for him to find you. She did not envy the rebel.

Charlotte expected Fawkes to compound on his threats, but he left it at that and fled up the trail. Charlotte spared one last glance around the circle, meeting Henry's eyes briefly before he looked away, and then sprinted after her mentor.

She ran until she stood again on the familiar bank, her small feet overlaying Fawkes' dried boot prints in the mud from an hour before. The young woman cocked her head, listening. The familiar thunder of hooves set her heart alight, even through the circumstances. It sounded like coming home.

The black horse and his dark rider burst into view, and this time, Charlotte was ready. She felt like she had been waiting her whole life for this, and a sense of peace overtook her. She held steady, legs splayed wide in a sturdy stance, watching the pair approach. Fawkes' hand reached out to her, but she hardly touched him as she leaped onto Ghost, as though they had practiced it a million times before. She settled in behind him and gripped his waist as they thundered away.

Once the rebels were a comfortable distance behind them, Fawkes slowed Ghost and dismounted. Charlotte felt a pang of regret that the ride was over so quickly, wanting to savor her one last moment with him before everything changed. The front of Charlotte's body felt the chill, and her arms ached with emptiness as her feet found the ground again.

The ride had pulled Fawkes' hood off, and he stood motionless yet windswept in front of her. She fidgeted, unable to achieve the absolute stillness her mentor accomplished as he separated his body from his mind. He simply waited for her to speak.

"Josephine is alive," she said.

"Yes, so you've mentioned. My question is, why would you believe such a thing? And who have you mistaken to be my wife?"

"There is no mistake. That man you saved—Stefan—did he ramble about a mysterious woman in the castle?"

Fawkes frowned. "No, but he was barely conscious when I dragged him out. I handed him off to the men waiting to take him just outside of Numencaster before making my way back to the walled city in Croantis."

"When Stefan started to get his strength back, and told the rebels the information that they needed, he also told them about a woman in the castle. Stefan reported that she was present when they interrogated him, but also that she had the gift of second sight. She also constantly screamed a name. That's why William was confused when Robin said your name." She took a deep breath. "The woman screamed for you."

Fawkes' legs buckled and he dropped down to his knees in front of her. "It can't be," he whispered. "Impossible. My wife died in a fire." Her story flipped his world upside down as everything he thought he knew was stripped from him. Charlotte reached out to run her fingers through unkempt blond locks, but the hand that shot up to her wrist stopped her before she could comfort him.

"How could I?" he asked her, eyes filling with tears. "Josie. My Josie. I didn't know, but oh gods!" He leaned forward and retched onto the grass between Charlotte's feet. "She is his prisoner. My wife has been screaming for me to save her." Tears mixed with vomit as Charlotte watched him break down. He scrambled back from her in horror and curled up into a ball.

Every part of Charlotte ached to touch him, but she didn't dare. It was wrong. She knew it was wrong to love him. Her own tears ran freely down her face as she watched his agony. She felt his devastation as if it were her own, and the desperation to ease some of his pain. But her heart couldn't take it if he stopped her from reaching out to him again.

"We'll save her," she promised him, voice cracking. "Both of us. We'll save her."

Fawkes didn't answer, drowning in his guilt. He stood up and yanked his cloak off. He threw it as hard as he could before sitting back down to think, cradling his head in his hands.

Chapter Thirteen

Once the shock and grief that accompanied the revelation waned, Fawkes tried to dismiss Charlotte again. Whether it was due to guilt from their relationship, or genuine concern for her well-being, she didn't know. It still stung when he tried to push her away, but she was expecting it this time.

"No," she said.

"Charlotte, I need to do this."

She raised her eyebrows. "And how do you think you're going to do it alone with an arrow-shaped hole in your shoulder?"

He looked at Charlotte with red-rimmed eyes, and she gentled her tone. He was too raw to be thinking clearly. "There's nothing for me to go back to," she reminded him. "I don't want anything to do with the rebels anymore, and Henry can't be reasoned with right now. Plus, Duke Belaq will try to hunt me down no matter where I go."

"This could be suicide."

She gave a harsh laugh. "Do you really think I expected to escape when I tried to break my brother out? All I knew was that I would never forgive myself if I didn't try something. Anything. That wasn't a life I could live, and I know you feel the same." She took a deep breath and plunged ahead. "Well, I wouldn't be able to live with myself if your solo mission to rescue

185

your wife went wrong. And I know you probably don't feel the same about me, but think about Josephine. Are you willing to risk her rescue on a gamble that you'll be enough? Just because you don't want me to help?"

Fawkes rubbed his face, as if trying to erase the tears. "I owe her more than that," he conceded. He shook his head in wonder. "Josie." Charlotte waited for him to gather his thoughts, and when he spoke again, it sounded like the Cloaked Shadow had emerged. "What else did you learn about her?" he asked, all business. The wall inside of Fawkes was rebuilt stronger than ever. Charlotte knew that by locking his emotions away and approaching this as any other contract, he might be able to make it out alive.

"Nothing else, really," she confessed. "Robin and William think she is just a rumor. They don't believe her existence could have been kept a secret for so long, because word of her powers would have spread. I only put it together because of what you told me about your wife and her gift."

Fawkes stood up and began to pace. "I've been in those dungeons more than once over the years. I have never seen the slightest hint of Josie, nor heard any whispers about her. I was her *husband*. I would *know* if she was there. Wouldn't I?" He looked to Charlotte, as if silently begging her to tell him that it wasn't his fault. That he couldn't have known. That it was all one big mistake. All the sins of his past would pale in comparison to giving up on his wife while she was still alive. After trying for five years to move on with his life, he struggled with the truth that he should have never mourned in the first place.

"If—and this is a big if—Josephine has been held

captive at Numencaster castle all these years, I doubt she would have been kept in the dungeons," Charlotte consoled him. "She might have been hidden elsewhere, her talents only recently employed in the king's castle."

Fawkes' expression darkened. "They have kept her from me. Whoever took her faked her death and made me believe she was burned alive. My wife was the gentlest soul I had ever met, and evil dared to touch something so pure. What have they been doing to her all this time?" His voice cracked in anguish, and Charlotte found herself wishing that Josie had really died in the fire, if only to spare the seer from suffering and imprisonment.

"Fawkes," Charlotte said, then hesitated. "We also need to be prepared for the possibility that your wife is no longer the woman that you knew."

"But she remembers me. She has been screaming my name. As long as a part of her still recognizes that she loves me, I can get her back."

But I love you, too, Charlotte wanted to say. It wouldn't change anything to say it out loud; it was horrible enough to think it. All speaking it out loud would do is ruin her already precarious bond with Fawkes. Somehow, she would have to force herself back to thinking of him as just a mentor instead of a man.

It was fine to promise herself that friendship would be enough in theory, but in actual practice, Charlotte found it to be impossible. When they sparred, even the touch of his body on hers sent her mind reeling. *Not yours, not yours, not yours*, she reminded herself to the beat of every punch.

At least Fawkes had finally relented, after much prodding from Charlotte, and agreed that two was better than one when it came to breaking into the most heavily guarded castle in the kingdom. They augmented their clothing and supplies along the way, but Charlotte knew how unprepared they were. Fawkes' shoulder refused to heal and it was compromising his fighting skills. Much to her surprise, Charlotte came close to besting him once. But even as her skills improved, Fawkes decided that Charlotte was to accompany him as a reinforcement, and only intervene in the direst of situations. Charlotte couldn't argue with his reasoning, considering she had never successfully completed a solo mission before. Still, she felt like she had gained a lifetime's worth of experience between that first time in Belaq's dungeon and the current situation they faced.

"And if you must choose between myself and Josephine, you have to get her out. Do you understand?" Charlotte nodded in agreement, though it made her sick to do so. If it was up to her, she would make sure Fawkes got out no matter what the cost, but she shuddered to think of the wrath it would incur. She would lose him anyway if that happened.

So instead of dwelling on the worst-case scenario, Charlotte threw herself into her training. Her body was the one variable she could control, and she needed it to be in peak condition if they wanted a chance of making it out of the castle alive.

Their progress was slow through Croantis, their exercises delaying them even further as they trained each day along the way. Fawkes had decided to take them directly north first, and then west over the border. "This route ensures that we will not cross paths with either the rebels or Belaq. Or whoever else the king has sent after me," Fawkes explained. Charlotte shivered, unused to such cold. "Once we cross the border, we will have to ride south, but no one will expect an approach from the north."

The landscape gradually changed around them—rocky steppes and barren plains taking the place of the lush forests and fertile lands that Charlotte had grown accustomed to. Walking across the alien land, she felt exposed and laid bare, like she couldn't hide any part of herself. She feared Fawkes could see her true thoughts and wondered how he felt about it all.

Gone was the man who had started to open up to her. Now, Fawkes exclusively channeled the Cloaked Shadow day in and day out. The persona protected him; it kept his mind on the mission and not on his wife's condition. He drove their training relentlessly, pushing his body further than Charlotte felt was safe in his condition. She could see how much his injury pained him with each movement, the wound re-opening countless times just as it had begun to heal.

Sweat stood out on his brow, a red stain blossoming on his shirt as he led her through different ways of fending off attackers that assaulted her from behind.

"I have told you a hundred times that you cannot flip me to the ground if you do not utilize my momentum."

Charlotte winced at the rebuke. "But you're bleeding," she reminded him. "It will hurt if you land on your shoulder—"

"My shoulder will be fine. That is not your concern. Your concern is flipping me to the ground. My concern is making sure that you know how to do it properly. You have to be prepared for any scenario once we are in the belly of the beast. Now, go again, and do as I say." The whites of his eyes were visible, but whether due to pain or his frantic obsession to get to the king's castle, Charlotte couldn't decide.

They had to walk a fine line between training enough and traveling quickly, but some days Charlotte thought he looked like a horse ready to bolt. She knew he would gallop Ghost to Numencaster in an instant if he thought there was the slightest chance he could break Josie out by himself. But he wasn't ready, and neither was she, and that would mean a death sentence for all three of them. So they strengthened their aching muscles and trudged their weary feet up unmarked paths, focusing on surviving the day.

Even as her world was in physical and emotional upheaval around her, Charlotte collapsed into her bedroll with a sigh of satisfaction every night. Nothing had happened how she had planned, but in some roundabout way, she had gotten exactly what she wanted— to be trained by the Cloaked Shadow. To find her own inner strength as she discovered what it meant to reach for the impossible. Her mind and body pushed her past the limits she set for herself so long ago. Everyone else—Fawkes, Josie, Belaq, Henry—faded into the background as she punched, kicked, and sprinted. She sculpted herself anew as she changed how she fit into the world.

Charlotte also watched herself change in Fawkes' eyes as he regarded her with new respect. She had gone from a young woman with all pluck but no skills, to a partner who would one day become his equal. Fawkes looked more hopeful for the outcome of their mission.

The day that master and apprentice crossed back over into Algonia, Charlotte could feel a change in the air. She could feel the differences between the two countries on her skin. Another world waited for her on the other side, ready to shock and test her. As they stepped over the invisible line, her senses suddenly sharpened and her body tensed with alertness. Fawkes did not have to tell her that they were back in her home country, a place that Charlotte now associated with pain, fear, and loss. It was all so achingly familiar yet horrible, and she felt the sudden urge to turn around and flee back to Croantis.

Fawkes seemed to have the opposite reaction. Now that they were within reach of Josephine, the magnetic pull he felt toward her drove him into a frenzy. Even when they rested at camp for the evening, he paced around the fire. Charlotte watched with a wary gaze, and wondered if his reaction was nerves, anticipation, or even fear. Possibly a combination of all three. Sweet Ghost tried his best to calm Fawkes with quiet nickers and nudges with a velvet nose, but he pushed the animal away. Nothing seemed to reach him as Fawkes paced and planned the most difficult and personal break-in of his career.

His whirling mind left traces on his body, the sleepless nights transforming into dark bags underneath his eyes. But through his turmoil, his face burned with pride on the night he finally declared Charlotte ready.

"You have come so far," he told her, voice rough with exhaustion. "You are incredible. You have surpassed all I had hoped you would become." Charlotte nodded solemnly at the praise, but her heart jumped at his words. As if his hands had a mind of their own, they reached out and cupped her cold, wind-chapped cheeks. "To have put yourself through this—for me—Charlotte, I am honored to know you. To have trained you." The facade of the Cloaked Shadow finally slipped, and he became Fawkes once more.

Charlotte was surprised to see the depth of emotion in his face and realized how much of himself he had been hiding from her since discovering that Josephine was still alive. To hear the words and see the loneliness on his face was shocking after weeks of purposeful distance between them. She wondered if it was crazy to think that underneath it all, this was still the man who had kissed her so passionately in Croantis. A man who yearned to connect.

She longed to lean in, to tangle her fingers in his wild hair and pull his lips down to meet hers. To continue what they had started before he left, and then what was interrupted when he reunited with her in the river. There was nothing to interrupt them here, and Fawkes' thumb brushing her cheek in gentle circles was doing nothing to dissuade her from her inappropriate thoughts.

But still, an invisible force held her back, and they simply stood frozen in the moment, two warriors acknowledging the fire and skill they both shared. The touch was innocent enough not to muddle things up with definitions of right or wrong, and Charlotte wanted to hold onto it forever. She wanted to bask in his pride for her, to soak up his words and forget for a moment why they were doing it all, because right then, she was the only woman on his mind. Charlotte couldn't feel her torn muscles, the aching cold, or her cracked skin. The warmth that rose up inside of her felt hot enough to burn her, and part of her wanted to go up in flames. But the scorch would consume both of them if she stayed silent any longer.

"I've become the person I've always wanted to be," she murmured, tilting her head away from his palm. "Thanks to you."

Fawkes shook his head slowly. "You have possessed it within you this whole time. I just helped to draw it out." He sighed and dropped his hand. "I have never met anyone else like you."

Charlotte's eyes widened at his words, and in an instant, they no longer felt alone as the ghost of another woman suddenly appeared between them. He winced, and the spell was broken. He stepped away, and it was all Charlotte could do not to grab him and bring him back to her.

Instead, she straightened her spine and said, "We are partners in this. You and me." *Even if we can't be together any other way.* It would have to be enough. It was too confusing to go back and forth between them. It was a relief to see the mask slip back onto Fawkes' face as he closed himself off and became the Cloaked Shadow once more.

Charlotte honestly believed that that was the last time that Fawkes would appear to her. It cost both of them too much when he slipped up and showed her his true self. Weeks of building a professional relationship had been undone in the course of a few stolen moments, and the awkwardness was palpable as they busied themselves with the camp. They could barely look at each other as they nibbled their jerky and stoked the fire. A cold snap moved in and a light snow began to fall, flakes tickling Charlotte's face as she huddled closer to the fire.

Once the flames faded into embers, Charlotte and Fawkes got ready for bed without a word to each other, their movements in sync. They curled up in their separate bedrolls, leaving a responsible amount of space between them. Charlotte rolled over, her back to Fawkes. She thought she heard him whisper, "Goodnight," but she squeezed her eyes shut and ignored him. She yearned for just a few hours of sleep, the freedom to not obsess about the man next to her for a time. *If only my teeth would stop chattering.*

****

Charlotte was hot. So hot she was burning up, her body slick with sweat underneath her blankets. She awoke with a gasp and tried to remember where she was. Blinding white shocked her eyes as she wrenched them open, only to shut them again immediately in pain. *Snow,* she realized. *It snowed last night. I'm outside.*

This realization only confused her further as she tried to wrap her head around why she felt so warm in the middle of a snowstorm. She heard a sleepy grumble behind her as a muscular arm tightened its hold around her stomach, clutching her until she was flush against a strong chest. His breath tickled her ear as he nuzzled into her neck, and Charlotte gently pinched herself to make sure she wasn't dreaming. He sighed contentedly while Charlotte froze, trying to figure out exactly why Fawkes was in her bedroll with her.

"Mmmmm," he groaned, vibrating from deep inside his chest.

He must be dreaming about something else.

Dreaming about Josephine. Tears stung her eyes at how incredible and safe she felt in his arms, contrasted with the pain it also caused to be so close to him while his heart belonged to someone else.

"Charlotte," he sighed, so softly she almost missed it. *Wait, he's dreaming about me?*

Under ordinary circumstances, Fawkes would have known the instant she awoke, thanks to the Cloaked Shadow's heightened senses. But Fawkes had been up for days at a time, injured, and had finally let his emotional wall crack last night. There was no way he would have purposely chosen to do this with Charlotte. *He probably has no idea what he's doing,* Charlotte realized.

He would be mortified if he awoke to find them in such a compromising position, and Charlotte didn't want to pile on any more reasons for him to feel guilty. Before steeling herself for the hardest, most selfless act of her life, she relaxed for a few more stolen moments against him. She let herself fantasize about what it would be like to wake up with him like that every day, but in a real house with a real bed. In a home they built together, in a new country, after escaping the traumas of their past. A fresh start. No violence, no blood, no pain. That was what she wanted for him. For them. But because they could never have that, she would have to settle for easing whatever pain she could now, and that meant preventing Fawkes from waking up the same way she did.

Filling her lungs with his scent, she carefully lifted Fawkes' arm off of her body and sat up, twisted away as she set it on her now-empty side of the bedroll. Praying that his exhaustion would keep him asleep just a little longer, she slowly slid out from under the blanket and into the frozen world.

"Don't tell him," she whispered to Ghost, the one witness to their unusual sleeping arrangement.

Ghost snorted at her, his breath rising up in clouds above his head. He appeared to be the only one completely unperturbed by the weather. The sweat had frozen on Charlotte's skin, and she looked back at Fawkes longingly.

Fawkes, feeling a gaze upon him, awoke with a start. He sat up and looked around for Charlotte frantically, his shoulders finally slumping with relief when he saw her standing next to Ghost.

As if reading Charlotte's mind, he scrambled to explain the situation. "I—ah—should apologize for this," he said, "but you were so cold last night. Your teeth were chattering in your sleep, and your lips were turning blue. It was the only way to keep you warm once the snow started falling." He cleared his throat. "I hope I didn't do anything to make you uncomfortable."

That was the most comfortable I've been in my entire life, Charlotte wanted to tell him. But it was clear he did not remember saying her name, or clutching her to him as if he was drowning and she was the only one who could save him.

"No," she said, turning away. "Nothing that made me uncomfortable."

****

Their footprints left clear tracks in the snow, but Fawkes said that it couldn't be helped. They pushed farther that day than any distance they had attempted before. Charlotte, having been declared ready for the mission, didn't need to stop at midday to train. There was nothing to do but push southward.

As they skirted a small farming community, Charlotte's thoughts jumped to Henry and the rest of the rebels, wondering if they were still in Croantis or if they had made the journey to Algonia already.

"Do you know what the rebels were planning?" she asked Fawkes.

"No. But once Josie is free, I have a mind to join them. That bastard of a king took my wife from me. He will pay."

If only Robin had known what it would take to get the Cloaked Shadow to fight for his cause, Charlotte mused. *It would have saved him a lot of trouble. If the revolution had such a powerful ally, it would be nearly unstoppable.* As it stood with Fawkes' rage, she almost expected him to try and assassinate King Otan himself once they rescued Josephine.

"You would go back to the rebels? Work with them?"

"Would you join me?" Fawkes asked. "Go back to your brother?"

"I don't know if I could." She tried to picture what a rag-tag family they would make— Henry, Charlotte, the man she loved but couldn't be with, and his newly rescued wife, all fighting for a cause she wasn't sure she supported. "All of this is dependent on whether or not we make it out of this alive. I guess I'll decide what I want to do if I make it out."

Fawkes stopped walking. "You do not have to do this. I never asked for your help."

"But you need it. I'm ready for this."

"Good. Because we will be in Numencaster in three days."

Chapter Fourteen

Numencaster Castle was unlike any castle Charlotte had ever seen. Its fortifications were visible even from a distance. She had vowed to stay by Fawkes' side through it all, but the longer she stared at the massive structure, the more she doubted their odds of success.

"How on earth did you get in the first time?" Charlotte asked her mentor, awed.

"I took a page from your book." He favored Charlotte with a small smile, the first he had cracked in the past three days of relentless travel. "I entered in through the sewer." She blushed, filled with pride that the legendary Cloaked Shadow had used her method.

The castle was more than twice the size of Duke Belaq's castle, with a wide moat encircling the outer wall. Turrets climbed upward into the clouds, while archers paced back and forth across thick parapets. The drawbridge was down, but at least fifty armed men guarded the entrance, and were in the process of thoroughly examining anyone who braved crossing into the fortress. *No wonder Fawkes had gone in through the sewers. There is no other weak point anywhere.*

From Charlotte's vantage point on top of a small hill, the town sprawled in front of the castle, surprisingly quiet due to the recent snowfall. A few citizens braved the wet and muddy trek, but the streets looked almost solely occupied by additional soldiers.

"King Otan has gotten even more paranoid," Fawkes said. "I gather he was not pleased with Stefan's departure."

"Do you think he knows the rebels are planning something?"

"He knows now that the rebels are organized enough to snatch a captive from his royal dungeons and not get caught. This frightens him. His Majesty resides under the same roof. I believe he has been sleeping with one eye open."

"Will we still enter through the sewers?"

Fawkes rubbed his stubble thoughtfully. "No. The king will expect it this time. I will have to create another plan."

"Well, Josephine isn't even being held in the dungeons, so they aren't our target location anyway. Where do you think she would be held captive? Not only will we have to break in, but we need to find her as well. We won't have time to search the whole castle before getting caught," she pointed out.

Breaking into dungeons to rescue prisoners they already knew were there was one thing. Trying to deduce where a mystery prisoner was being held, within the entirety of the castle, was another challenge altogether. She would have preferred the dungeons. At least that was familiar territory.

"She might be inside one of the towers," Fawkes said, mostly to himself. "Her existence has been kept a secret for many years. It would make sense if she was locked up, out of the way. But the question is, which one?"

"Well, which side of the castle is the dungeon

under?"

"The back of the castle, on the south side."

"If Josephine is brought down secretly to question prisoners in the dungeon without anyone seeing her, then she is probably smuggled through a nearby passageway. They keep her far enough out of the way so she is hidden, but close enough to use her when they need her. It has to be the turret on the right, at the back of the castle."

Fawkes began to pace. "Deductions aren't enough to go on. We need someone with first-hand information. We will only have one chance at this. We cannot waste it."

Charlotte touched his shoulder with a gentle hand, forcing him to still. He seemed painfully thin for his normally strong build. The stresses of their journey combined with his injury had taken a disturbing toll.

He looked at her with blue eyes that swallowed his face in the single-minded, wide-eyed panic of a trapped animal. "I should have known she was there the first time," he said. "I should have saved her weeks ago. How did I not know?"

"Stop punishing yourself. You barely escaped with your life after rescuing Stefan. There wasn't time to go wandering around the castle looking for her, even if you had known she was there."

"With all this extra security now, getting to her will be close to impossible." His voice was wracked with guilt.

"You have me this time. We'll get to her," Charlotte promised. Taking a chance, she stepped forward and wrapped her arms around his waist in a comforting embrace. She felt him sag against her, allowing himself a moment of peace. It wasn't a romantic embrace, and nothing like how Charlotte felt when she woke up in his arms in her bedroll. This was simply a symbol of human connection, a promise to be by his side no matter what they faced. "We made it here. Now we watch and wait, and come up with a plan, together," she said.

****

It was easier said than done. Charlotte and Fawkes observed the activity in town and around the castle for two days, and were nowhere closer to formulating a plan of attack. They searched for a hole in the defenses, but the security around the castle was ironclad. As Charlotte wished for a way inside, she never expected that their chance would come at such a cost. It started at midnight with the first explosion.

Fawkes had been keeping watch while Charlotte slept. Both of them had been on high alert so close to the castle, trading off sleeping while the other kept a close eye out for wandering villagers or possible rebel forces. Thus far they had remained undetected within a few miles of the town.

Charlotte heard the boom as it wrenched her from a dead sleep. She was up and at Fawkes' side in an instant. "What was that?" she asked, ears ringing. His gaze was fixed toward the town, where an orange fireball lit up the night.

"Something caught fire. Something big."

The edge of town was burning. The wind picked up, and the screams of the townspeople reached Charlotte's ears. The fire licked the night sky as it gathered fuel, feeding itself as the wind tossed it higher.

"Was it the granary?" Charlotte asked.

"Could be. It was on that side of town."

"How could a granary explode like that?"

The smell of scorched material invaded her nose, tickling the tip with the acrid scent of something she couldn't quite place. "Cannon powder," Fawkes said, answering her unasked question. "I haven't smelled it since I was halfway around the world. Years ago. It is so rare..." He tapered off, confused.

Charlotte looked at him, horrified. "The rebels? Is this their doing?"

"This was not an accident."

As if in agreement with him, a second explosion rocked the village, this time in the center. "They're attacking the people!" Charlotte said.

"This is our opening," Fawkes said calmly. All of the stress Charlotte had seen in his face during the last few days was gone and replaced with a controlled certainty. The Cloaked Shadow finally had a plan.

In a whirl, the black cloak was on, covering his face as he prepared to ride into the chaos. Charlotte swallowed back her fear and leaped up onto Ghost's back, settling in behind her mentor. As they galloped toward the flaming village, cries of agony and terror welcomed them. People swarmed the streets, running around in pure panic. The more level-headed were trying to drag the critically wounded out of harm's way, and others tried to put out the fire with ineffective buckets of water. Children shrieked and babies screamed while mothers frantically called their names. Still the fire spread, pushing everyone back as they fled from the scorching heat and the blinding smoke.

Fawkes urged Ghost faster through the streets, dodging the inferno. As they made their way deeper into the town, Charlotte saw soldiers charging from the castle, ready to protect their king's property at any cost. Fixated on the two fires consuming the town, the armored men ran past the horse without stopping. Charlotte watched as a badly scorched woman reached out to clutch a soldier's arm, but he shook her off and kept going. The woman fell to the ground and didn't get up.

We should help them, she thought, wondering how she could be in the midst of this tragedy and not do something to help the people. Who had she become? So many of them were going to die, but Fawkes depended on her to push aside the guilt. The fact that she and Fawkes were using an act of terrorism to their advantage made her ill.

With a sharp turn, Fawkes steered into an alley and dismounted, motioning for Charlotte to stay put. With his back up against a wall, he pulled out his dagger and waited until a confused soldier ran past. In a blur, Fawkes jumped on the unsuspecting man from behind and slit his throat in one fluid motion. Fawkes was off the soldier before the body hit the ground, dragging him by the feet back to where Charlotte waited.

This was the first time she witnessed him kill in cold blood, and she felt the Fawkes she thought she knew slip further away. He cared about nothing else other than Josephine's life. Everyone else was expendable, including himself.

Fawkes must have seen the shock on her face, but he chose to ignore it. "Strip the armor and put it on," he ordered. In a daze at all the blood and violence around her, Charlotte felt like she was in a dream. *This is what it takes,* she reminded herself. *You made a promise.*

If she was going to survive tonight, she needed to channel her own inner Cloaked Shadow and push her humanity away. Holding back her revulsion, her surprisingly steady fingers began unbuckling the heavy chain mail from the sweat-soaked body. By the time she finished, Fawkes had killed a second soldier and was stripping off another set of armor next to her.

"Get dressed. Hurry," he urged. The metal clothing weighed a thousand pounds as Charlotte did her best to put it on correctly. If not for her newly-strengthened muscles, the mail sheet alone would have buckled her knees. The helmet was wet inside, and the armor stank with fear from its previous owner.

Feeling like she was trying to move through water, Charlotte clumsily remounted Ghost. The steed held steady as Fawkes did the same, his cloak tucked up underneath his arm as he took on the guise of a captain in the king's army.

Ghost dodged bodies and debris as they made their way toward the castle. Once the trio approached the drawbridge, both riders dismounted. Fawkes whispered into Ghost's ear, then gave him a slap on the rump. The horse headed in the opposite direction from the fires, and Charlotte hoped he had been told to run far away and stay out of harm's way.

The stereotype of military obedience and calm control was nowhere to be found outside the castle. Soldiers screamed orders that were barely heard above the turmoil as they scrambled to get organized against an enemy they couldn't see, much less fight directly.

One captain was at the center of it all, standing at the edge of the drawbridge. "Cavalry, stay with me! Infantry, down into the streets! Contain the fire; lead the people to safety at the church. These are King Otan's people, and we will protect them! We will protect Algonia! The rest of you, circle the castle. No harm will befall the king." He caught sight of Fawkes and Charlotte approaching. "Oi, you! Get down to the village! That's an order!"

Charlotte felt her skin blister before she heard the blast. She was thrown forward onto the bridge as a wave of heat washed over her, and then a *boom* rendered her temporarily deaf. With ears ringing and soot clouding her eyes, her hands scrambled to find Fawkes. His body lay prone on the ground, almost on top of the knight who had just been shouting at them. She grabbed his shoulder and flipped him over to check his breathing. His chest still moved, and his pulse was strong. If it hadn't been for their helmets, Charlotte shuddered to think what would have happened.

She risked a glance behind her and found the origin of the blast. A wagon filled with hay used to occupy the space where a blazing fire now reigned. It had been placed innocently close to the moat, and then detonated in front of the dispatching army.

A warning to the residents of the castle of what is to come. The rebels want to send a message, and blowing up the king's front yard shouts their intentions loud and clear. The wood beneath her began to rumble. *They're raising the drawbridge,* she realized, horrified. "Fawkes!" she shouted, though her own ears were still ringing so loudly she couldn't hear her own words. She took off his helmet and slapped his face. "Get up! We need to move!"

Pain flickered across his face, and he grabbed his injured shoulder. Charlotte saw the red stain spreading underneath the chain mail. The blast and the fall had torn it open once again. There was no time to assess the damage, though, because they were about to be unceremoniously dumped off the bridge.

Charlotte caught Fawkes' cloak just as it came close to sliding into the moat, while using her free hand to haul him to his feet. They limped their way inside the castle as the drawbridge rose behind them. The army's focus was over the wall and assessing the damage, so two wounded impostor soldiers did nothing to draw their attention. Charlotte moved slowly and purposefully, keeping her helmet on and her eyes down as she helped Fawkes past the throng of soldiers awaiting orders in the courtyard.

Once she steered them into a shadowed hallway, the two of them slumped against a wall to catch their breath. "Help me get this off," Fawkes grunted. "I can't breathe."

"But our disguises—"

"I can't breathe," he repeated. "We will move faster without all this on. Take yours off, too. We have an hour at best to locate Josephine and get out before the army regains control of the situation."

Charlotte helped Fawkes remove his armor before turning her attention to her own. "Will the rebels continue the attack?"

"Three explosions are a message," Fawkes said. "But I do not think this is the entirety of their attack. I think that this was only the beginning. However, I doubt they will do anything more tonight."

Though her mind whirled, Charlotte didn't press Fawkes further. Once her heavy armor was off, Charlotte felt so light she could fly. "Which way to the far tower?" she asked, and handed him his cloak.

"This way," he said, and they melted into the shadows.

****

The castle was surprisingly empty and quiet. Charlotte guessed that after the first explosion, all the nobility were ordered to remain in their rooms for safety. The lethal pair padded silently down dark hallways, only pausing whenever a harried guard ran by, using their training to remain invisible.

Though the castle was freezing cold, Charlotte sweated with adrenaline and anticipation. Every fiber of her being was on high alert, waiting for a surprise attack or someone to raise the alarm. There were no further explosions in the village, so their window of opportunity shrank with each passing second.

Charlotte stuck close to Fawkes, her lungs burning as they picked up the pace, weaving in and out of small alcoves, and sometimes doubling back if Fawkes felt they went the wrong way. The most important direction for them to move was up, and they took the servant's stairs two at a time whenever they came across a promising passageway.

Farther back into the castle was the older section, built centuries ago. It lacked the fanfare and grandeur of the great hall and throne room near the castle entrance, but the rear of the massive building held a classic allure. It gave no hint of the horrors that lay just a few floors underneath it. Prisoners were tortured and killed in the king's dungeon, all while nobles and courtesans traversed the smooth stone passageways high above, unable to hear the screams.

"We're almost there," Fawkes murmured to her,

shaking Charlotte from her dark thoughts. Charlotte couldn't see any indication that they had reached the tower that Josephine most likely resided in, but she trusted her mentor's instincts. They were in a dead-end hallway, with intricate tapestries lining the walls. The light from a single torch at the far end illuminated their way.

"Start looking for the door," Fawkes ordered. After a moment's hesitation, Charlotte realized what he meant and began lifting the dusty curtains of fabric. While silencing a sneeze, Charlotte suddenly knew exactly which tapestry the door was behind. She motioned for Fawkes to follow her until she reached a tapestry that looked almost brand new, and most importantly, free of dust. A tapestry that had to have been moved more than the others in the recent years.

Fawkes pulled the fabric back to reveal a thick wooden door, completely smooth except for a keyhole. He knelt down and pulled a small pin from his belt, not unlike the one Charlotte had hidden in her hair the night everything started.

Fawkes' hands shook as he fumbled with the pin. *His wife is just beyond this door*, Charlotte thought, overcome with tenderness as she looked down at the legendary Cloaked Shadow, reduced to just a mortal man over a thing as simple as a locked door. She knelt down next to him and put her hands over his to steady them. They felt ice cold, but their trembling stopped at her touch. With renewed confidence, Fawkes jiggled the pin and the door opened with a creak.

The dark, winding staircase in front of them was all that stood between Fawkes and his wife now. He took slow, methodical steps while Charlotte followed behind, not daring to touch him. This moment was his alone. Whatever awaited Fawkes at the top of the stairs would either set him free or destroy him, but there would be no moving forward until Fawkes had an answer.

Charlotte was selfishly torn between wishing that the rumors had been about another seer and hoping that the room was empty. But for the sake of her mentor, she hoped he would find a truth he could live with at the top of the tower.

A soft glow of light reached Charlotte's eyes just as she thought the tower couldn't possibly get any higher. Charlotte heard a gruff voice, "Yer Majesty? That you?", then a deep groan as she watched Fawkes sink his dagger into yet another unsuspecting guard. She stood with her back pressed against the curved wall as Fawkes kicked the body down the stairs, but not before taking his keys. The body tumbled past her feet and into the darkness.

Killing the guard sharpened Fawkes' focus. Murder brought the Cloaked Shadow into control, and nothing could stand in his way. The mission was all that mattered. This time, when he put the key in the lock, his hands did not shake. Charlotte stood back as he opened the door and walked in to meet his fate.

Chapter Fifteen

As she watched the man she loved step past the threshold, Charlotte remained frozen in place. After all of the planning, the training, the what-if, she was back to feeling like a helpless young girl. She had done all she could, and she could follow Fawkes no further. He had made his choice, and against all odds, they had reached Josephine. The tiny hope she had been holding onto—that the room would be empty, or it was the wrong woman—faded the longer she waited in the stairwell.

The absolute quiet, however, started to unnerve her. *Something's wrong*, she thought, and she forced her feet to move. Following Fawkes was a compulsion she couldn't shake, as much as she wanted to be able to gracefully let him go. Charlotte stumbled through the doorway and almost crashed into Fawkes, who remained transfixed at the sight of a woman staring out of a narrow window.

The woman wore a white sleep shirt, her black hair tinged with blue from the moonlight. It tumbled freely down to her knees in a wavy curtain. She hadn't turned around at Fawkes' arrival, and it appeared Charlotte's presence didn't bother her in the slightest either.

Charlotte risked a glance at Fawkes, whose eyes were filled with tears. She watched his throat work up and down as he swallowed the words he was unable to speak. *So it's really her,* Charlotte thought. There was a certain peace in the realization. There could be no back and forth with her and Fawkes anymore, and in a way, she was relieved. She wanted to bury the possibility so deep it could no longer torment her. But before she could, Charlotte needed to help him one more time.

Charlotte grabbed Fawkes' hand and gently tugged him forward. The tears that had pooled in his eyes finally fell, streaming down his cheeks as he let the woman from his present lead him back in time to greet the woman from his past.

Fawkes looked at Josephine like she was a ghost, and he seemed afraid to touch her. Charlotte gave his hand a reassuring squeeze while her own tears ran down her face. Then she released him and stepped back.

The dreamy reunion between husband and wife turned into a nightmare the second Fawkes touched Josephine's shoulder. Charlotte watched as the contact ripped a destructive path through the waif-like woman, transforming her into a shrieking banshee.

Hair and fists flying, Josephine turned and attacked Fawkes like a rabid animal. She clawed at him with long fingernails, landing bloody scratches on his skin as he tried to restrain her without hurting her.

"Josie! Josie! It's me. It's Fawkes. You're okay. I'm here," he yelled above the screams. Her battering refused to slow, so Charlotte stepped in and grabbed Josephine's arms from behind and pinned them to her sides.

Blood oozed from a particularly nasty scratch on Fawkes' cheek, but he gave it no notice as he looked upon Josephine in agony and wonder. "What did they do to you?" he murmured, reaching out to stroke her face. He pulled his fingers back just in time, as Josephine's teeth gnashed too close for comfort.

Josephine struggled against Charlotte's hold but wore herself out quickly. Her body sagged and her head fell forward against her chest. "Do to me, do to me! What does anything do to one? Chitter-chatter, pitter-patter. Like underground birds in winter. Cold. Cold. So cold," Josephine ranted. Dropping too fast for a surprised Charlotte to catch her, Josephine sat down on the bare floor. She hugged herself, mumbling, and refused to look at either Fawkes or Charlotte.

Fawkes lowered himself to his haunches in front of Josephine. Charlotte followed his lead and did the same. "I'm not going to hurt you, Josie," Fawkes said. "Not even going to touch you. I just want to see you." He choked back a sob. "You are here. And alive."

His tears must have reached something deep inside of Josephine, because her ranting and rocking suddenly stopped. She looked straight at him and cocked her head, as if the sound was familiar. Her hair fell to the side, revealing an empty eye socket that Charlotte hadn't noticed before. The gaping hole was a dark shadow in an otherwise pretty face. It seemed bottomless, reflecting the depths of her hopelessness inside. It held horrors and secrets neither one of them could begin to comprehend.

Josephine's intact eye twitched back and forth between the two faces in front of her. A long scar ran though the eyelid, from her eyebrow to her cheekbone. Charlotte wondered if Josephine had done it to herself. *Did she try to claw her own eyes out?*

The small room surrounding them held very little.

There were no utensils, sharp objects, or anywhere with which to hang a rope. A bare mattress lay on the floor. The only allowances Josephine had been given were books. A modest stack of books lay in the corner, with a fine layer of dust over them. How many times had she read them before her sanity left her? Charlotte doubted they had been touched in quite some time, and now stood as a sad reminder of who Josephine used to be. What a mind she had, and now that brilliance had been undone by torturous years.

"That's it," Fawkes murmured, entranced as recognition flashed across Josephine's face.

"Fawkes?" she whispered, mouth agape. She reached out a hesitant hand and cupped his cheek before her hand trailed down his scar in wonder. Charlotte could barely watch the tender moment exchanged between them, but she couldn't look away. Josephine had them all under her spell.

Now that Josephine seemed to understand that they weren't hallucinations, her sanity steadily gained the upper hand. "You're here. You're alive. I've called for you, night after night. You finally heard me. I knew you weren't dead, no matter what they told me. I knew you would come to free me."

"Our home—the fire. I thought you died. When I found out you were alive, nothing could keep me from you. I had to come and save you."

Josephine shook her head. "My dearest Fawkes, my sweet husband. You are here to free me. Not to save me. I cannot be saved, not after what I have done."

Confusion rendered Fawkes silent as he tried to discern what Josephine was telling him. Charlotte, though she hated to intrude on their moment, grasped her true meaning instantly. "No one has done something so horrible that they cannot be redeemed," Charlotte assured Josie. "They forced you to use your gifts, right?"

Josephine nodded, tears filling her single, dark-brown eye. Fawkes grabbed her hand, and this time, Josie did not pull away. He leaned toward her in earnest. "It was their fault. The people who took you, who forced you. Whatever you had to do, it was not your fault."

"I see them all," Josephine said, retreating back into herself. She focused on something outside of reality. "Every one of them that I condemned. Every person who died because of what I did not have the strength to keep secret. Their suffering, and their screams. People sentenced to death because of what I saw them committing in the future, actions that had not come to pass. And they didn't understand as they went to their graves. Names, names, names! All have run together in my head. They will not give me a moment's peace. Their numbers have grown so I cannot hold them off. They will consume me."

"No!" Fawkes shouted, vehement. Josephine flinched at his outburst. "We will get you out of here," he promised. "We have to move quickly."

"It's too late," Josephine said calmly. "But it is for the best. It is what I want."

"It is not too late. Come," Fawkes ordered, gathering her up in his arms. Josephine relaxed in her husband's arms, and gazed at his face, as if memorizing it. Her face glowed with love for him as she allowed herself this embrace, as if it was the only thing she had been waiting for.

"They are coming up the tower," she told Fawkes. "There are too many soldiers. They have come for me. But I will no longer give them what they demand. Fate forced me to wait, and now I see why. My greatest wish came true, to see you one last time. Now I am fulfilled. But I must pay retribution, the souls demand it. I only wish I could have been stronger for you, my sweet husband."

Fawkes shook her roughly. "Josie, you are not making sense. You have been the one to suffer, and King Otan will pay retribution, I swear to you. Now that I have you, we can restore you to health. Together."

Josie looked at him with proud resignation. "That was never your true purpose for coming here. I've just had another vision. It is for me to tell you that they will do it again, murdering hundreds for their cause. It is your purpose to know it, and to stop it. You must stop the senseless violence and protect the innocent. This is my last gift to you. You've pulled me out of the darkness long enough for me to do what I must. To be of sound mind as I take my final journey. This has been your last gift to me."

"Fawkes..." Charlotte said, fear gripping her as she started to put the pieces together, of Josephine's possible intent.

"Your cloak," Josephine said, interrupting Charlotte and drawing Fawkes' attention back to her. "You've worn it well. The fabric tells many stories, some good and some bad. But a different redemption is in your future, and we must diverge." Fawkes' wife ran her hands over the dark material, and he shuddered under her touch. "I sewed it to keep you safe, to keep you hidden from prying eyes. I wove my magic and my love for you into it. It held you when I could not." Her fingers paused at his chest, just above his heart. Josephine's gaze darted from her husband's face to Charlotte's, and she gave her a soft smile.

"Take care of him," she whispered to Charlotte. Josephine shuddered, blinking as she tried to refocus. "My hold in this reality is slipping," she said, addressing both of them. "I don't have much longer before my mind disappears again."

"I'll bring you back to yourself as many times as it takes. Nothing will ever hurt you again," Fawkes vowed.

"Do not weep for me; rejoice that I will be free. Promise me." Josephine's hands dropped to Fawkes' waist, drawing him in even closer in their embrace. "You have already mourned me once. Do not do it again. We have been given the gift of closure and goodbyes. The time for sadness has passed."

"Josie, I do not understand what you are talking about, my love. If this is the madness speaking, we will find a way to cure it." He cradled the back of her head in his hand, as if reassuring himself that even though her mind might disappear again, the woman he loved would still be in there somewhere.

Josephine broke the embrace and stepped back, and alarm bells starting ringing in Charlotte's head, while Fawkes looked hurt and confused at Josephine's sudden withdrawal. Charlotte saw the silver flash of the dagger, pulled from Fawkes' belt, a moment before Fawkes did. She cried out a warning. *"No!"*

Both Charlotte and Fawkes lurched toward Josephine, whose gaze was locked on Fawkes with a contented smile on her face. An instant after the dagger was raised, too quickly for them to stop her, Josephine plunged it into her own heart. A small sigh escaped the seer's lips as she tumbled to the floor.

Fawkes embraced Josephine an instant before she hit the stones, blood pooling beneath them, soaking his cloak. With the exception of the hilt protruding from her chest, it looked for all the world like his wife was merely asleep. The haggard pain that defined Josephine's face had vanished. The girl that Fawkes had married so long ago gracefully took over Josephine's body as it was freed in death, pushing away the remnants of a mad and tortured woman.

"Josie. Wake up, Josie," Fawkes sobbed. "I just got you back. I cannot lose you again! Why, why, why would you do this?"

Charlotte wanted to offer words of comfort, but no sound emerged from her open mouth. She had tried to stop it. Why hadn't she knocked the dagger from Josephine's hand? Why hadn't she been quick enough? The warning signs were there. Charlotte had known that something bad was going to happen and had tried to warn Fawkes. A million alternative scenarios flooded her brain as she watched her mentor cradle his dead wife. If only she had been better, stronger, faster.

Regret hit her like a punch to the stomach. Instead of helping the man she loved, she had only succeeded in bringing him unimaginable pain. *It's all my fault*, she thought. She had told Fawkes his wife was still alive, helped bring him here, and then stood idly by while Josephine killed herself. And now there was nothing Charlotte could ever do to make it right, and she would never forgive herself.

She couldn't move away from the tragedy in front of her. Fawkes seemed to have forgotten Charlotte was there as he stroked his dead wife's face. His tears slowed, and a numbness overtook his features. Both Fawkes and the Cloaked Shadow were nowhere to be found, and Charlotte didn't recognize the man with the thousand yard stare.

A muffled shout from the stairwell snapped her back to herself. Listening hard, she could hear the heavy steps of multiple men climbing the tower. Josephine was right—the guards were coming for the seer, and had no doubt stumbled upon Fawkes' unfortunate victim at the bottom of the stairs.

Separating herself from her panic, she analyzed the facts of their situation. Save for Fawkes' dagger, and a small knife hidden in her boot, they had no other weapons to speak of. The rest were in a pile of discarded chain mail on the other side of the castle. She could determine no other way in or out of the tower but down the stairs. They were cornered. She had no idea how many soldiers were on their way up here, but knew that she and Fawkes were already outnumbered. With the Cloaked Shadow in play, they could possibly stand a chance, but one look at Fawkes told her that his alter ego was long gone. He wouldn't even put up a fight if a sword was pointed at him. In fact, she suspected he would welcome it.

That left Charlotte, alone with mere minutes to come up with a plan to save them. The barren room around them held no answers, and she bit her tongue to keep from letting out a frustrated scream. She paced their small confines, looking for anything that might help. She approached the single window and looked down from their dizzying height. *The moat*, she realized. *It's right below us.*

The tower jutted out just enough over the water below, its depth a mystery. Standing at the window made her knees tremble and her palms sweat, and she couldn't look down for long.

The clinking echo of armor and steel grew louder, and Charlotte was out of time to doubt herself. Pulling the knife from her boot, she gripped the hilt confidently and smashed the thick blade into the center of the window. The shock of the impact reverberated up her arm, but the glass held.

Cursing, she dropped the knife and shook her arm to get the feeling back. Small cracks spider-webbed out from the origin of the impact on the window, giving Charlotte hope that with enough force, she could shatter the glass altogether. She repositioned for another assault, briefly wishing she held Fawkes' dagger instead of her knife, but she couldn't bear to pull the dagger from Josephine's chest. Plus, Fawkes would kill her for attempting it.

Aiming her second strike at the same place as her first, the glass cracked audibly. After a third strike, the window had no chance. The glass shattered and fell, most of it falling into the moat below, but a good portion landed on Charlotte. Fragments sliced her clothes and any skin that was exposed, making shallow cuts that dripped and stung.

She hardly felt the damage, though, as she strode over to where Fawkes still lay on the ground with Josephine. "Fawkes, we need to leave. Right now. You have to say goodbye to her." Charlotte wished she could offer more words of sympathy, but it would have to wait until they weren't in the middle of enemy territory.

He looked right through Charlotte. His face was void of any feeling, like he had completely closed himself off from the outside world. His grief had turned him into a hollow shell as the past repeated itself.

But from that grief, the Cloaked Shadow had been born. Charlotte needed to tap into that, find the part of Fawkes who had created the Cloaked Shadow out of necessity, and access it immediately. No amount of shouting, slapping, or pleading would do it. She needed to reach the primal place inside of him that could still feel something, and nothing was more primal than fear. Fear for someone he cared about, who was still alive.

Fear for her. Which meant she had to force herself to face her own greatest fear and hope that it would be enough for Fawkes to remember what she meant to him. Or had meant to him, at one point. It was a literal leap of faith, one which could bring Fawkes out of his shock but also provided the only means of escaping the tower. But Charlotte couldn't just push him out; he wouldn't survive a fall in his catatonic state.

"Fawkes," she coaxed. "Look at me. You need to follow me." His once-unfocused gaze sharpened on her as she walked backward to the broken window, as if sensing the danger in her actions. Charlotte backed up until she felt a breeze whip through the gaping hole, sending shivers up her spine. Every nerve in her body screamed at her to run back to safety, to take her chances fighting the army coming up the stairs. Anything was better than inching closer to a deadly drop.

Charlotte turned and braced one foot on the ledge,

her vision threatening to tunnel. Her stomach clenched and her entire body trembled violently. She glanced back over her shoulder, but whether it was to see if her plan was working, or silently beg Fawkes to stop her from jumping, she didn't know. Fawkes had let go of Josephine's body, but still remained squatted next to it. Charlotte's danger had produced a subconscious reaction in him, but he still looked lost.

The young woman gulped, tongue heavy and thick as she tried to form the words that might be her last. She meant to tell him to come after her, or that they needed to get out right now. All other words died on her lips as she struggled to reach deep inside of him. "I love you."

Then she jumped.

Chapter Sixteen

Once her legs propelled her off the ledge, Charlotte didn't have time to wonder if Fawkes followed. Suspended in the open air, she surrendered herself to fear and let it flood through her. The singular emotion raced through her veins, pushing out all other thought as it filled her. She accepted its presence—there was nothing within her power to do anything otherwise. She embraced it, and it no longer held the power to paralyze her. Her fear could be remolded, repurposed. So she turned it into pure adrenaline, and took ownership of her body again.

Time slowed during the fall as Charlotte took in every detail around her. There was peace in her weightlessness, and the closest she would ever come to flying. Why had she let her fear of heights rule her? She almost wished she could fall forever, to revel in the wind on her skin and the grace of her floating limbs dancing. She had never felt anything like it before. What if her greatest fear had masked her deepest desire—a way to achieve absolute freedom of body and mind?

There was simplicity in having only two options— she would either survive the impact, or she wouldn't. If she didn't survive, then she wouldn't be alive for it to matter. She heard a voice scream, *"Charlotte!"* above her, and decided that she would much rather live.

She snapped her legs together, tightening every muscle in her body as she hit the water at an angle. Her feet entered first, slicing through the water like the dagger had sliced through Josephine's heart. The water hardly slowed her down as she rocketed toward the bottom of the moat, bracing herself for the inevitable impact that could break her legs.

Instead, her feet touched nothing, and the water buoyed her back to the surface. With lungs already starting to burn, Charlotte forced her numb legs to kick as she crawled with desperate strokes for the surface. Everything ached, her body too battered and bruised to register the extent of her injuries.

With a gasp, Charlotte filled her lungs with smoky air. The nearby blaze assaulted her senses, which had been in the blissful dark and quiet of the moat just moments before. She was almost pulled under the water again as a dark figure plunged into the moat next to her.

Fawkes. He had jumped for her. He had left death behind and come after Charlotte. His fighter's heart had found reasons worth staying alive, turning him away from the temptation of joining Josephine in death.

But Fawkes was still badly injured, and Charlotte didn't intend to save him from certain death in the tower only to watch him drown instead. She took a deep breath and dived back under the surface, groping blindly for his body.

She stretched her arms out as she kicked downward, wondering why he hadn't started floating to the surface yet. Then she realized, horrified, that he still had his cloak on. If Fawkes had been knocked unconscious upon impact, combined with heavy, waterlogged fabric, there was a very good chance he was at the bottom of the moat.

Panic seized her, and she almost inhaled a lungful of rank water. It was going to be impossible to find him in the cloudy, dark sludge. Charlotte forced her body still, though every part of her mind urged her to move, to act, to do *something* while Fawkes was drowning.

Her own heartbeat echoed in her ears, and she tried to channel the instinct that Fawkes always told her to listen to. *Your body feeds you information constantly,* his voice rang in her ears, a memory from a lesson during their journey back to Algonia. *You have to empty your thoughts and listen to what it is telling you. Do not try to analyze it, just use it.*

Charlotte felt a tingle in her left fingertips. Without questioning it, she lunged that direction and caught a fistful of fabric. Relief quickly turned to fear as she tried to pull him to the surface, and he dragged her down farther.

Almost out of air by this point, Charlotte used a few more precious seconds to locate Fawkes' neck. With a yank, she released the clasp and the weight fell away from his body. Her mentor's identity and legacy, stripped and lost forever.

Charlotte grabbed a limp hand and struggled for the surface. Spots pricked her vision, urging her to give in to unconsciousness. Her kicks grew weaker, and her strokes were ineffective, treading water instead of moving upward. It never occurred to her to cut the dead weight of Fawkes loose. Just as her body started to shut down, the wrist she still gripped twitched. Then she blacked out.

****

Blue. Charlotte was drowning in blue. An attempt

at inhalation resulted in a hacking cough, followed by a stream of vomit, before Charlotte realized the blue she was drowning in was Fawkes' concerned gaze and not the brackish water.

He helped her roll to her side and up onto hands and knees as she threw up the contents of her lungs and stomach again and again. When she finally caught her breath, she collapsed with a moan back onto the ground. Charlotte could hardly believe that the solid ground underneath her was real. After taunting death with her aerial leap and then again under water, she never wanted to leave the earth again.

"Can you sit up?" Fawkes' voice sounded far away.

"No," she answered, groaning.

"It is not safe here. We have to move."

"I can't." Charlotte's body didn't even feel like her own anymore. She had never been in this much physical pain. Her body rebelled against her for pushing it too far.

A hand reached down to stroke her forehead, and Fawkes' face appeared above her once more. She fought back tears at the sweet, simple gesture of comfort. *I just want to rest. Don't make me do any more.*

But the man staring at her wouldn't allow her to give into weakness. "My arm," Fawkes said. "I can support you, but I can't carry you." He looked distraught, but Charlotte couldn't tell if it was a reaction to her own dire condition or the memory of his wife's suicide. It had to be the suicide.

Charlotte closed her eyes and let out a resigned sigh. "Slowly," Fawkes ordered. He positioned his hands behind her head and helped ease her up into a seated position. Charlotte realized they were still on the banks of the moat. The town still blazed, heating her when she should have been shivering from her ordeal. The uncontrollable fires shielded the two outlaws from discovery, but their position was still vulnerable. Thankfully, there were no soldiers nearby, as Charlotte debated whether she could even crawl away, much less fight.

Fawkes, careful not to jar her, looped his hands under her armpits and hauled his apprentice to her feet. She swayed unsteadily and braced against him. "I have you," he assured her. Wrapping his uninjured arm around her, the battered couple staggered across the castle grounds. The movement helped to clear Charlotte's head, and she grew stronger with each step. By the time they reached the edge of the gardens, they were leaning on each other for mutual support. It was as much an emotional need as a physical one as they both tried not to think about the nightmare they had just witnessed.

The sound of the village grew fainter behind them as they retreated from the castle. Charlotte allowed herself a moment of awe that they were both still alive. But she left the castle a different person than she was when they entered, and Fawkes, she feared, would never be the same again.

Everything had gone so much worse than any scenario they had planned ahead of time. Josephine's suicide flashed through her mind every time her eyes flickered with exhaustion. She had wanted Fawkes to be happy, that was all. Charlotte accepted her role in causing Fawkes' pain, knowing that no amount of regret would encourage his forgiveness. He was all hers now, but broken in ways she couldn't fix.

They pushed onward until Fawkes stopped, looking around for something only he could see. Charlotte tensed, trying to ready herself for a fight, but that action alone sent her head spinning again. Fawkes winced as he moved the fingers on his injured arm to his lips and whistled low and clear.

Ghost burst forth from his hiding place in the trees, galloping toward his master. The horse slowed as it approached them, sensing that the riders were not interested in leaping onto his back. His velvet nose nudged between them and he let out a concerned whinny.

"We will be okay, ol' boy," Fawkes murmured, and Charlotte dared to hope that maybe Fawkes was not as far gone as she feared. Turning to Charlotte, he gestured for her to mount first. He helped as well as he could, but Charlotte had a feeling his shoulder injury was worse than he let on.

Once on top of Ghost, Charlotte swallowed the urge to throw up. The rocking motion as Ghost fidgeted did nothing beneficial to her stomach. Fawkes mounted up behind her, stifling a groan of pain. "Away," he ordered the horse. Ghost took off in the opposite direction of the castle.

"Where are we going?" Charlotte asked.

"Anywhere but here."

****

Charlotte must have fallen asleep astride Ghost, because when she opened her eyes, nothing looked familiar. "Are we heading for the border?"

"No."

The arms around her were cold and clammy, accompanied by a blood soaked sleeve. "We need to stop," Charlotte said. "I have to take a look at your arm. We can't go much farther like this."

"I am fine."

"No, you aren't. I can tell, and I'm not even looking at you." The body against her back shivered, proving Charlotte's point. "I didn't drag your arse from the bottom of a moat to watch you die slowly from blood poisoning."

There was no answer behind her for a while, until he whispered, "You should have let me die there with her."

So that's it. We are going to have it out, right here. If Fawkes was determined to fight with Charlotte before taking care of himself, so be it. But the sooner they got everything out in the open, the better chance she had of breaking through to Fawkes.

The conversation needed to be face to face, so Charlotte halted Ghost and slid off the horse. The ground rose up to meet her much sooner than she was expecting, and she stumbled. Without a moment's pause, Fawkes was off his mount and at her side, steadying her.

"I'm so sorry, Fawkes," Charlotte started. "I never imagined...If I had known..." The right words wouldn't come, and tears filled her eyes. "Josephine was incredible. Strong. Ferocious. And I could see how much she loved you."

"I had the power to save her while she was suffering. But I failed to search to the end of the world for her. I gave up on her. And then I didn't get to her in time," Fawkes ranted. "Now the woman I loved was torn from me. Not once, but twice."

"You brought her back to herself in the end," Charlotte said in a soothing tone. She winced, realizing how her words sounded trite and condescending.

"How could she leave me when we found each other again?" The look in his eyes begged Charlotte for answers she couldn't give. A glassy sheen of sweat coated his skin, two bright spots burning in his cheeks. Illness already ravaged through Fawkes' body, and he wasn't in his right mind to process the events of tonight. "Why couldn't I stop her?"

"It was her choice, Fawkes. And she decided she couldn't live the rest of her life haunted by what she had done. She thought it was her way to happiness, her way to redemption. You brought her peace."

"I brought her *death!*" he exploded.

"It was what she *needed*," Charlotte shot back. "A way to escape, to set the time-line of her existence right. I don't think she was supposed to survive that fire, and she knew it. The very fact that she still lived, upsetting the natural order of the world, drove her mad. She was forced to use her gift against her will, with no means of escape until you came for her. I think she was truly dead when you mourned her, when you rebuilt yourself from her ashes. The woman you loved disappeared five years ago, and you were never meant to get her back." At those words, Charlotte sucked in a gasp. She had gone too far, and she knew it.

His eyes widened with hurt, and he whirled around and started walking away. "Fawkes," she pleaded, "you wanted to live. You made a choice, and you chose to jump."

"You forced my hand."

"You wanted to save me. There is a part of you that lives for the fight, and I need to you keep fighting that battle inside. Josephine sacrificed herself, to fulfill her own destiny and yours. You did not belong together anymore, and she knew it. You both had different paths to redemption."

"I am on the path of revenge, not redemption."

Charlotte chased after him, jumping in front to block his stride. "Were you even listening to her? Josephine didn't want this for you!"

"We were happy," he choked out. "And they took her away, locked her up, and used her. The king will pay for what he has done. I cannot rest until then."

"Josephine begged you to save people, not kill them."

"But King Otan as good as killed my wife himself. The rebels have their wish. I will no longer stand idly by."

The word 'rebel' suddenly brought to mind Henry's face, coated in soot as flames danced in his eyes. Charlotte's baby brother as a part of the hellish attack on the city. While pushing her humanity aside to survive the night, she had refused to put a face to the rebels who had senselessly murdered countless innocent people.

Had Henry actually plotted to commit mass murder? Her instincts told her that Henry wasn't capable of that. *But I ignored the people dying around me to get inside the castle. By focusing only on the mission, I lost sight of myself.* Who was this girl who ignored the suffering of children? Had the same thing happened to Henry? Was Charlotte in any place to judge both Fawkes and Henry for their actions? Her own morality walked a knife edge as she made more and more allowances, excuses, and justifications for the men she loved.

Now Fawkes was talking about joining the rebels, a path that led to aiding and encouraging these acts of terror. What he was talking about went beyond seeking revenge for his wife. Charlotte needed to redefine her own boundaries of right and wrong and figure out if she could stand by Fawkes through it all. Deep down, she was scared she was fast approaching a point of no return, or if she had indeed already crossed a line along their journey together.

She had been willing to defend herself and attack those who meant to do her harm. Charlotte would have killed the soldiers who threatened her mother without a second thought. She was willing to do anything for Henry to get him out of prison. But to premeditate the slaughter of others who had done nothing malicious— Charlotte could not wrap her head around it. Innocents were always the true victims of war. Most people cared not for politics, wanting to be left to their business and their families. That was not a crime to die for.

Charlotte pictured Robin on the throne, having achieved the very goal that the rebels worked toward for over twenty years. Nothing would change within the country but the man who wore the crown. Robin wanted power for the sake of power, hidden behind the gauze of revolutionary thinking. That was not a good enough reason, in Charlotte's opinion, to cause upheaval and massacre in Algonia. The cost of a rebel victory was too high for her to stomach.

Fawkes hated killing, but he hid it under the guise of apathy and disinterest in politics. He killed only when necessary, and Charlotte just couldn't see Fawkes joining the fanatics and helping to plan murder on a massive scale. But how much of a leap was it, really, to go from using the brewing civil war for his own financial gain, and joining up with the cause? The reason handed itself over to Fawkes in the form of his dead wife, and rage now blinded him to reason. There was no point in arguing with his decision now, because nothing rational she said would reach him.

"You are right to be angry. There is nothing in the world to take away the pain you feel right now. I only ask that you sit and rest, just for a while," she said.

Fawkes shook his head. "There is no time. We have to reach Robin and his people." He moved to stagger back to Ghost, but Charlotte spoke up. "I can't go any further right now," she told him, realizing that his concern for her well-being was the only thing that could permeate his single-minded grief. Truth be told, she could probably have pushed herself a bit more before she dropped, but Fawkes didn't have to know that. Her mentor's stubbornness was going to get him killed, and she wasn't above being overly dramatic to prevent it.

Fawkes sighed. "I think we have put a safe enough distance." He looked longingly back toward the direction they had come, the direction of the castle. "What will they do with her body?" he wondered aloud. Then his knees buckled, and he pitched into Charlotte's arms. He clung to her and sobbed, finally giving into his grief. Charlotte cried for his pain, wishing she could ease some of it and take the burden off of him. She cried for the unfairness of it all, for both her own lost innocence and Fawkes'. For all the people in the town who had been in the wrong place at the wrong time. For her brother's future, and the choices he had made. For the violence that seemed to follow Charlotte wherever she went. And for the fact that there was no good choice, no clear side to choose, in the war that had erupted.

Where do we go from here?

Chapter Seventeen

Charlotte awoke with Fawkes still in her arms, his body shivering while his hair dripped with sweat. His eyes stayed closed as she disentangled from him and then rolled him onto his back so she could get a better look at his shoulder in the pre-dawn light.

Pulling the neck of his shirt down, she let out a hiss. The wound had been reopened more times than she could count, and now it looked worse than ever. The flesh was angry and ragged, and Charlotte could feel the heat rising from it as her fingers danced over his skin. Fawkes groaned and mumbled unintelligibly. His body reeked of sickness, and Charlotte was at an utter loss.

Insecurity taunted her. *Josephine would know how to heal him.* Fawkes' wife still haunted Charlotte, even more now that the woman had died a second time. *Well, I'm alive and she's dead. She chose to die. I chose to live. Measuring myself against her does nothing useful,* she told herself. Charlotte's determination sprung her body into action.

Leaving Fawkes wrapped up in as many extra blankets as she could find from Ghost's saddlebags, Charlotte scoped out the area, searching for enough dry firewood to keep a blaze burning for hours. She then busied herself stripping the damp outer layers of bark. Water would not be an issue, as there was plenty of snowfall to melt to keep Fawkes hydrated. No new snow had fallen, though, and Charlotte wondered if their trail from the castle was obvious enough to lead any unwanted visitors to their makeshift campsite.

Her meager knowledge of medicinal plants did not prove helpful while surrounded by the wet, cold winter. She couldn't identify anything useful under the blanket of white.

Charlotte briefly considered returning to Desmund's cave, the one place she had felt truly safe since leaving her old home. He would know what to do to help Fawkes. The old man had done it before, when the Cloaked Shadow appeared outside his dwelling, barely alive and with a neck wound that would have killed a lesser man.

Desmund would have the tools, books, and facilities to restore Fawkes, but instinct told her that Fawkes wouldn't survive that journey. They were weeks outside of and too many miles from the border. There was nothing surrounding them, except if Charlotte chose to return to a burnt and ravaged Numencaster. But physicians there would be plenty busy with their own people, and an outsider with a fever and an infected wound would be considered a lost cause.

The only viable option was to try to break Fawkes' fever herself. In order to break his dangerously high temperature, Charlotte needed to stop the infection from spreading.

Once the fire was roaring, the last worry on Charlotte's mind was attracting attention. Fawkes had grown worse in mere hours, and they were running out of time. She could not afford to be cautious anymore.

He was delirious, alternating between shouting at ghosts and sobbing quietly to himself. He thrashed naked in his bedroll, chapped lips white amidst his red face.

Stripping Fawkes had been clinical rather than sexual, with Charlotte fighting back tears when she saw how many scars crisscrossed his body underneath fresh bruises and welts. Though she knew her own body looked no better underneath her clothes, it was something else to see the extent of their ordeal written out on the skin of a person she loved. Fawkes was weaker than she had ever seen him, in both body and mind. It was no wonder that the infection chose this time to pounce.

He called out to Josephine many times, which Charlotte expected. She focused on trying to make him more comfortable while keeping his head and limbs from flailing and injuring himself. During a particularly bad spasm, Charlotte could not hold Fawkes down with her arm strength alone. Without thinking, she straddled herself over him, her careful weight keeping him flat on the earth.

"Charlotte!" he cried, eyes still rolled back, but startling her half to death. "Charlotte, Charlotte," he whimpered.

Hearing her name on desperate lips, Charlotte finally conceded that waiting any longer might kill Fawkes even faster than what she needed to do. She steeled her resolve while waiting for Fawkes to calm down underneath her. The shock and pain she was about to impart on a fragile body was something she hadn't wanted to resort to, but there was no other choice.

Carefully climbing off of him, she pulled the knife from her boot and thrust the blade into the glowing coals. Waiting until the metal glowed red-hot, she removed the smoking knife by wrapping Fawkes' discarded tunic around the hilt.

When Fawkes had been shot in the back, the arrow had gone almost completely through his shoulder. The head lodged itself in the front, in the thick muscle that roped between his chest and arm. Fawkes was forced to push the arrow through all the way before breaking the head off and pulling out the shaft. Charlotte needed to address both sides of the wound in order for her plan to work. She decided, after much consideration, that it would be better to turn Fawkes over and start with his back. Plus, it might be easier if she didn't have to watch the agony on his face as she administered her primitive doctoring.

Charlotte returned the blade to the fire with a hiss before gently turning Fawkes onto his stomach. The wound looked better from the back than at the front. She would seal it up on this end before tackling the infected flesh on his chest.

"This is going to hurt," she whispered to him. "But I have to do it. It's the only way to save you. I know right now you probably don't want to be saved, but it's in my hands. And I'm selfish. I don't want you to die. For this to work, you need to fight the poison in your blood."

Charlotte reached back into the fire and pulled the knife out. Steam rose from the red-hot blade and dispersed into the cold air. She swallowed audibly and braced herself for the scent of burning flesh. Lining up the tip of the knife with the jagged hole of his wound,

Charlotte plunged it into his back.

Fawkes howled and bucked his head back, which Charlotte dodged to avoid a head-cracking collision. She held on and kept the blade inserted in the wound as it burned away the rotted flesh, sealing off the hemorrhaging veins on the inside. Without warning, she yanked it back out and thrust it back into the fire to reheat.

Beneath her, Fawkes whimpered, but lay still, as if his involuntary movements had cost him too much strength. Charlotte was thankful she didn't have to see his face. She needed to close off the surface of his wound, too, and had to lay the blade flat against his skin.

It was so much worse than plunging the knife inside, because she had to watch as the metal burned off the festering skin and blistered instantly. Fawkes cried out before twitching and falling silent, unconsciousness carrying him away from the ungodly pain. *If I work quickly, I can flip him over and fix the hole in his chest before he wakes back up.*

Teeth gritted with determination, she did the same doctoring to his chest as she had done on his back. She moved efficiently, without the slightest tremor in her hands. The infected flesh was worse on the front, requiring more than two cauterizations both internally and externally. Though his skin was now black and blistering, Charlotte preferred it to the dangerous, angry red it had been before.

Wishing she had freshly-laundered linens to bandage him up, Charlotte settled on ripping up the cleanest looking fabric she could find from their gear. She rubbed and packed fresh snow into the wound first to help with the swelling. Fawkes started to stir with regained awareness at the icy contact, so Charlotte hurriedly wrapped the strips of fabric tightly from under his armpit, across his chest, and around his back.

"It's all done," she murmured, stroking sweaty hair back from his forehead. Her method of treatment was one of last resort, and she knew that Fawkes' recovery would be fighting against all the odds. She had done the best she could, and she hoped with everything she had that it would be enough.

She stayed up by his side all day and into the night, battling against her own exhaustion. She watched him obsessively for any sign of improvement but found none. She poured as much water past his lips as she dared, but most of it ended up trickling down his chin. Fawkes seemed to stay the same, not getting any worse, but at the same time not healing like he needed to. He cried out in more feverish dreams, and Charlotte gave up trying to make sense of his ramblings.

Fawkes was caught in a state of limbo, with death and life pulling at him on either side. Josephine was on one side, and on the other, Charlotte refused to let him leave the land of the living. She needed to remind Fawkes why he should stay, to fight against the temptation to exchange pain for peace. Touch and love would remind him of what he would be giving up if he gave into the infection.

Charlotte stripped off her clothes, shivering in the freezing night air. Grabbing fistfuls of snow, she scrubbed the grime off of her body as best she could, the snow bath leaving her skin pink and fresh. Goosebumps pricked her body as she pulled back Fawkes' blankets and settled in next to him, skin to skin. Her breathing was slow and even, and she felt his rapidly pounding heartbeat decrease just a fraction. The hitch that had been in his breath for two days disappeared as he relaxed into Charlotte. She clutched him, willing him to stay with her. "I love you. Be strong. I love you. Be strong," she repeated, until she drifted off to sleep.

When Charlotte awoke and felt Fawkes' skin on hers, she thought for a terrifying moment that he had died in his sleep. His skin felt so much colder than what she had grown used to, and it took the feel of his chest rising up and down for her to realize that his fever had broken.

He slept soundly in her embrace, without thrashing or fever dreams. Charlotte pulled back from him and deftly loosened one of his bandages to peek at the wound underneath. It seemed to be scabbing over the way it was supposed to, without a halo of infection surrounding it.

"I can feel that." A hoarse voice interrupted her prodding. Fawkes eased from his side onto his back, and fixed Charlotte with a clear-eyed stare.

"Welcome back," she said.

"It's good to be back."

"How do you feel?"

"Like I was dragged over hot coals."

"You're pretty close to the truth. Are you in pain?"

"My shoulder feels like it was pulled off my body and then reattached. Other than that, very weak."

Charlotte propped her head up onto her palm. "Do you think you can take some food and water?"

Fawkes licked his papery lips. "How long was I out for?"

"Over two days." Charlotte's revelation caused a jolt of surprise through Fawkes' body, and then a wince of pain crossed his face.

"I don't remember what was real and what was a dream," he confessed. "Did anyone come across us while I was unconscious?"

"Not yet," Charlotte reassured him. Her relief at seeing Fawkes alive and on the mend was tainted by the anxiety that had been rolling inside of her while they had been sitting ducks. It was nothing short of a miracle that no search parties had stumbled upon them. A thin layer of fresh snowfall had fallen a few hours ago, covering their tracks, but she was sure that the king's men were widening their search.

Fortunately, no one in the castle had seen Charlotte and Fawkes, and the discovery of Josephine's suicide didn't point to them. The king was hunting for the rebels who attacked his city, not the Cloaked Shadow. But the king had lost his strongest advantage, and without his seer, he was leading the charge blind. Charlotte needed to feel out Fawkes' mindset, to see how he was coping, and to find out if he was still set on revenge against the crown. However, that was a discussion that could not be held on an empty stomach and would have to wait until after she prepared their breakfast.

Suddenly aware that both she and Fawkes were naked under the same blankets, she wondered how to disentangle herself from an uncomfortable situation. *I've done nothing wrong*, she told herself. *He did the same for me.* Only the first time it happened, they had both been clothed.

But as everything else lay bare and exposed

between them, no secrets, shame, or hidden parts of themselves, it was almost appropriate that they were naked. Every other boundary had been crossed during their time together, so why should she feel ashamed about being seen without her clothes? If there was anyone in the world she was actually comfortable with seeing her naked, it was the man she trusted with her life. He knew her body, how she moved, every muscle. They had just awoken together, skin to skin, a rebirth as Fawkes decided to live. For Charlotte, that was more intimate than anything she had ever shared.

With that in mind, she started to maneuver out from the heavy weight and warmth that enveloped her, bracing for the snap of cold air that would hinder her as she struggled to put on clothes.

"Where are you going?" Fawkes asked, just as she pulled back the blankets.

"You need to eat to build your strength. We can't stay here much longer—"

Fawkes interrupted her escape and pulled her back to him. Gently resting his forehead to hers, he stared straight into her eyes. "Thank you, for saving me." This wasn't the same man who, in a fevered frenzy, sobbed and vowed revenge; whose grief over reuniting with his wife only to have her die again consumed him. Something had happened to Fawkes while he dreamed, something that healed his mind and soul at the same time his body recovered.

"What happened to you?" Charlotte whispered.

"Josephine," he said, never taking his eyes from Charlotte. "As I lay between life and death, she came and spoke to me. She showed me what our life would have been like, another reality, one in which we were happy. And it was wonderful. I lived my whole life with her in an entirely different future. When it was over, she kissed me and left, and I felt complete. She gave me peace. And I understood that somewhere else, she and I had lived our lives without tragedy, and another version of myself was content. Part of me wanted to stay, but I did not quite fit. It was not right. I realized I belonged here, now, that I needed to be here with you."

Charlotte was pretty sure her heart stopped beating, as she willed him to continue his explanation.

"I cannot explain it," he went on. "Josephine's death feels like it happened long ago, and I mourned her and loved her in another time. A part of myself is alive with her in that other world, and this part of me belongs here with you. I do not need to carry her with me anymore in this life."

Charlotte tried to wrap her head around what Fawkes said, but his ramblings confused her more than reassured her. She pulled her forehead away from him, unwilling to believe what he said was true and that he had come to terms with Josephine's death. Part of her waited for the fall out, for the slap in the face that would come when Fawkes realized that he couldn't be with Charlotte and instead drowned himself in guilt again. Unwilling to risk her own heart in case he was still delirious, she simply stared at him and said, "Okay."

But she had to admit, Fawkes really did seem changed, like a weight had been lifted from him. There were no traces of the Cloaked Shadow within him as Charlotte scrutinized his smile. He actually smiled at her. *Maybe the fever damaged his brain.*

Reading the doubt in her face, Fawkes reached out a gentle hand, resting it on her cheek. "You are the future I was meant to have, in this world." The anger that Fawkes had been holding onto, the edge that made him into the infamous Cloaked Shadow, had dissolved when his fever broke.

Unable to settle on the right words, Charlotte leaned in for a chaste kiss. Charlotte wasn't deluding herself. They had come so far together, but still had miles to go before they could rest. After everything they had been through, it took both of them facing death to bring them here. It was not a happily-ever-after moment, but it felt like the start of a new way of life. She allowed herself a small moment of bliss to chase the bad thoughts away.

Fawkes had been achieving his revelations through fevered dreams the past few days, but Charlotte had been turning over the events of the tower nonstop in her mind. The memory refused to be laid to rest, and Charlotte felt like there was something important staring her right in the face.

It all came back to Josephine. Cryptic as she was, Charlotte felt like Josephine had been trying to warn them that night. It had been overlooked, due to the fact that it preceded a violent suicide. What had the seer told them? Something about 'They will do it again and murder hundreds', and that it was their duty to stop it. *Protect the innocent*, that was what Josephine had urged.

All these theories would have to wait. "I love you," Charlotte said.

A smile broke out across his face. "I was wondering if I had imagined that," Fawkes said. "When you jumped from that tower…" He shuddered and pulled her in close again. "How did you know that would be the only thing to reach me?"

"Because you knew how scared I was to jump, and I did it anyway."

Part of Charlotte waited for Fawkes to say 'I love you' back to her, but another part of her hoped he would wait. Her initial confession had been due to extreme circumstance, and in light of Josephine's suicide and near-death escape, she knew the timing wasn't appropriate. So she settled for another kiss, then leaped up to tend to the fire before Fawkes could pull her back down. They needed to eat and move as soon as Fawkes felt able.

He let her go with a sigh, laying back down and already exhausted again. "Rest," she told him. "I'll wake you when breakfast is ready." She turned her attention to pulling on her clothes. She felt Fawkes' attention on her but didn't acknowledge it. *Not now*, she thought.

Whether or not avenging Josephine was still on the agenda, Charlotte had a nagging feeling that their outlaw duties were not over yet. After everything she had witnessed, Charlotte could not, in good conscience, walk away into the sunset with Fawkes. There was his redemption to consider, not to mention her own, for the parts she had played.

Chapter Eighteen

"I still reach for my cloak," Fawkes confessed to Charlotte as they prepared for bed that night.

Despite all of Charlotte's anxiousness, they had decided that Fawkes should rest for one more day. Though every instinct screamed at her to get moving, to move him prematurely might cause him to lose the precious ground he had gained toward full strength. He had slept much of the day, waking only for food and water when Charlotte stroked his forehead. The brave face he wore didn't fool Charlotte; she knew how much pain he was still in.

"I'm sorry I had to cut it off," Charlotte said. "I know how much the cloak meant to you. It was a part of you, especially because Josephine—"

Fawkes cut her off. "I would rather the cloak lay at the bottom of Numencaster's castle moat than my body."

"Am I right in assuming that Josephine wove whatever special magic she possessed into it?"

He sighed. "I have wondered that for a long time. I do not know exactly what she did to it, but when I put it on, I felt protected."

"She wanted you to be safe," Charlotte said. "Both in the physical and spiritual world. With the cloak, I think you were invisible not only to her, but to any other seer, in order to protect you. No one could use mystical means to harm you. That's why you were able to work undetected for so long."

"I think she kept much of her talent a secret from me," Fawkes mused. "I had no idea she was capable of so much. But somebody did, and that is why they took her."

"It wasn't just her protection that made you successful. You developed your own skills, talents that any espionage agent would be envious of. She enchanted the cloak, but it was you who made the Cloaked Shadow a legend."

He laughed bitterly. "And look where those skills got me. I knew nothing of my wife's suffering, and I am weaker now than I have ever been before."

"Maybe," Charlotte said. "But you aren't alone now. Combined, we have greater strength than you possessed while working unaccompanied, thanks to the training you have invested in me. We can stop what's coming."

"Stop what's coming? What do you mean?"

"Never mind," Charlotte backtracked quickly. "I don't know yet. I've been thinking about what Josephine said. Let me sleep on it. It might make more sense in the morning."

"I expect I will be strong enough to travel tomorrow," Fawkes said, as he welcomed her into their bedroll. When exactly this unspoken agreement had occurred, Charlotte didn't know, but it felt right, so she didn't question it further. She slid into his arms as though it had been their pattern for years instead of hours.

She tried to stay awake to guard Fawkes while he slept, but the exhaustion of caring for him and the constant vigilance over the past two days had taken a toll. *Just a few hours of sleep. Ghost will warn us if he hears anyone approach.* In a moment of weakness, Charlotte closed her eyes, and her landscape changed.

****

Charlotte hurled through a burning building, running as fast as her skirts allowed. Black hair tangled in her eyes. She didn't recognize the hallway, but somehow she knew where she was going.

"Can't let them catch you," a voice said inside her mind. "Just grab the book and get out."

It was then Charlotte realized that the body she occupied was not her own, and she was trapped inside, along for the ride. She attempted to stop her feet, but they were not under her control. With nothing left to do, she got comfortable in her vantage point to watch the events unfold.

She pushed a door open into what appeared to be a study. It was yet untouched by flames, but smoke poured into the small space. Charlotte felt the heart of the body she shared hammering with fear. "Just leave," Charlotte wanted to tell this woman. "Get out. Nothing is worth this." She felt a strong kinship with the woman who had such determination, and couldn't help but fear for her life, even though she knew it wasn't real.

A thin finger scanned the spines on a stack of books, searching for the right one through the haze. Through the stranger's eyes, Charlotte's gaze fell onto a familiar cover. To Charlotte's great surprise, she was able to read the title—The Magick of Herbs. "Oh no," she thought. "This is Josephine. I'm inside of Josephine." Her host's deft finger continued past the book that would one day end up in Desmund's possessions.

Charlotte was experiencing the fire that destroyed Fawkes' home and marriage, at the exact moment in time that his life changed. The crackling of burning wood grew louder as Josephine tarried in the study, acrid smoke burning her eyes as she searched for the book that she hoped would save her life, and her husband's.

In triumph, the woman held up a small, black book she found hidden in the back of a shelf— To Punish and Curse. Charlotte felt Josephine's pang of regret at what she was about to do, but it turned into resolve when she heard a taunting voice.

"Come out, come out," a man's voice sang, as he ambled comfortably through the fire. No other voice could set Charlotte on edge quite like that one, and she knew instantly it was Belaq. Josephine also knew the duke, though Charlotte could see in Josephine's memories that she didn't know his name yet. She knew him only as a traveler who had sought her out a few days prior, to help heal a small injury he had received during a hunt.

Josephine had been wary of him, mostly due to the fact that her husband was away from the household. The moment she had touched Belaq's blood, she had seen his true self. She had a shocking vision of his violent past and sent him away. However, Josephine's abilities piqued the interest of the duke, which Charlotte knew from firsthand experience was a dangerous thing to do. Drawn by Josephine's talent, an infatuated duke returned for her, and this time he had been prepared.

Though Fawkes had given hints about Josephine's

abilities—her second sight, her healing skills—from Charlotte's point of view inside the seer's mind, Josephine had only told Fawkes about a fraction of her talents. She kept much of herself hidden from her husband, helping people when she was able but careful not to go far enough to scare anyone. People were afraid when women had too much power.

But now, by pulling out her book of curses, Charlotte could see that Josephine meant business. Belaq appeared in the doorway, staring at her with bloodlust in his eyes. Knocking the book of curses out of her hand, he landed a blow across the seer's face. Reeling back, Josephine tried to land a few feeble blows of her own.

Inside, Charlotte screamed at Josephine, trying desperately to take control of the body, to move weak arms and legs into the fighting patterns that Fawkes had drilled into her over difficult months. But Josephine knew none of those defenses, and without her magicks, she was powerless against Belaq's bigger and stronger frame.

The duke laughed at her struggle, brushing her hands away as though she were a buzzing gnat. Grabbing onto Josephine's long hair, he yanked her to him. Charlotte could feel Josephine's disgust and horror and understood it all too well.

"You'll make a fine present for the king." He spat into her face. "I think you're just what he's been looking for. An actual seer." Josephine bucked against his hold, but Belaq never loosened his grip. "And I get to be the one to deliver you." Satisfaction showed on Belaq's face, and Charlotte knew him well enough to know that he was trying to estimate how much favor he

would earn with the crown for making such a crucial discovery that would aid the underground war against the rebels.

"But do you want to know the best part?" he whispered into her ear, breathless with thoughts of what was to come. "I can have all the fun I want with you on the way to the castle. No one is going to be searching for you."

Fawkes' name was on Josephine's lips, to cry out that her husband would save her, but she couldn't risk putting him in danger. Belaq had to believe that she was alone, otherwise he would kill Fawkes or make him suffer as a way to control her.

So she swallowed her scream, and allowed Belaq to drag her from the burning house. Everything started to fade to black when Josephine's inner voice spoke directly to her. "Charlotte," she said, scaring the observer half to death. "The next attack is coming. You have to stop it."

Where? How? Charlotte tried to ask, but she was pulled from Josephine's body and lifted up, watching from above as the nobleman pulled the brave woman into the forest. Charlotte was carried away with the smoke.

****

Charlotte jolted awake, looking frantically around their camp for any signs of an intruder. She found none but pulled herself out from under the blankets anyway. The frozen ground around her was undisturbed, and Ghost was quiet. However, she still couldn't shake the feeling that she was being watched.

Maybe it was Josephine watching her, urging her to complete the mission assigned by a dead woman.

Charlotte realized that she had only been asleep for a few minutes, although it seemed like hours. She was more awake and alert than she had been in days. Her mind was refreshed enough to try and untangle the mess of clues the seer had given her.

The dream had been a message, she was sure of it. Josephine had entrusted Charlotte with her most terrifying memory for a reason. Fawkes had been given a glimpse of an alternate future, while Charlotte had been given a vision of the past. How did it all come together to shape the future in this world? Was the fire the key? Did the clues point back to the ruins of Fawkes' home? Was Josephine trying to show her something within the books? Questions spun in Charlotte's mind as she tried to find the connection between her own experiences and Josephine's life. The deceased woman had felt a kinship with Charlotte for a reason.

Nothing looked familiar in the dream, except for the book and the duke's leering face. Josephine suffered through what Charlotte narrowly escaped. Belaq was the link between the two women. *Whatever attack Josephine has been trying to warn us about, Belaq is somehow going to be involved.*

A rush of certainty filled her as that thought fell into place. She needed to go back home. Going back was the only way forward for her and Fawkes. The moral gray in which Fawkes lived his life was no longer a viable option. He had been pulled from the shadows when the cloak had been cut from his body, and now he needed to step into the light. Charlotte would be by his side and help him navigate his path in the sun.

She never expected to return home. The thought of

going back to the place where her mother died and her brother had been imprisoned forced a cold sweat to surface. She would, however, enter the village as a much stronger version of herself than the scared girl who ran away.

Charlotte was tempted to wake Fawkes to share the key points of her dream with him, in just enough detail to tell him she had figured out their next mission and not enough to traumatize him. Before she could wake him, Ghost let out a quiet nicker.

Charlotte's body immediately stilled, ears straining for any clues in the muffled, white wilderness. If Fawkes had been in top form, he would have been up and at Charlotte's side without hesitation. But pain and recovery still dulled his senses, entrusting Charlotte to take care of their security, so she was on her own to deal with a possible intruder.

We should have left today, she thought, wishing she had listened to the instinctive need to hide them farther from the castle instead of using Fawkes as an excuse to stay put one more day. The clean up after the attack was probably under control by now in Numencaster. No doubt King Otan had ordered his soldiers to comb the area once it was clear that a second attack was no longer imminent.

Ghost had detected either a soldier or a rebel near their camp. A few weeks ago, Charlotte would have hoped it was a rebel, but now she was equally apprehensive about facing either. Watching the rebels blow up women and children did not instill her with faith that they were sane and stable.

Maybe it's Henry out there, she thought wildly, before she could squash the unwelcome reminder of her brother back down. Even if it was Henry, she had no idea what she would say to him. Not after the attack that he helped to carry out. Had he known what was going to happen? The boy she knew would have been viscerally against that method of warfare. But the man he was becoming, the same Henry who willfully participated in torture, might have rationalized it as an act for the greater good.

After a few breathless moments, Charlotte was almost relieved when the man who stepped into the firelight was not her brother. Charlotte would have to save the sibling's confrontation for another time, and instead deal with the wide-eyed soldier in front of her.

He appeared to be alone, and very frightened, if the shaking sword he held in front of him was any indication. "H-halt. In the name of King Otan!"

Fawkes might have been at less than full strength, but there was no way he would sleep through a surprise visitor. Sure enough, out of the corner of Charlotte's eye, she watched him sit up and assess the situation in seconds. He stayed in his bedroll and watched her.

A quick scan with her senses determined that this boy was currently alone, sent out to scout and report back his findings. The soldier seemed determined, though, to prove his pluck and directly confront the suspicious travelers. He wasn't much of a threat, as Fawkes had obviously deduced, but Charlotte needed to ensure that the boy didn't bring the rest of the army down onto their heads.

Charlotte cautiously circled the fire, until she stood protectively in front of Fawkes. The soldier crept closer, sword ready to attack. "You-You're just a woman," he said, shocked.

She could almost hear Fawkes smirk behind her. "I'm sorry to do this to you," she told the boy, and nimbly leaped onto him, knocking the sword to the ground before he could reel his arm back to swing it. Aiming her fist at his nose, she popped him quickly, blinding him with tears and blood. Automatically, the boy's hand flew to his nose, and Charlotte swept his feet out from underneath him. He landed flat on his back, and Charlotte heard his breath exhale with a whoosh. She was on top of him in a flash, yanking her knife from its hiding place in her boot.

Lining up the blade to his throat, she hesitated at the smoothness of his skin. Not a hint of stubble graced his ruddy cheeks, and she realized just how young he really was. Images of Henry as a boy, the bumbling little brother following her around, flashed in front of her.

She sighed, then using her fist wrapped around the hilt, clocked him across the top of his head instead.

"Well done," Fawkes said.

Breathing hard, mostly due to adrenaline rather than actual exertion, Charlotte crawled off the boy. She looked at her mentor with more than a little bit of pride. He had taught her to disarm a man and render him unconscious in mere seconds.

"Instinct took over," she said, making her way to Fawkes. "How are you feeling?"

"Well enough to travel, I would wager," he said. "We are lucky it was just the boy who found our camp. We need to move—more people are nearby."

Charlotte nodded her head in agreement. "I know where we have to go."

Fawkes arched an eyebrow. "Where is that?"

"Home. To Duke Belaq's lands. I'll explain on the way."

"What are you going to do about that one?" Fawkes gestured to the boy. "He will tell his superiors that he saw us. You know what we have to do."

"Fawkes, I can't."

"Then I will do it for you," he offered, standing up.

She hesitated, torn between what she felt was right and what she felt was safe. "No, that's not what I want. You heard Josephine. The souls of those she sentenced haunted her. She wanted redemption for you, Fawkes, and that starts now. Plus, I can't kill him. He's younger than Henry. He is just a boy."

"Charlotte," he said gently, "he will be able to identify us."

"Let's leave him here. We can leave the fire going so he doesn't freeze to death. We can be long gone before he wakes up. And who is to say he will even report us? I cannot live with sentencing everyone we come across with an execution."

He sighed. "You know this is dangerous."

She almost laughed at him. "You mean what we've been doing all this time hasn't been dangerous?"

"Fine. We will leave him, though it is against my better judgment. But I trust you, and he is your captive. This is your decision."

The pair busied themselves readying Ghost as quickly as possible. The extra day of rest seemed to have restored new life into Fawkes, reassuring Charlotte that it had been worth the cost to stay longer. She took advantage of her burst of energy and packed them up in record time.

The rush of taking down the soldier so efficiently

still coursed through her veins, and she itched for action. The feeling of power, and the calm certainty that she would survive the fight, was intoxicating. There had been no room to doubt herself, and she had proved to Fawkes exactly what she was capable of. To know now that she had the ability within her body to overpower others, to render them helpless at her feet—how was she ever going to walk away from it?

It's no wonder Fawkes chose this particular career path, she thought. As the Cloaked Shadow, he had gotten to relish in besting others without necessarily relishing in the kill.

But Charlotte had to be honest with herself. As she held the knife to the boy's throat, the temptation to cross her own moral boundaries had been strong. If he were older, or hadn't resembled Henry to such an extent, a part of her deep down wondered if she would have gone through with slitting his throat. The instinct that had reared up as she protected both herself and Fawkes frightened her.

"Which direction to the dukedom?" she asked Fawkes, as he mounted up onto Ghost with very little of her help.

"South, then west." He grunted. "We need to ride long and hard, and hopefully outrun anyone who might find our trail, thanks to our friend back there. And on the way, you are going to explain to me why we are returning to your former home."

"Redemption," she said, and settled in behind him. "Point Ghost in the right direction, then lay back on me and rest," she instructed. Much to her surprise, he did so with little protest.

Chapter Nineteen

Along the journey home, Fawkes and Charlotte pooled their knowledge. Fawkes agreed with Charlotte that the rebels were most likely going to attack Duke Belaq and slaughter hundreds of his people. With such a 'success' at Numencaster, Robin probably felt unstoppable.

In her gut, Charlotte knew that Belaq was going to be the target of the next attack. The message had hit her loud and clear after Josephine's warnings and her subsequent nightmare.

"But how do we know they won't attack other villages on the way?" Fawkes countered with his own assumption.

"Because I know Robin. This is personal, especially after what happened in Croantis. The rebels are sending messages to the most powerful men in the kingdom, men that they hold responsible for a number of offenses."

Once they neared the duke's lands, Charlotte and Fawkes doubled their caution. Both the king's army and the duke's private forces roamed the region in impressive numbers. Even as they dodged the soldiers, Charlotte hoped that the army's presence would at least slow down the rebels as well. It would make it more difficult to transport the materials they needed for another attack while under such scrutiny. The rebellion's network of spies and allies was vast, but this time they lacked the element of surprise.

"We will approach through the forest," Fawkes decided. "The soldiers will avoid it at all cost. However, we will need to be on guard in case of a run in with the rebels. It is likely that they are camped within it to remain close to the village."

"They aren't afraid of the Cursed Forest?"

"Who do you think has been spreading rumors about the forest for years? The rebels have always used it as a sanctuary within Algonia, even before the Great War. The stories about it are not true." Fawkes considered a moment. "Well, most of them, anyway."

"Do you think we will come across Robin and the rest, before they attack?"

Fawkes shook his head. "By the time we reach Belaq's castle, I predict they will have already infiltrated the village."

"I just can't believe Henry would go along with something like this." Charlotte tried to will away the tears that flooded her eyes. "If only I could find him. Talk to him. He knows these people. They are neighbors who helped raise us, friends who worked at the castle and in the stables. My brother would never hurt them!"

"Charlotte, the brother you knew is no longer the same person as Henry is now. You have known this for a while. You need to be prepared to deal with the possibility that he is forever changed, thanks in part to Robin's influence. I need to know, though, how you plan to confront him once we arrive."

"We will stop the mass murder, Fawkes, and then I'll finally get Henry out of Robin's clutches."

Charlotte braced herself to broach the other point of contention that hung heavy between them. "And what will you do with Belaq?"

Fawkes stiffened, pulling on Ghost's reigns involuntarily. "I will kill him, if the opportunity presents itself. He deserves to pay for what he has done."

"But you will not seek him out? For revenge?" Charlotte prodded. She needed to hear him say it; that Fawkes' first and only priority would be to save the people of her village, and not abandon it in order to pursue the duke and make him pay for his sins. Even though she felt that Belaq deserved whatever was coming to him, he was not the focus of this mission.

Fawkes sighed. "My foremost duty will be with you to help stop the rebel attack." That promise would have to be enough for her.

The forest loomed ahead of them, dark and foreboding, but oddly comforting at the same time. It wasn't as frightening as Charlotte remembered it being the first time around. Now, she approached the Cursed Forest knowing that this was the last time she would enter her homeland. Whether she left or not was contingent on surviving the mission. Either way, she knew it would all end here, and she would never make the journey into her village again.

Fawkes was still weak, but gaining strength in spite of their relentless traveling. His fever never resurfaced, and he was gaining some of the mobility back in his arm. Charlotte cleaned and changed the bandage nightly, now that Fawkes would let her near the injury. Thick scar tissue was sure to develop, and she wondered if it would forever hinder his fighting prowess. She suspected Fawkes feared it, too.

"Now you just need a matching injury on your leg," she told him one night, as they camped in the Cursed Forest just outside of Charlotte's village.

Fawkes looked at her, confused. "Why would I need that?"

Charlotte ran a light finger down the raised gash from his temple, then down to the scab on his shoulder. She felt the gooseflesh raise on his exposed chest in the cold night air. "So you'll be balanced," she teased. "And then I can trace a path through your scars it all the way down here—"

His hand shot out and grabbed her wrist before she could dip too low. "Charlotte," he warned, voice low. "Not here. It is too dangerous."

They hadn't dared light a fire in days and had already skirted a few of Belaq's patrols that had been brave enough to enter the forest. There was still no sign of Robin or his men, but they needed to be on high alert at all times. Fawkes hadn't been keen on the idea of…distractions.

Charlotte knew that he thought about it just as much as she did. The fleeting moments of affection between them were urgent and raw as they raced across the kingdom. Heated kisses, hands that strayed too far, embraces that would have inevitably led to something more, but the timing was never right. They hadn't even been able to share a bedroll since the boy soldier had stumbled upon their camp outside of Numencaster. Now that Fawkes was healing, they slept in shifts or not at all, and pushed to cover as much ground as they could to get to the dukedom in time.

Charlotte and Fawkes planned to sneak into the

village at first light and gather information. Ideally, they would locate the rebel forces and stop the attack. But dawn was an eternity away, and the sunrise could very well mark their last day together if things went wrong. Charlotte used Fawkes' grip on her wrist to tug him closer. "Don't do this to me," he warned.

"What, this?" Charlotte rose up onto her tip toes and leaned in, brushing feather-light kisses across his jawline. "Or this?" She moved her mouth down his neck, receiving a vibrating groan from his throat onto her lips. He didn't move away from her, though. His body remained perfectly still as Charlotte explored his skin, unwilling to stop her but stoic in his stubbornness not to give in.

He drew a shuddering breath as Charlotte wound her free hand to his waist. "Why do you insist on torturing me?"

"Because who knows when I'll get the chance to again," Charlotte murmured. Strong hands closed around her shoulders and pushed her away. Fawkes' eyes flashed dangerously in the dark as he stared down at her with a frown.

"I will lay with the woman I love, but not here, in the dirt, in the cold. Right now is not our last moment."

The woman he loves? Charlotte stared at him in shock, but Fawkes didn't seem to notice. "Now stop distracting me," he said. "You are making it very hard to remember that. You sleep first. I have first watch. We will move into the village before dawn."

Awash in Fawkes' confession, Charlotte didn't feel the sting of rejection. *Had he truly meant it?* He had said it in such a matter-of-fact way, like she already knew it, like he had said it a hundred times before.

As Charlotte settled into her bedroll, Fawkes' words turned over in her mind. After her dramatic outburst before jumping out of a tower, maybe it was sweetly simple that he had told her so offhandedly about his feelings. There would be no deep conversation the night before the mission, with whispered pet names and fervent promises, no desperate love making like it would be their last night on earth.

They just were together, having discussed tactics and mapped out the village for most of the day. They needed to have absolute focus if they were going to get their 'right moment' someday.

****

Charlotte's turn for watch came all too soon. Fawkes woke her with a gentle kiss on both eyelids, before landing one on her mouth as she eased out of her deep slumber. Stifling a yawn, she asked, "Anything to report?"

"All is quiet. Wake me if anything happens," Fawkes said, and they switched places.

Charlotte watched him fall asleep instantly as she stretched stiff muscles. She hoped she wouldn't have to wake him soon, because every extra bit of sleep would help his shoulder heal. She stood up and paced around the campsite, trying to stay warm and alert. If she sat down now, the grogginess would overcome her.

Her circles around the camp grew larger and larger, spiraling out as she stayed sharp for anything unusual. It felt more proactive than just waiting for an enemy to stumble upon them. After the boy soldier got the jump on her, Charlotte promised herself that it wouldn't happen again.

As her radius expanded, she began to notice signs of human interference—disturbed foliage, misplaced soil, and the occasional hoot of an owl that reminded her how unnaturally silent the forest had become. A force seemed to be pulling her; it felt familiar yet frightening at the same time. Giving Fawkes a glance over her shoulder to reassure herself that he was all right, she decided to follow her instincts. It was obvious that she wasn't alone, but whoever stalked the forest appeared to have turned around just before their camp. It looked like the track of a single person, but she couldn't be sure.

Crouching behind a thick trunk, she watched and waited for a sign. Her breath was deep and even, helping to steady the knife in her hand. While listening hard, a rustling sound prepared her for action. Leaping around the tree, she bowled into a dark figure and knocked him to the ground. A surprised yelp escaped his lips, echoing through the quiet forest. Charlotte's knife found the stranger's throat and the blade nicked the skin.

"Don't kill me! Please don't kill me, Fawkes." The body she held captive trembled under her hands, but didn't struggle to get away. Charlotte pulled away enough to let the scarce moonlight filter through the trees and illuminate her captive on the forest floor.

"Charlotte?" her brother said in disbelief. "How—how did you—I thought you were the Cloaked Shadow!"

Charlotte was on her feet in an instant, scanning the trees. "Henry," she said, not looking at him. "Where are they? Where are Robin and the others?" It took everything in her to keep from sprinting back to Fawkes to make sure he was safe.

"They left me to stay here in the forest, until it was time. Said I would get recognized in the village. I've been here for days waiting for them to come back." He shivered. "I was looking for food, and I thought I heard voices earlier. I kept getting turned around, you know how the forest has its ways…"

Charlotte did know, and she suspected that the forest had a hand in pushing her to find her brother. Before she greeted him with open arms though, she needed to know the truth. "Henry," she said, face stony. "Did you know about the attack in Numencaster? What they were going to do?"

He swallowed audibly under her scrutiny. "Yes," he whispered, eyes downcast. "But I didn't know it was going to happen like that. The screaming—oh God. It was so much worse than Robin said it would be. He said it would prove a point, make them pay attention to us. Encourage others to join the fight against the crown. But Robin had this weapon—some kind of powder, I'd never seen it before. It didn't just make noise."

"No, it didn't," Charlotte said, disgusted.

"How do you know?"

"Because I was there. I saw what you and your rebel friends did. How could you, Henry? All those innocent people—children, even!"

"I know!" Henry burst into uncontrollable tears. "I don't know how it all happened. It was so fast—"

"Did you even try to stop them?"

"It was too late," he mumbled. "The kegs had already been set. Charlotte, I didn't know what they were going to do, I swear it!"

"You are a coward," she told him. "And now

you're here, about to do it again. To our home, Henry! To the people we know, who helped raise us."

"I don't know what else to do, but Duke Belaq deserves it, Charlotte. You know he does." Henry's tears slowed, and a burning hatred flamed in his eyes. "Robin promised they would only bomb the castle this time. They are only going to try and kill Belaq. He said it was for our protection. After what we did to Belaq in Croantis, he was never going to stop hunting us. The duke is going to track us all down and kill us—that's why we have to do this."

Charlotte stared at him incredulously. "You really believe that Robin will only set the castle to explode? You really think that he isn't going to put cannon powder all over our village, and watch the whole community burn? Robin is only about himself, Henry. Now he has a taste of the destruction he can cause, and he is going to want to do it again. He wants people to fear him because he thinks that will make his transition to power that much easier."

"He won't, Charlotte." Her brother begged her to understand. "He said that the king's town was just a test run. Robin said that we would only bomb the duke's castle this time. The one before was supposed to be practice before a real attack on the king's castle and—"

"And you what? Commit regicide?"

"It is for the good of the kingdom! There can be no progress while that tyrant holds us back. Why can't you understand?"

"Because how much death and destruction will have to happen before Robin gets what he wants, only to turn around and rule worse than King Otan?"

Henry shook his head, trying to come up with an

answer. Charlotte's brother was lost and confused, caught up in events and political schemes that he couldn't hope to comprehend. He trusted too easily, fell too quickly for Robin's promises of a better life for everyone. "Belaq deserves to die, Charlotte," he finally said, as though that was the answer to everything.

"Yes, he deserves it, but what is the cost you are willing to pay for his death? Is vengeance worth the lives of those who did nothing wrong to you?" Even as she said the words to Henry, part of Charlotte wanted to leave the bombs in the castle, to let the duke burn for what he did to her brother, her mother, and Josephine. Duke Belaq would get what was coming to him in due time, but there had to be another way besides causing untold damage to the village.

Trying to reason with Henry was getting Charlotte nowhere, so she switched tactics. "Where are the powder kegs, Henry?" *I just need to stick to the facts.*

He hesitated. "I don't know for sure, but I know where they might be. Robin knows that I worked in the duke's stables. He asked me for ten possible places around the castle that would be secluded. I don't know which ones he picked to hide the powder in."

Ten locations? And spread out all around the castle? Finding the rebels and the kegs would take ages. "When are they coming back for you, Henry?" she asked.

"I think they will fetch me when the sun comes up. They told me to wait three days. I'm to help light one of the kegs, Robin promised. He knows I deserve to help kill the duke."

How on earth did the rebel leader expect to smuggle powder-filled kegs into a guarded castle? Did he have someone on the inside, a member of the duke's staff to help him? It would be a logistical nightmare.

Or maybe, the voice of reason whispered, *Robin intends to blow up the village again, just like last time. There are no kegs in the castle.* Charlotte needed to talk to Fawkes before explaining her theory to Henry, which would be about as effective as banging her head against a wall.

"If you aren't going to help stop this, Henry, will you do one thing for me, as I am your sister?"

"What is it?"

She noticed he didn't agree right away. Promises between family were no longer unconditional. "Don't tell Robin that Fawkes and I are here."

Her brother furrowed his brow, considering his own terms. "I won't tell him if you don't try to stop us."

"We won't go to the castle," she lied, "but we will be in the village. I don't trust Robin with our people."

Her false promise assuaged him, and even appeared to alleviate some of his guilt at participating in another attack. Her obvious distrust of Robin finally brought out some of Henry's insecurities about the rebel leader. "You really think he would do that?"

She nodded. "Don't tell Robin we are here, and we will make sure he doesn't attack the village. When they come for you, we will follow you to where the rebels are."

"But don't interfere with the attack on the castle," he warned.

Lying through her teeth, Charlotte said, "Of course."

"Then I won't tell them you're here. I want to do right by our family, Charlotte. This is for us. Being back here, knowing what we've lost because of the duke, it makes me so angry. Do you understand?"

"More than you know," Charlotte answered. Henry seemed determined to finish what he had started with the duke back in Croantis, and beating Belaq within an inch of his life still wasn't enough retaliation for killing their mother. *At least some of Henry's conscience remains*, she thought. *He wants to protect the lives of innocent people. But his desire for the duke's death overshadows the voice within him warning against blind trust in Robin.* Henry's willingness to forgive the rebel leader for Numencaster proved his naïve desire for vengeance without collateral.

Now, Charlotte needed Henry's naïveté to work in her favor to get herself and Fawkes in a position to defeat Robin. "We will be right behind you tomorrow," she promised. "Just don't look back. Don't tell them anything. Wait on the edge of the forest until they come for you."

"Robin wouldn't lie to me," Henry mumbled, as Charlotte turned around to head back to Fawkes.

"Goodbye, Henry."

****

When dawn broke, both Fawkes and Charlotte waited, hidden, for the rebels to come and retrieve Henry. Ghost remained back at their campsite, as they decided on stealth on foot versus speed through the village. They watched as Henry paced nervously, just outside the tree line. For the thousandth time in her life, Charlotte prayed for her brother to keep his mouth shut.

Robin himself did not journey to the forest, which did not surprise Charlotte. Instead, two other rebels that she vaguely recognized exchanged quick words with

Henry. After a conversation that was too low for her to overhear, they flanked Henry and headed for the village.

"Wait a while longer," Fawkes cautioned. "Their trail will be easy enough to follow. We can't risk being seen, or they might start the attack early." Fawkes had agreed with her plan when Charlotte burst into the campsite the night before, so frantic to share crucial information that he thought they were being attacked. After whirling around and finding no threat, he calmed down enough to hear the details of their first real lead. However, he had voiced his doubts about trusting Henry, and Charlotte was sadly inclined to agree with him.

Charlotte's first instinct was to tie Henry up in the forest and prevent him from being involved at all, but she couldn't make her brother's choices for him. He was entitled to a certain amount of sovereignty, even though she just wanted to protect him from the world. It wouldn't be fair to Henry, and it certainly wouldn't be right for Charlotte to take on that role. Just as she forged her own path in life, so must he. These past few months had hardened her brother, changed him in ways Charlotte would have never imagined. She chastised herself for always underestimating him. She just hoped he wouldn't let her down this time.

So with a hood pulled down low over her face and Fawkes at her side, Charlotte made her way to the village. There was a role reversal this time, with Charlotte remaining disguised while Fawkes was brazenly uncovered. No one would spare him a second glance, other than innocently assuming he was a traveling stranger. *The benefits of a secret identity,*

Charlotte thought, as she gripped the brown fabric.

Charlotte's heart ached at the familiar sights and sounds of her village stirring and preparing for the day. It was like stepping back in time to observe a younger version of herself. The idea that all she had known as a child was going to be blown sky high, possibly in mere hours, made her panic.

Fawkes, sensing her discomfort, gave her hand a reassuring squeeze. "It looks different from the last time I was here," he said.

"I was thinking the opposite. It feels the same; it is me who feels different."

"When I was here last, it was just another contract. Just another mission standing between me and payment. But now I see it as the place you grew up, the place that gave me you. Lands that are owned by such an evil man somehow produced the person I have been yearning for without knowing it. It brought us together."

Charlotte sighed. "Growing up, I never thought I'd leave here. Once I left, I never thought I'd be able to return. I never thought I would want to come back, especially after my mother." Conflicting emotions rolled inside her, and she felt pulled in countless different directions. Ghosts of her past, memories, alternative futures…everything surrounded her, the what-ifs threatening to drown her.

"You are no longer that person, Charlotte," he told her, as they crept through the quiet streets. "You fought long and hard to be the person you are today. Nothing can take that away from you."

She couldn't respond as her heart rate quickened, realizing the familiar route they walked. Through the twists and turns of the rebels' trail, they had ended up in the last place Charlotte would have expected Robin to hide out. Henry couldn't have led them here, could he? Fawkes and Charlotte had turned onto the street that her old house still stood, and watched as Henry ducked in through the doorway of their childhood home.

All at once, Charlotte felt grossly violated. She heard Fawkes' intake of breath next to her, as though he too couldn't believe what he was seeing. These murdering intruders were no better than the soldiers who had dragged her mother from that very home. But just as the streets were washed clean of her mother's blood, there was no hint on the outside of Charlotte's simple wooden home tying it to anything sinister within.

Her brother must have offered up their dwelling as a meeting place for the rebels. *He knew, and he didn't tell me.* Charlotte saw red as she struggled to keep from bursting inside and dragging Henry out by his ears. She wondered what other crucial information he had kept from her for fear of how she would react.

"They are gathering," Fawkes whispered, eyeing the house from their hiding place. "It is happening soon, possibly tonight."

Over the next hour, Charlotte watched from her vantage point as a dozen other men slipped from the alleyways and into her childhood home. How they all fit inside, she had no idea, but there had to be a good reason to convene in such an uncomfortable space.

She saw the occasional soldier patrolling the streets, but Duke Belaq had not increased his security like she assumed he would. *After such a brutal attack on the king's town, and Belaq's bad blood with the rebels, he has to know that he could be next.* Even the village residents seemed uneasy, as though they felt it in the air that something was wrong. Citizens spoke with muted tones, shuffling outside only to throw glances over their shoulders and return home again.

Where is the duke's army?

Charlotte shivered, muscles aching from remaining in one position for so long. "Do we approach?" she asked.

Fawkes also sensed that something wasn't right, but he was waiting for the last piece for it all to come together and make sense. "They are all inside," he murmured, thinking out loud. "That means everything is already in place. Why risk a meeting? Unless something has gone wrong. This is not a replicate attack. The duke has not increased his forces." They reached the same conclusion together. *The duke is waiting for the rebels to make the first move, for them to show their hand before he shows his.*

"There's Robin," Charlotte pointed out. "And Henry." Her little brother trailed after the redhead leader, looking distraught. The rest of the men poured out of the house and scattered quickly, running in all directions to different parts of the village. "They're going to do it now?" she asked, confused. Attacking the village in broad daylight was risky.

"Something has them spooked," Fawkes said, eyes never leaving Robin as the rebel pushed Henry into the same alley Charlotte's mother had been dumped in. Robin appeared to be fed up with Henry's blubbering, and laid a slap onto his face. Shocked, Henry immediately stopped crying. Charlotte watched as Robin laid an encouraging hand on Henry's shoulder, speaking earnestly to the impressionable young man.

Henry's shoulders slumped as he bowed his head, scuffing the dirt with his feet. The boy nodded as Robin spoke, before meekly following him out of the alley and down the main street.

"That's not the way to the castle," Charlotte said. "There are definitely no bombs in the castle, are there? Robin lied to Henry."

"Yes," Fawkes agreed. "Robin does not have the ability to get into a castle as heavily guarded as the duke's. I believe the only powder kegs are placed throughout the village. Robin intends to attack the people again."

"We have to stop it!"

"Robin will die before he gives up the locations of the bombs. Henry knows nothing. We have to go after the other men and see if they will lead us to all the other storage places."

"I can't just let my brother go along with this madman."

"I know. That is why you will follow Robin and Henry to their location, and I will track down the others. One of them will talk. I will move as fast as I can to disable the kegs. Do you know how to render cannon powder useless?"

Charlotte shook her head.

"Get it wet," he instructed. "Do not let anyone with oil or flame get near it." He pulled her to his chest in a rough embrace. "Be cautious," he said. "I have a feeling stopping the attack is not our only objective today."

"I love you, Fawkes. Be safe."

He raised one eyebrow and favored her with a grin, looking almost giddy in the face of such dangerous odds. Charlotte knew that feeling now herself, the rush of adrenaline before combat. "The Cloaked Shadow has been preparing his whole life for this moment," Fawkes said. Then he kissed her hard and left.

Chapter Twenty

While tailing Robin, Charlotte almost lost him a few times before catching a glimpse of his shocking red hair. His sneaky movements evolved into bold strides through the village streets, as though the time for caution had passed. He grew more reckless with each step. His frenzied movements told of a man unconcerned for his own life. His first plan had gone off without a hitch right in the king's front yard, and he had walked away unscathed. Charlotte wished she knew what it was to feel that invincible.

A yet unknown factor had spooked Robin into moving up the time line, but the air of confidence surrounding him suggested that minor inconveniences could be overlooked. One of those inconveniences came in the form of a very reluctant young man trailing behind him, trying to keep up.

Henry hadn't tried to reason with Robin, as far as Charlotte could tell, since the slap laid on him in the alley. He stayed on Robin's heels, but his head remained on a swivel, as if trying to find anyone who could help him stop it. *He's looking for me to save him. Again.*

She followed the pair until they ducked into the blacksmith's shop on Market Street. A horrible thought struck her. *A bomb in there would cause the most damage to the village.* The rebels had a limited supply of cannon powder. The smithy was the perfect central location and provided the most volatile environment. Fawkes would hopefully stop the other bombs from going off, but she knew that they would only be the smaller, less devastating ones.

Charlotte crept up to the shop. Peeking in through the window, she saw Henry lunge for a hammer while Robin busied himself lighting one of the forges. Her brother was about to do something stupid and get himself killed. There was no time to lose and no time to formulate anything more than a basic plan as she vaulted through the window.

Somersaulting on the ground, she was on her feet in an instant, standing between her brother and the power-hungry rebel leader. Robin spun around in surprise to face a furious Charlotte alongside a hammer-wielding, former rebel. "Traitor!" he spat at Henry, ignoring Charlotte's presence.

"I'm the one you should be worried about, Robin," she told him calmly, redirecting his attention.

"What, you think you're going to stop this? Nobody stands a chance against me. I am on the side of the righteous. The will of the people is with me."

"The same people you're going to blow up?" Charlotte had been waiting for this confrontation since the rebel attack at Numencaster. She desperately needed to understand how Robin justified an attack on his own countrymen. He was a coward, willing to blow up the guiltless and hide in the shadows, running away before he could be fought face-to-face.

"They need to know that their king is weak! He cannot protect them, therefore he cannot lead them. The nation will crumble without strong men, like our revolutionary men."

"And you believe you deserve this power? After everything you have done?"

He shrugged. "A small sacrifice for the greater good of the country."

"Well, how about I sacrifice *you* for the greater good of the country?" Charlotte took a step closer to his grinning face, the whites of his eyes revealing his madness. Charlotte was astounded at his logic. *He thinks he is saving his homeland by murdering it.*

His sudden cackle made her jump. "Oh, I would like to see you try. I knew you would be trouble; I knew you were hiding something. If only I knew you had such a close relationship with the Cloaked Shadow, or should I say, *Fawkes*, I could have put you to much better use. There's nothing like a little external motivation to get employees to do what you want."

"Don't you dare threaten my sister!" Charlotte felt Henry move behind her, and her arm shot out to catch his, keeping him in place.

"Henry," Robin sighed. "What happened to you? You were my most promising young revolutionary. You have more reason than anyone to punish the duke. He doesn't deserve his life of privilege and power, Henry. He is not a protector of his people. I can make you the new duke. But we have to do it my way."

"By setting off powder kegs all around the village?" Henry's voice shook with rage and hurt, finally glimpsing the truth under Robin's charismatic visage. The man he had looked up to and trusted had betrayed him with his lies, and was now threatening his only surviving family.

Robin looked at Henry with pity. "You haven't

figured it out by now? I had hoped the one I picked for my protégé would have had a sharper mind."

Charlotte looked back and forth between them in confusion. She needed the complete story before she launched her attack. What had she missed?

"This is the only bomb, Henry," Robin continued, eyes glittering. "The others were just decoys. It should keep Belaq distracted for long enough. He wants the powder. His men have been searching for it all over the village. He thinks we don't know, that he was so clever to dress them in plain clothes. He doesn't realize that we have been trained to spot a military man through any disguise. They will be sorely disappointed to find kegs of dirt to haul back to their psychotic master."

Charlotte felt like her throat was being squeezed. "So why hasn't he killed you yet?" she asked.

"If he did, he would never be able to find the largest stash of the most powerful weapon in the kingdom. It has taken years to collect, smuggle, and bribe our way to build this great symbol of our revolution. No, he would rather risk the attack in order to get his hands on my cannon powder. And while he is looking in all the wrong places, I am about to show him that power we wield is greater than his."

That means Fawkes is looking in all the wrong places, too. It also left Charlotte, alone, to face a crazed revolutionary and a violent duke who would probably show up any minute. Charlotte needed to find the powder and disable it before either Robin or the duke could get to it. Otherwise, this battle of wills between Belaq and Robin was going to have an explosive ending.

The whole thing made her head spin. Belaq knew

about the impending attack. Robin knew that the duke knew, and yet everything had been allowed to get this far. The fate of an entire village was the stake in their game. Everything was coming to a head, and the smallest spark would ignite what had been building for years. This was beyond a political statement, and it would only get more personal when Fawkes showed up. Charlotte was positive Fawkes would find them, once he figured out that there was no real cannon powder in the first location.

"You are going to tell me where the powder is hidden in here, Robin," Charlotte said, voice low and menacing.

"I think the time for conversation is over," Robin said, slowly walking backward. "Clever girl, to keep me talking. Make me waste precious time. If only your brother was half as clever as you."

Charlotte needed to get Robin out of the smithy and away from wherever the powder was hidden. One wrong move and they could all go up. He would not go down without a fight, though, and Charlotte couldn't risk accidentally setting off the explosion.

She turned to her brother, who still held the hammer in his shaking hands. "Henry," she said, gently tugging at the weapon until he released his hold on it. "Go outside. Get as many people to clear the area as you can. Quickly and quietly. Don't cause panic."

"I'm not leaving you here with him!" Henry said.

She regarded him with a level gaze. "I can take care of him, Henry. But just in case I don't, you need to save these people." Tears filled his eyes. "Go, now," she ordered. He must have sensed the iron will in her tone, because he turned and ran from the building. She hoped Henry would evacuate at least the part of the village closest to the coming explosion. That left Charlotte and Robin alone, facing off as he squirmed his way to the back corner of the smithy.

Charlotte tested the weight of the hammer, weighing it with her hands as she tossed it back and forth. It was not a graceful weapon, not like the precision of a knife edge. It was not a weapon of the shadows, a silent killer, and effective with a whisper of sound. No, the hammer was brutal. A weapon that needed its master to swing it with fury in order to deal a killing blow. It could crush a skull beyond recognition, a weapon that immersed the attacker in the smell and feel of the kill. It was as personal as an attack with bare hands, only fueled by more rage.

But rage that burned within Charlotte was controlled for the moment. It allowed her to assess her foe with razor-sharp precision, to focus on her training rather than let loose.

"Where is the powder, Robin?" Charlotte asked again, as she stalked toward the rebel with her weapon. Her prey pushed on a wood panel within the shop, and it opened to reveal an escape hatch. *Of course*, she thought bitterly. *Robin loves his escape routes*.

"I'll be seeing you," he said, as he crouched down to dart through, holding his dagger in front of him. "On the other hand, maybe not."

Charlotte was torn, debating in a split second whether or not to chase the rebel or spend extra precious minutes looking for the powder in the blacksmith's workshop. The decision was made for her, however, when Robin suddenly reappeared, backing away from a knife-point at his nose, his own weapon turned against him.

"Fawkes!" Charlotte shouted, when she saw the second figure come into view. "The powder is somewhere here. Robin hid all of it in here, the other barrels—"

"Were just decoys, yes," Fawkes said. "I came to look for you as soon as I realized. Made it easy to find, with all the fleeing people."

"Belaq is on his way, I'm sure of it. He wants the weapon," Charlotte said. "You get Robin to talk; I'll start looking." She began overturning tables, testing the floors, and examining every nook and cranny in the shop.

"You're never going to find it," Robin said. "Give up and get out, otherwise we will all die."

"So you are willing to let other people die for your cause, but not you?" Fawkes said, moving the knife over to Robin's temple. "Coward," he said, and sliced.

Hot blood and screams filled the air as Robin clutched his ear, or the gaping hole where his ear used to be. Fawkes grabbed him by the collar and hauled him back up to his feet. "Let's try this again. Charlotte asked you a question." The Cloaked Shadow had made a reappearance, even without the cloak itself. Cold, calm, collected—Fawkes allowed his alter-ego to take control of his body and get things done. Charlotte hoped he wouldn't take it too far and lose himself, but she had to admit, she was relieved to see him.

Robin just whimpered, blood gushing through his fingers as he tried to stem the flow.

"How much time do we have, Charlotte?" Fawkes asked. "I need to know how slowly I can kill him."

"I don't know, I don't know!" she said, frantic.

Fawkes turned his attention back to his captive. "Here is the thing, Robin. I do not mind dying. I do not mind killing you. But I will be damned if I let you kill that woman over there." He turned back to Charlotte when Robin refused to react. "Charlotte," he said, "get as far away from here as you can. Run."

If she wasn't so stressed, Charlotte would have rolled her eyes. "I'm not abandoning you, or my village. We can get him to talk."

Fawkes slashed a vertical cut down Robin's jaw in response, almost identical to the scar down his own neck. *"Where is it?"* he bellowed.

"Taking all of my fun, I see." Duke Belaq appeared in the doorway, flanked on one side by the biggest soldier Charlotte had ever seen, who held Henry by the throat. "Look at my good fortune. Everyone I wanted to see, all together at once. I think because I started with the boy so many months ago, I should begin with him here, no?"

Henry thrashed in his captor's grasp as the massive soldier raised him off the ground. Charlotte reacted viscerally, abandoning her search and launching herself at the men. "Charlotte!" Fawkes yelled, and all hell broke loose.

Charlotte's hammer smashed down on the soldier's arm, which released her brother at the sound of bones shattering. Belaq ignored her, making his move on Fawkes and Robin. Unconscious, Henry fell to the floor, but Charlotte had no time to check on him. The soldier was reaching for his sword with his good arm.

Charlotte ducked the first swing of the sword, dropping to the ground before retaliating with her hammer. Two quick blows to the knee caps and her aggressor was down, screaming in agony. She had disabled a man more than twice her size without a second's hesitation. It wasn't a conscious decision to use the minimum amount of force to achieve the maximum amount of debilitation without striking a killing blow. It was due to instinct, from the lessons that had been pounded into her over and over.

When the soldier hit the floor, Charlotte was already up on her feet and moving to help Fawkes. Her mentor faced off with the duke while trying to hold Robin captive between them.

Belaq could have come with an army, but instead he faces us alone. He wants to savor this moment, to have all the glory to himself. After the torture the duke had survived in Croantis, he would not give anyone else the pleasure of killing Robin and Henry. Belaq didn't appear to be feeling any long-term effects from his injuries, and Charlotte wondered how he had healed so rapidly. Besides some discolored bruising on his face, it was impossible to see the ordeal that the Duke had suffered.

"The famous Cloaked Shadow, I presume," the duke said, as they circled each other, sizing up their opponent.

Robin, whose face was pale with blood loss, swayed a little on his feet in the center, but that wasn't going to stop him from trying to save his own skin. The rebel leader saw his opening as Duke Belaq distracted Fawkes, who seethed with barely contained fury at the man who destroyed his wife. Robin tried to make a break for the hidden passage only to find himself restrained by the duke this time.

"It appears we have the same objective with this

one—pain," Belaq told Fawkes, holding his own dagger to the rebel. "I've been thinking about this for a long time." The duke's face split into a gleeful smile, reveling in the thought of bloodshed rather than the ticking time bomb somewhere in the shop.

Duke Belaq ran his knife over Robin's face, and Charlotte shuddered with the memory of his cold blade against her skin in Croantis. She stood at the ready next to Fawkes as Belaq held the rebel as a shield between them. Charlotte was certain that if Belaq wasn't holding Robin, Fawkes would have been on him in an instant. The rebel was a reminder of their true purpose— finding the powder. Everything else was just a distraction.

Belaq, though, seemed to think he had all the time in the world. He started making small nicks in Robin's already-bloody flesh. "You think you can threaten my home?" he murmured to Robin, almost lovingly as rivulets of red streamed down. "You do not get to decide who lives and who dies in my dukedom. That is up to me. Do you know what I have done to rebuild my family name? You will give me this weapon, and no one will dare speak ill of the Belaqs—past, present, or future. We are a strong and powerful house, and even the king will fear us."

The powder was not going to transfer from one madman to another if Charlotte had anything to say about it. Robin grew more frantic as he struggled against the duke's grip. "Help me!" he begged Charlotte and Fawkes, deciding that they were the lesser of two evils.

"Then tell us where it is," Charlotte said calmly.

"It is already activated. If we wait very much

longer—"

"All the more reason to confess," she said.

Robin grunted as another cut sliced his face. In that moment, he seemed to realize that no matter what happened, he wasn't going to get out alive. For all of his bluster and talk of sacrifice for the revolution, Robin truly hadn't planned on dying. After his years of careful planning, escapes, and successful attacks, he had started to believe he was truly invincible. But this final plan was going to be the death of him, whether at the hands of the duke, the bomb, or the Cloaked Shadow. He had gone too far this time, and no one was coming to save him, not even Henry.

Charlotte saw regret flash across Robin's face as his eyes darted over to the lit forge. All at once, she knew where the powder was hidden, and exactly how much danger they were in.

Fawkes, so in tune with his partner's presence, felt Charlotte tense. He followed her line of sight to the flames, and his jaw clenched in understanding.

Cannon powder was in Fawkes' realm of expertise, and he would have to be the one to safely disable it without blowing them all up. That meant leaving Charlotte to take care of Belaq, the only man she had ever faced whose skills rivaled Fawkes' own. The fight would be the greatest test of her skills, with the greatest repercussions. One wrong move, one bump into the forge, could send them all sky high.

Charlotte rose up on her toes, ready to bounce into action. Belaq narrowed his eyes at her, and she could see him scrambling to decipher what had just changed in their holding pattern. Charlotte and Fawkes' silent link facilitated their countdown to action. At the same time, Fawkes moved with graceful purpose toward the forge, and Charlotte stepped in front of Belaq and Robin to take his place.

"It appears I do not need you after all," the duke said to Robin, and with a practiced motion, slit the rebel's throat. The dying man's sputtering gasps as he clutched his throat sickened Charlotte, but she held her ground. The fresh spray of blood on her clothes didn't make her woozy—it only sharpened her focus and her determination not to be the knife's next victim.

In front of her stood the man who had driven Charlotte down this path, but she was not the same girl who trembled in fear at his mere presence anymore. As she stared at Belaq, the smiling faces of two beautiful women flanked him. Both had died at his hands, degraded and tossed away like they were nothing. The appearance of Charlotte's mother and Josephine gave her strength for the fight to come. The sudden certainty that she was going to win fell over Charlotte like a blanket. *Or a cloak.*

Charlotte didn't let herself turn around to see how Fawkes handled the cannon powder. Was it fair for her to take the revenge that Fawkes so desperately wanted, to take his place in this fight? But Fawkes had not killed anyone since Josephine told him his new path, and Charlotte was not about to let him start now. Fawkes' mission was of broader scope than the one assigned to Charlotte, but her sacrifice would be just as poignant.

The duke smirked at her, Robin's blood dripping from his fine clothes. He moved toward her as she stood frozen in place, as though he expected her to react the same as when he cornered her in Croantis. What

Charlotte was really doing was preparing herself for the inevitable, for the shift in mentality that came when planning a killing blow versus a disabling blow. The one she landed would have to be the end of Belaq.

He lunged for her, dagger whistling past her ear as she nimbly dodged his thrust. She backed away, dancing on her toes like she and Fawkes had danced a hundred times before. He hardly saw the hammer in her hand as a worthwhile threat, especially considering he held the wicked-sharp blade. The longer Charlotte held his attention, though, the more time she gave Fawkes to finish his task.

"I remember you are quick," the duke said, undeterred. "Unfortunately for you, I'm going to have to be quick as well, as much as I would love to savor this." He rolled his eyes over her form, leering.

Her adversary readied for another assault, but Charlotte read the duke's plans with easy clarity. In underestimating her, he fought lazily, and gave everything away a split second before he attacked. Charlotte was hardly out of breath after ducking and diving around four more attempts on her life. The duke appeared to be saving his energy for what he thought was his true opponent—the Cloaked Shadow.

The duke was never going to get that far, though. Charlotte was going to make sure that this ended here and now, with Belaq's blood on her hands instead of on Fawkes'. In order to protect the man she loved, she would sacrifice her own innocence.

Belaq finally realized that he was not dealing with the same Charlotte from before, and he switched tactics. He flew at her in a whirling fury, his decades of fighting expertise apparent, and she didn't move fast enough. Searing pain shot through her side as the dagger opened up a gaping wound on her torso. Ripping the breath from her lungs, it took all of her strength not to double over. Her torn blouse revealed jagged flesh on her left side, pulsing with heat.

Through the haze of her pain, she felt Fawkes' eyes on her, distracted from his task at hand. *No*, she thought, *I can do this.* She straightened up, and took on her fighter's stance, readying for another attack.

When he saw that she was not going to go down easily, Belaq let out a feral snarl. "I'd rather kill you with my bare hands anyway," he said. He threw down his knife and charged at her.

Belaq bore down on Charlotte like a bear, trusting in their size difference to save him from any real damage. And if she did get in a lucky hit, well, Belaq was determined to take her down with him. Charlotte's opponent was beyond rational thinking, his ferocity overwhelming any self-preservation instinct.

As Belaq closed in on her, Charlotte flashed back to training with Fawkes in the snow. He was yelling at her to flip him to the ground as they repeated the exercise over and over. *Use my weight and my momentum against me,* Fawkes chided.

Taking no heed of her abdominal injury, muscle memory took over and Charlotte forgot to fear for her life. She had faced this attack a hundred times before. She dropped her hammer to the floor.

The duke was in front of her one moment, and then he was soaring through the air behind her. Time slowed as Belaq hung in space, limbs flailing before he hit the ground. The earth shook with the force of the impact, knocking the air from his lungs and cracking his skull.

In a split second, Charlotte was on top of him, weapon in hand. But when she reached across the floor for her hammer, her fingertips closed over Duke Belaq's knife instead, and now Belaq's own knife was at his throat. His eyes widened in surprise. A girl who hardly weighed anything straddled him and had managed to get the upper hand. The dark eyes that bore into Charlotte's were not her mentor's blue ones. This gaze was not filled with approval and pride as she bested the man underneath her. These eyes were filled with loathing and rage, reminding Charlotte that this was not a training exercise.

Belaq had no breath to speak, but it didn't stop him from reaching up and grabbing Charlotte by the throat. As his fingers began to tighten, Charlotte drove the knife into his neck, twisting the blade as a fountain of blood spurted over her hand and into the dirt. The duke's lungs tried to work with a bubbling wheeze as he inhaled through the hole in his throat. He did not look afraid or in pain, just confused, like he had entered a new reality. He was trying to understand a world in which a woman could beat him.

His fingers loosened from Charlotte's neck and limply grasped for purchase on his own throat. He tried to grip the hilt of the knife, but it was slick with blood. Belaq's struggles grew weaker as he tried to comprehend his position.

Charlotte felt this all with cool detachment as she waited for the end, calm as his body bucked beneath her. Once the light left Duke Belaq's eyes, the enormity of her actions hit her with full force. As much as she knew he deserved to die, the duke's limp body didn't bring her the sense of peace and closure she was hoping for. Instead, she just felt empty. It was over.

Blood would be forever on her hands, branding her soul. It wasn't how she thought it would be, and the memory of the violent struggle would forever haunt her dreams. But Charlotte had made her decision; a decision to take Belaq's death upon her own conscience instead of Fawkes'. Giving up his revenge against Belaq had put him on the path toward something greater and better. Charlotte loved him enough to give him this gift, even if it meant crossing an irreversible line in her own life.

She had sacrificed a part of her innocence she never realized she had until it was gone. Would she grow to resent Fawkes for putting her in this position? For leading her down this path? Would his love be enough for her to shoulder this burden for a lifetime?

All these thoughts crowded her mind as she stared at her bloodied hands. Then she looked up, and her gaze met a deep blue stare. Fawkes was waiting for her to move, to speak, to take any sort of action first. As soon as she tried to get off the duke's body, all the adrenaline left her system.

Seeing Charlotte's muscles fail her, Fawkes swooped down and pulled her into his arms. At the contact, Charlotte burst into tears of relief. She was alive, and so was Fawkes. Against all odds, they were still standing. Charlotte pulled her face away from where it was buried in his neck to look around the room. Robin and Belaq's bodies lay near the previously lit forge, blood cooling in puddles on the floor. Near the doorway, Charlotte saw the soldier still writhing and groaning on the ground, unable to stand due to his crushed kneecaps. Her gaze fell on the last body, which had not moved.

"Henry!" she cried, and let go of Fawkes to run to her brother. She dropped to sit on the floor, pulling Henry's head into her lap as she sobbed for him to wake up. Charlotte stroked his face while Fawkes hastily searched his body for signs of life.

"He's breathing," Fawkes confirmed, and Charlotte let out a sigh of relief.

"How long until he wakes up?"

A low moan answered her question as Henry started to stir. He looked up in confusion at his sister's worried face. "What happened?" he asked.

"I did what I had to do," Charlotte said.

Chapter Twenty-One

Fawkes and Charlotte extracted enough cannon powder hidden within the forge to have destroyed half the village. A thorough sweep of the rest of the smithy revealed extra caches of explosives and oil hidden within false panels in the walls. The forge itself, though, was the real genius of Robin's plan.

As they collected the dangerous material, Fawkes explained how Robin had rigged a slow-burn fuse underneath the top of the forge. The cannon powder had been stashed within, and then the fire was lit on the surface, gradually building the heat and pressure inside. Robin had placed a collapsible shelf underneath where the coals sat, designed to give way once the surface was hot enough. This method of delayed detonation would have given him enough time to get far away before the cannon powder ignited. The extra powder and oil hidden throughout the building was supposed to magnify the effects of the blast radius. Fawkes' careful disarming of the forge prevented the shelf from collapsing, saving everyone.

Fawkes and Charlotte decided to leave the bodies of Belaq and Robin where they lay, miraculously the only casualties of what could have been a mass murder the size of which the Kingdom of Algonia had never seen.

"The rest of the duke's men will be here soon,"

Fawkes warned. "We need to smuggle the powder out of here and hide it until we can transport it from the village." He turned to Henry, who still rested on the floor, and continued. "There will be a manhunt for all the rebels involved, especially once word gets out that the duke is dead."

Henry staggered to his feet. "I have to find them. The other revolutionaries. I need to help them."

Charlotte stared at her brother in disbelief. "You can't be serious," she said. "They were just about to murder hundreds of innocent people!"

"That was Robin's plan," Henry said. "But not everyone was for it. There are a lot of us within the faction that didn't agree with it. They didn't want to do it. Robin forced them."

"Like he forced you?" Fawkes raised an eyebrow.

"No." Henry turned bright red and looked at the floor, swaying a little. "I did it for revenge. I thought we were going to blow up the duke's castle, not the village. Robin kept it a secret to get me to do what he wanted."

"Henry, they are violent extremists! I've been trying to get you away from them for weeks. You cannot go back to them," Charlotte said.

"But I need them, and they need me," he said, sounding like a petulant boy. But then, under Charlotte's frustrated gaze, Henry straightened up, giving his sister hints of the man he was becoming as vestiges of his childhood fell away. He spoke to her with renewed confidence. "I have come to believe in what the revolutionaries are fighting for, Charlotte, even if I don't agree with how they were doing it. They showed me that there are a lot of problems in Algonia and how I can be a part of changing it. I am a part of something bigger for once in my life. I belong with them."

"I can't be a part of that, Henry, I just can't." Charlotte reached out to grab Fawkes' hand, presenting a united front. "We can't be a part of that." *Besides, in the political game, there is only a choice between the lesser of two evils.* As it stood, Charlotte could not, in good conscience, choose either side.

"We need to leave," Fawkes concurred. "All of Algonia will be looking for us. Not even Croantis will be safe. We do not have time to argue with him."

Charlotte nodded sadly. She let go of Fawkes' hand, and moved to stand in front of her brother. "I don't understand it, nor do I think this revolution is something you want to be a part of, but you have to make your own decisions. Just do not ask me to bear witness to these choices." Her heart ached too much to say the words—*You will always be my baby brother, but I cannot follow you down this road anymore.* Fawkes was her family now, and she belonged at his side.

Though Henry was right in front of her, Charlotte could not reach out to him. Her brother was the one to close the gap between them. "Thank you," Henry told her. "For everything. I've lost track of how many times you've saved me." His arms wrapped around her, uniting them across the divide for one last time. Tears squeezed from Charlotte's eyes as she held him tight, and she ignored the fresh flow of blood from the wound in her side. There would be time to heal later.

Fawkes reached forward and clapped Henry on the shoulder. "Believe in what you must, but take care not to let it consume you. Do not let your past control you. Move forward." Henry nodded seriously, and Fawkes continued. "If we get word of any more rebel violence upon civilians..." He didn't need to complete the sentence for the implication to be understood. Charlotte hoped it would never come to that.

Henry gulped. "Take care of my sister."

Fawkes gave Charlotte a tender look. "She has always been the one to take care of me."

Epilogue

Charlotte stared at the horizon. The shores of her homeland shrank in the distance until she could barely see them. She felt Fawkes' arms wrap around her waist from behind, shielding her against the sea breeze. He held her close, careful to avoid her nearly-healed scar. She allowed herself to relax against him, and the reality of their freedom set in.

With their volatile cargo currently sinking to the bottom of the sea, it no longer held the power to harm anyone. Charlotte felt a weight lift from her shoulders. They were on their way, she and Fawkes together, leaving their painful pasts behind. The ship struck out for faraway lands with names she had never heard of, places where they could find a fresh start.

"You are beautiful," Fawkes whispered into her ear. A delighted shiver ran down her spine. It had been a long time since she had felt so at peace. They weren't running from something for once—they were running toward something greater. The air of possibility surrounded them, whipping up their hair with the spray off the ship.

"I'm ready for our adventure," she said, turning to land a playful kiss on his cheek. Her lips landed on the deep dimple in his smile. A green cloak graced Fawkes' shoulders—vibrant and rich, the color of life. She rested her cheek on it with a sigh.

Wherever they ended up, they had agreed to use their abilities for those in need, for good instead of for profit. Plus, she couldn't imagine giving up her training. It had become a part of who she was. Fawkes was well on his way to healing both on the inside and on the outside, and Charlotte was determined to help him attain redemption. Helping people was a good place to start. With this purpose in mind, they had boarded a ship to the other side of the world.

Fawkes nudged a calloused finger under her chin and raised it up gently. Butterflies tried to escape Charlotte's stomach every time he gazed at her like that. Eyes that matched the sea and sky, encompassing Charlotte's whole world, looked at her with such love it took her breath away. The Cloaked Shadow was forever gone, and in his place stood simply Fawkes, and he leaned in for a kiss.

A word about the author...

Taylor Hobbs writes romance novels while living aboard a sailboat with her family. To learn more about her books and adventures, please visit https://cannonstocruising.com/